Photo by Brenda Tucker

Michael Calhoun Tucker is an extraordinary storyteller! In his first book, *The Crackers: The Legend of Jessie B. Tucker*, his prowess as a writer comes alive as he weaves the historical facts about the family's legends and myths into a compelling novel. Filling in the gaps lost to history, Michael takes you on an adventure only he could create. Part fiction, part fact, completely entertaining, Jessie B. and his extended family are Michael's story.

Born and raised in rural central Florida, he's lived and absorbed the very fabric of the Crackers. Michael embodies the voice of his Scots/Irish and Creek Indian ancestors in this exciting novel, and entwined in his storytelling are lessons of the spirit and the heart, reflecting this complex man and his unique style of writing.

The Crackers

The Legend of Jessie B. Tucker

The Crackers

The Legend of Jessie B. Tucker

Photo by Michael Calhoun Tucker

MICHAEL CALHOUN TUCKER

ISBN: 1517056004
ISBN 13: 9781517056001

Dedication

In Memory of

Geneva Mae Young Tucker
She gave me life.
Then she showed me how to live it.

Acknowledgements

To my wife, who for twenty years told me to stop telling her about my stories and sit down and write! She never stopped having faith, or giving encouragement.

To my two daughters Callie and Meghan, who think I can do anything.

To my friends who reviewed my story, for their wonderful feedback and encouragement.

I read somewhere once: when you make a commitment, the universe conspires to make it happen.

The universe brought me this wonderful person named Raven Dodd.

With her knowledge of writing and publishing (and patience), she has turned my story into a real novel.

Thank you, Raven!

Preface

You've read about how the west was won. This book is about how the wild and uninhabited middle of Florida was tamed! *THE CRACKERS: The Legend of Jessie B. Tucker* is a story about four families who fled Georgia during the Civil War and headed south. They were successful farmers who did not own slaves and who felt that the war was not about them, but Sherman was burning Georgia, and they decided to start new lives in Florida or risk losing their families. It turned out that the war followed them south, and the four men had to join the fight in Florida or lose any hope of keeping their homesteads and settling down.

Although this story is a novel based on historic facts about the events that happened to my ancestor, Jessie B. Tucker, it is not just a history of occurrences during and after the Civil War. It is about the lives of these white families from Georgia that came crashing together with a band of Creek Indians. Jessie is left for dead in the Everglades, having been shot by a Seminole scout for the Union Army and is rescued by three Creek braves. The subsequent meeting of Jessie B. Tucker and Two Worlds, the ancient spiritual leader of the Creek band, sparked the merging of whites and Indians that changed the lifestyle and landscape of Central Florida.

There were plenty of laws in Florida after the Civil War, one of which was that all Indians had to live on the reservations. It took the wisdom and courage of Jessie B. Tucker to lay down his own law and defend it, in order to protect their white and Creek families from vicious outlaws, warring Indian tribes, angry ex-soldiers who had lost everything, and white families that had been torn apart, who were hostile to any red man.

Last but not least, this story is about the love that held these white and Creek families together. Against all odds, these unlikely partners prevailed to create a new life and help to launch the second largest cattle drive in the Union, leaving a legacy that lives on many generations later. My hope is that you will fall in love with these characters and enjoy being introduced to the magical events that shaped a new world. If so, I will have succeeded.

Thank you,
Michael Calhoun Tucker
Naples, Florida, September, 2015

Part One
Two Worlds

Two Worlds by Brenda Tucker

One

Woman of the Wind slowly rose from her fur bedding, giving the joints of her old body enough time for her to stand. As she pushed back the hide that covered the opening to the lodge she lived in, she looked back at her son and his wife still sleeping. It was two hours before the light of the sun would hide the huge orange ball of the harvest moon, which reflected off the water of the lake, creating the effect of two moons. Walking carefully, she made her way across the short distance to the lodge, where her husband now lived alone. It had been several years since she had left him to live alone in his medicine lodge, where he communicated with their ancestors. He no longer belonged to her; he belonged to all the people of their small tribe. Two Worlds and the people who followed him lived as their ancestors had always lived.

Reaching the lodge she hesitated, trying to slow down the pounding of her heart and the tightening in her chest. She didn't want the sadness that was about to overwhelm her to keep her from doing what she knew she must do. As she pulled back the skin that covered the opening, she let out the breath she had been holding and leaving the entrance open, she stepped inside. In the soft light of the moon and the glowing coals of the dying fire, she saw her husband sitting dressed only in his loin cloth, smoking from the long stem pipe. She knew he had not slept and wondered how long he had been back from the world of his ancestors.

As she fought to control her sadness, she took a robe, made from pelts of the small Florida red wolf, which hung from a lodge pole. Holding the robe that she and the other women in the tribe had so meticulously cured and sewn, she waited. In one smooth motion, Two Worlds rose to his feet. No one knew his real age; he had been here long before the others were born. The robe reached to his ankles as she draped it over his aged and slender shoulders. Two Worlds stood silently as she took the deer hide bag, in which she had placed the medicines to help him on his final journey. Reaching to where he had been sitting, she picked up the pipe and the bag of tobacco mixture. She added them to the medicine pouch and then placed it over his head to hang from his shoulder. Now she felt no pain in her old bones as she knelt down and lovingly placed Two Worlds' moccasins on his feet. Rising, she walked to his staff, which hung from leather strips, knowing he would need it on his long journey.

As he reached out to take the staff, which was wrapped with fur and feathers, his thin hand covered hers. Holding her hand, he spoke for the first time.

"I have had several wives in this lifetime and have lost sons to battles, but you have taken away the pain from their loss by giving me another son, who has the wisdom and courage to lead the people into the new world. Placing his hand to her aged cheek and looking into those eyes of wisdom and strength, he said, "You have all the things to give that any man could ever ask for. Do not feel sad for me; you have made my time here with you a time of pleasure."

Placing her hand over his, she was finally able to speak. "My sadness is not for you going to meet your ancestors; my sadness is for me and all of your people who will no longer have you in our lives."

She stood, looking into his knowing eyes, and cherished the feeling of the moment, for she knew it would be the last. As the moment passed and his hand slipped softly away from her face, she turned and picked up another bag that held dried food she hoped he would eat. However, she knew that he had probably eaten his last meal, and with a heavy heart, she placed the soft strap over his head to hang from his other shoulder.

Taking one last look around his lodge, he walked to where a roll of hides hung from a different lodge pole. Removing it, he placed the leather strap around his shoulder and stepped outside. Seeing the giant orange ball starting to slip behind the water of the lake, now done for the night, he started on his final journey to take his long awaited turn to be with his ancestors. Reaching the top of the slope, he turned and looked back into the valley that held the water of the lake. He took one last look at the lodges of his people and the wooden houses built under the shade of the huge water oaks. As he turned to continue his journey, he saw Woman of the Wind standing at the bottom of the slope near the water's edge, where she had followed him in silence. Lifting his staff and acknowledging her, he turned and disappeared.

Two

Two Worlds had been traveling for several hours. He was in no hurry as he observed the deer standing at the edge of the tree line, watching him as he slowly made his way toward his final resting place. They showed no fear as he passed within fifty feet of them, and he smiled to himself further on when the huge male panther appeared from behind a myrtle bush. The panther, matching his stride, reached over to touch his hand with his moist nose and sniff the robe he wore. Two Worlds smiled again as he gently laid his hand on the soft fur of the panther's huge head. He kept it there for several minutes until they entered a stand of red gum trees and came upon a small spring of cool bubbling water, where they stopped to rest. With the panther crouching beside him to lap the cool water, he knelt and scooped water into his hands. When he had quenched his thirst, he leaned back against the trunk of a large red gum tree. Watching the canopy of red and orange leaves fluttering in the gentle breeze, he sensed the advancing cold winds that would soon strip the leaves from the branches, leaving them bare. He knew it was the right time for this journey.

Two Worlds traveled slowly, often stopping to rest as his old body tired easily now. He had eaten nothing in the two days since he had left the valley and his people. He rested at the top of a ridge and looked out across the vast expanse of pickerel grass, dotted with small lakes. The lakes were fed by hundreds of small springs that bubbled up from the rivers beneath the earth where he stood. Memories flooded his mind as he again recognized the land where he had grown up as a young boy, following his grandfather. He was raised by his grandfather after his father and many others died from the disease brought by the white man. His grandfather had been a medicine man and counselor to the chief of a large tribe in the Creek Nation, before the white man had made war on his people. He had watched his people being killed or driven from their land, as more and more of the white men became greedy for the lush land that the springs and rivers had created over time.

Two Worlds stood for a long time, letting the memories flood his mind and take him back many moons, before he started down the slope to join his grandfather and his ancestors. A small smile creased the wrinkles of his aged skin as he savored his memories and made his way to the nearest lake, surrounded by a few water oaks. Under the shade they provided, he and his traveling companion drank the cool water and rested before taking on the last stretch of the day's journey. They were still crossing the open plains of lush grasses when darkness began to descend upon them.

As the darkness pushed the last of the sun behind the horizon, Two Worlds gathered small dead limbs and built his fire out in the open, so he could see his ancestors in the stars. He then took the drinking gourd from the leather pouch, where Woman of the Wind had placed the dried food. Two Worlds needed no food now; his only need was to reach the place where he would join his ancestors. Dipping the gourd in the clear cool, water of the creek that flowed from lake to lake, he drank until he had quenched his thirst. Leaving a bit of the water in the bottom of the gourd, he opened the leather pouch and removed a small, thin pouch, filled with dried powder. Shaking a little of the powder into the gourd, he took a twig and stirred until it had dissolved, and then in one quick motion, he poured the liquid into his mouth and swallowed.

The huge panther lay at the outer edge of the fire light and remained alert, listening to the chanting as his master spoke to their ancestors. The panther too had lived long past his time. The fire had died out by the time the panther rose and made his way to where Two Worlds slept, to lie next to him and rest.

Three

It was late afternoon the next day when Two Worlds and his silent companion reached the edge of a large forest. The panther silently accompanied Two Worlds as he entered the forest, following a faint trail that led deeper into the canopy of shade from the tall yellow pines. Dotted here and there were patches of red gum trees and large clumps of palmettos, in which the large diamond back rattlers loved to make their home. The forest was alive with birds; the blue jay's chattering, letting the forest know that there were strangers entering their home and red cardinals calling to their mates to stay close. Two Worlds heard a loud rat-a-tat-tat above him and looked up to see the largest of the wood peckers, opening holes in the dead standing trees and looking for a meal of grub worms. Slowly, he moved deeper into the woods where it was shaded from the sun and felt the difference in the coolness of the air. Darkness came earlier in the thick woods and he knew he would not reach the end of his journey today. Two Worlds kept moving in search of a place he was very familiar with, and he knew that he was close when he stopped for the night and built a small fire.

The sunrise was just beginning to light up the forest as the sleek brown cat watched the old man rise slowly to his feet. Two Worlds knew his strength was weakening, although his stride seemed to quicken as they drew closer to their destination. He knew that they were almost there now as the familiar scene began to unfold around him. Two Worlds and his companion stopped at the edge of a huge, ancient sink hole. The hole was a quarter of a mile across, over sixty feet to the bottom and held the history of his past. Two Worlds had first been brought here by his grandfather, long ago when he was a young boy.

When they arrived, Two Worlds found the peace he had been seeking all his life, now flowing through him and giving him new strength. Leaning against his staff, he started down the barely visible path, the panther following silently behind him, listening to the soft chanting as Two Worlds spoke to his ancestors. Reaching the bottom, he stopped next to a small bubbling spring, which was no more than two feet across and surrounded with lush green grass. In his mind's eye, he could see new born fawns safely feeding on the grass. The huge cat leaned forward next to the old man and together, they drank for the last time from the cool pure water of the spring.

The sun had not yet passed overhead, when Two Worlds pulled back the branches of the oak tree that hid the opening to the cave. Stepping inside and feeling the cool air, he stopped and waited on the big cat to join him. Memories and emotions flooded him as he walked into the huge cathedral that was at least twenty feet high and forty feet across. There were several smaller cave openings, some tall enough to walk in standing up and some only big enough to crawl in. Taking his time, he stopped at each opening and looked at the skeletons of his ancestors, lying on dirt shelves. On the ground next to them, were the bones of their panther companions. Moving slowly, he finally came to the one where he recognized the spear and war the shield of his grandfather.

The robe and the hide pouches had mostly disappeared. Walking across the cave, he looked down on the shelf that had been carved into the wall years earlier, waiting for him. Observing his final resting place, he knew he wasn't ready yet. He had one more thing he had to finish. Two Worlds gathered small dry sticks of wood, placing a few on top of his fire starter and lit a small fire within a circle of rocks. Sitting with his legs crossed, he sat the bundle of fur across his lap. He had kept the bundle with him ever since his grandfather had died and left it in his care. Untying the leather straps, he unwrapped the soft fur covering that held the smooth ancient skin, which showed the drawings that told the history of his people. He ran his fingers gently across the figures, remembering the stories told by his grandfather, until he came to where the stories ended. Now he would add the history of his time along with the remaining tribe. He hoped that one day his son would pass on more stories of his people.

Two Worlds reached for the hand stitched bag, in which Woman of the Wind had placed his pipe and tobacco. Thoughtfully, he filled the bowl of the pipe with the tobacco mixture, then picked a small twig from the fire and with its flame, lit the pipe. He inhaled several puffs before he laid it beside him. Reaching back inside the skin, he took two small gourds of dye that Woman of the Wind and their son's wife, Waiting Owl, had made from the wild berries and lichen that grew on the bark of trees. Removing the stoppers, he set them on the ground in front of him. Looking in the open bag, he removed two five inch pieces of palmetto stems that had been cut and made into sharp pointed sticks, to use when adding his story to the ancient skin. Feeling the effects of the pipe smoke, he thought about where to start as he added a few more sticks to the fire. As his mind soared back into the past, he decided he would start with the vision that had brought them into the white man's world. Picking a palmetto stem and dipping it into one of the bowls of dye, he began to bring their story up to date.

The Vision

In an ancient hidden cave, steam rose up as the old medicine man trickled water over the hot rocks in the fire pit. A tattered deerskin covered the small obscure entrance, creating total darkness in the cave that was little more than a small alcove. Calling on the wisdom of his ancestors to guide him, Two Worlds had fasted for three days awaiting the vision. As he began to soar free of the steam filled cave, he saw the small band of people as they journeyed across the land, reaching the edge of the great waters that had no end. There, they built a village. He saw the stranger walking among them until the great winds of destruction came from the endless waters, scattering the village and people across the land.

Listening to the wails and cries of the survivors, the old man's body sat motionless as his spirit followed the people across the land. Circling, he watched as the stranger brought the survivors together, preparing them for the long journey to a new world. The survivors built great fires to carry the spirits of their dead loved ones to their ancestors. He watched his people carrying their burdens of grief as they followed the stranger across many rivers to a land of valleys and lakes. Here, among new people, they started new lives far beyond their understanding.

The Indian Story

Two Worlds led his people through the glades into the Ten Thousand Islands, always looking for the place from which the vision would begin. They had been traveling for more than three weeks. The travois, pulled by the horses they still had with them, were loaded with their meager belongings. Red Sun, Eagle Hunter, and Silent Stalker were scouting far ahead of the people, vigilantly searching for signs of slave hunters and roving Seminoles. The Seminoles were hostile toward the Creeks because they would not join them and fight their war with the white soldiers. There were only twenty Creek men, women, and children who had chosen to follow Two Worlds and his vision.

It was late afternoon, and the sun's rays reflected off the choppy waves of the Gulf of Mexico. The sun began its decent into the western sky as Two Worlds passed beneath several large gumbo limbo trees, growing along the edge of the spring fed stream. The stream flowed into a one hundred foot wide inlet with long stretches of beach on either side of its mouth. Small islands, surrounded with oyster bars, dotted this shoreline of the Gulf. Good, he thought to himself, this is the place I saw in my vision. He turned and gave thanks to the four winds.

The people began to unpack the animals and set aside the tools needed to begin the building of their new village. The next morning, they started clearing the area where the lodge of their medicine man, Two Worlds, would be built, circled by the other lodges. Two Worlds instructed Red Sun to take Four Bears and Silent Stalker and scout the surrounding country. They would be gone three or four days, to make sure there was no danger from whites farming in the area and to look for game for the village. The people would now wait for Two Worlds' vision to begin

Part Two
The War

Photo by Michael Calhoun Tucker

Four

It was late August. Heat shimmered from the short, brown grass that covered the Everglades, and it looked as if it would explode into flames any second. Only the thousands of cabbage palms that dotted the open plains could survive the heat. The diamondback rattlesnakes, who normally basked in the heat, had found shelter under blown down tree trunks or were sharing holes with gopher tortoises. The tortoises had dug their holes deeper than normal, trying to find some coolness in the depths of the earth. The panthers and bobcats sought what relief they could find, lying under trees or in the top branches, which were laced together to form a shaded shelter inside the long narrow hardwood and cypress hammocks. Some hammocks were more than two miles long and a mile wide, running north and south, parallel with the water flow that worked its way slowly to the Gulf of Mexico.

Small Florida deer had abandoned all feeding for the day and lay camouflaged in the palmetto thickets, not daring to go into the strands where they would be too tempting a meal for the panthers. A lone red wing hawk sat on a limb, feasting on a young rabbit that had been foolish enough to try crossing from one palmetto thicket to another. The only things moving were several buzzards slowly circling at 2000 feet, anticipating the smell of their next meal to be brought up on the rising wind current. All kept watch for thunder heads that built up every day late in the afternoon, bringing hope of rain that would bring only temporary relief from the heat. Hot air battled the cool air moving inland off the ocean. Most of the time the cool air was turned back after moving no more than three miles inland from the gulf.

Jessie Tucker sat on his horse within the thick oak strand, miles inside the Everglades, watching the black clouds that were moving in from the coast. Seeing the clouds build up, he waited for the lightning show that would surely come. Sitting quietly on his horse, he saw the small group of Union soldiers, who were trying to find some relief from the sun. They stayed in the shadow of the tall oak trees that made up the mile wide strand as they led a string of mules, loaded with supplies coming from the east coast. The Union Army was loading supplies brought by ship, to be carried through the Everglades to the west coast for their soldiers. The soldiers were moving down from Georgia, slowly taking over Florida as they traveled south.

Jessie's shirt clung to his back, and sweat trickled down his temples as he leaned forward and patted the neck of his horse, whispering quietly in his ear to keep him quiet. The soldiers were no more than 100 yards from his position, and even though they were quite noisy with occasional braying from one of the mules, the soldiers were jumpy and nervous, and Jessie didn't want to be seen. He watched the soldiers swatting mosquitoes; their shirts were soaked with sweat. Hell's country, they must have thought, where it never got cold enough to kill the mosquitoes. The heat was unbearable to the northern soldiers, and snakes were everywhere, waiting for someone to take a wrong step.

Jessie saw his horse's ears turn back as he felt the skin quiver under his hand on the Marsh Tackie's neck. It was a short, stout animal that was perfect for the thick wooded Everglades. The army had bought these rough little horses from the Indians. Jessie trusted his horse; it was like a watch dog, always letting Jessie know when something was near, even before Jessie could hear or see anything. Several times since they had taken up company, it had warned him of danger in heavy thickets that had turned out to be a bear or some wild hogs, either of which could be deadly in heavy brush. He leaned down and patted the horse on the neck to calm it. The horse didn't normally stay nervous once Jessie let it know that he understood and recognized the warning. However, this time it kept quivering and flicking its ears.

"Easy boy, I see them," he whispered in its ear, "just be still and we'll be ok."

Jessie sat quietly, taking off his hat and wiping his brow; his blue eyes missing nothing. He thought about how he had gotten here while he waited until the last Yankee soldier passed. Then turning his horse, he started to slowly ease out of the back side of the oaks. He headed for the small mobile camp, hidden in a cypress strand no more than two miles away where he had to meet up with his small band of twenty soldiers. A few of them were professional soldiers, but most of the men were like him, countrymen and farmers, men new to soldiering. They were volunteers for the Confederate Army and helped to stop the supply lines flowing in from the east coast to feed the Union Army. They will be nervous and restless he thought as he was their best scout and had been gone too long. As he traveled the edge of the cypress strand again, he thought about how they all had gotten into this mess.

Jessie Tucker had volunteered five months before, along with John Campbell, Dave Kersey, and Bill Walsh. All of them were pushed down out of Georgia where their farms had been taken over to grow food for the languishing Confederate Army. By this time the war was going badly, and the Southern Army had barely enough food and clothing to give the soldiers who were fighting Sherman. Sherman was burning his way across Georgia and the men wanted out. Tucker, Walsh, Kersey, Campbell, and several other small farmers were from around Blackshear, Georgia, a town about eighty miles south of Atlanta. The town was in Sherman's path and in a panic, in fear that Sherman was bringing his hellfire and destruction their way.

The farmers gathered at the farmers market outside of Blackshear, on a long, flat platform alongside the railroad tracks, where they used to sell their produce to shipping companies. Several of the farmers wanted to leave and go south to the central part of Florida. It offered isolation, no farms, no industry, and no slaves. The plantation owners talked about loyalty and keeping their way of life, trying to convince everyone to stay and fight. Jessie and the other small farmers owned no slaves and wanted nothing to do with the war. Their loyalty lay with their families' safety; protection from what the war was bringing. After the meeting; Jessie, along with John, Dave, and Bill, squatted in the shade of a large pine tree at the end of the long platform, discussing their options.

Jessie spoke first. "My father gave up the small piece of land he sharecropped on in Tennessee, brought our family here and homesteaded the piece of land we have been farming since I was ten years old. Both parents and a sister are buried here and the last thing I want to do is give up my farm, but I will not put my family in danger out of stubbornness. My thought right now is to gather my equipment and move my family south into Florida and find new land where they will be safe." Jessie looked around at the other men and waited to hear what they had to say.

John took a long, deep breath and letting it out slowly, spoke with anguish in his voice. "My family has been here for two generations, logging and cutting trees into lumber, but I agree with Jessie. I will not put my family in harm's way. Jessie, if it is your decision to leave, I will sit down with my family and talk this over with them. My gut feeling tells me life is about to change as we know it. I will get back to you in a couple of days."

Dave Kersey stood and walked in a circle as the others waited for him to make his decision. Stopping and turning to face the others, he said, "There are only Martha and me since we can't have children, but the years we have spent here were only possible because of the help we have gotten from our friends. I don't know what is going to happen here in the future, but I think both of you are right." Looking at both Jessie and John he said, "Martha and I will be ready to go when you are." He turned and with his shoulders bent from the burden of his decision, he walked to his wagon without waiting to hear any more.

Jessie watched the anguish wash over Bill Walsh as he came to the same conclusion as the others. Bill spoke slowly, knowing that what he was going to say would change the lives of his wife and their two girls and put them into a situation over which he had no control. The thought made his stomach knot up in fear. He looked from Jessie to John and gave a slight nod of his head. "I will be ready within a few days. I have to go home and talk with my family now." He stood up to leave.

"I will see you in a couple of days," John said to Jessie as they followed Bill to their wagons.

Five

Belle had put Horace and Jenny to bed and was drying the last of the dishes when Jessie and Ed came in from the barn.

"Sit down and I will pour you both a cup of coffee," Belle said, as they came through the door. Setting three cups on the table, she folded the dish cloth, lifted the coffee pot from the stove and filled the cups. Settling in her chair, she looked at Jessie. "I have watched you ever since you came home from town today, walk around drawn up and heavy footed like you were carrying the world around on your shoulders. Whatever happened in town today must have been pretty bad if you can't talk about it. But if it involves the rest of this family, I think you should talk to us about whatever happened."

Jessie took a slow sip from his coffee cup and looking into Belle's and Ed's eyes, he set the cup down and laid his burden on the table as he explained what he and the other families had decided. Finishing the story, he looked into Ed's eyes and saw the fear and uncertainty and knew there would be a lot of questions arising from his childrens' fears. Looking at their faces as he described the situation and his decision, he thought about when his father had done the same thing, leaving Tennessee for Georgia and how bad he had felt. Looking into Belle's eyes, he knew that the weight of all that was going to happen would not be his to bear alone. He would never love her more than he did at that moment. The lonely chain of responsibility fell away from Jessie as they sat drinking their coffee and discussing what was to happen next. It was the right thing to do, but Jessie hated leaving his home and knew everyone felt the same way.

Belle, heartbroken at the thought of leaving her home, never hesitated but started making a list of the things she could pack in their two wagons. No one would ever see the tears she would shed in the middle of the night; nights when she would slip out of bed and walk through each room, tears sliding silently down her cheeks. Remembering the joys and pains of childbirth, she thought about her three children, brought into the world in this very house.

The fireplace, with a thick slab of hickory for the mantle, held all the treasures she and the children had gathered and cherished. Small arrowheads, a lucky leg bone from a rabbit, a kerosene lantern to light the room and in the center, a picture of her and Jessie at their wedding. She removed the picture, walked to the window and held it up to the moonlight. Their faces were illuminated, and Belle thought she saw Jessie's eyes twinkle in the picture like they did in real life. Her heart grew stronger; it didn't matter where they lived as long as she had Jessie by her side. Smiling, she slowly brought the picture to her lips and kissed his image. Holding the picture to her heart and moving silently across the room, she placed the picture back; the tears were gone. Jessie was right and she knew it; they would move to Florida and start again.

Jessie and the other families spent the next week putting together what each one could carry to start a new life, hopefully without this war. Jessie sold all the equipment he could not carry, along with the farm for twenty cents on the dollar, to his neighbor Dan Sutton, who owned the plantation joining his property. Dan thought he was foolish to leave because the war would end before it got to them. Jessie thought Dan Sutton was a fool, to think the war wasn't coming to them and took what money he could get.

John Campbell, Bill Walsh, and Dave Kersey stood under the tall gum trees, little more than a mile south of Blackshear, waiting as Jessie and his family caught up with them. Jessie felt the silent uncertainty from the families as he took the lead and started south, following what roads they could find as long as they continued south.

They had been traveling for more than a month, slowly working their way south and finding ferries to cross the larger rivers. They were not sure how far they had traveled into Florida when they came to a small settlement called Brooksville. It was late afternoon when they pulled their wagons up under the live oaks next to a small spring lake at the edge of town. The four families set up a camp big enough to stay a while until they could find out where they were and where they wanted to go next.

Ed, Jessie's son and Frank, John's oldest boy, had taken the smaller boys to gather firewood for the cooking fires and the coming night. The women discussed what food to cook and what supplies they were going to need if the settlement had anything left. The families had found little food in other small settlements because everything was going to fight the war. They had lived mostly on wild hogs, deer meat and turkey that they hunted as they traveled.

The men sat together around the small fire while the women were washing the dishes and watching the kids play along the water's edge. After the supper of wild hog, poke salad they had made after finding the weed growing around the lake, and cornbread cooked from their short supply, they saw a wagon with a horse and rider on each side approaching from the road leading to town. The men stood up as the wagon came to a halt.

The large man sitting on the wagon seat and driving the buckboard said, "I am Charles Whitman, the mayor of this settlement, and this is Captain McKay," he said, nodding to his left. Looking to his right he continued, introducing the third man. "This is Captain Albritton of the home guard squad. Did you men come to join the fight?"

"I didn't know the fighting was going on this far south," Jessie spoke up. "That's why we left our farms in Georgia and came south."

"There has been fighting going on along the coast for the last year and a half," Captain Albritton replied. "We can barely get supply boats through the Yankee barricades. We could surely use you men here to protect our home front."

"Are any of you cowmen?" McKay asked.

"No, we are farmers," Bill Walsh said, "except John here, and he's a lumberman and none of us know about cows."

"We are headed away from this war," John said. "We stopped to find out where we are and see about some supplies before we move on."

"Well, we are going to need farmers and lumbermen when this war is over," Whitman spoke up. "You'll find no supplies here. We can barely feed the people we have left." Looking around at the women coming up from the lake and seeing the wagons loaded with equipment, he added, "I wish you luck."

McKay rode his horse closer to the men. "If I wanted to keep my family safe and out of this war, I would head more east and south. The closer you stay to the Gulf of Mexico, the more fighting you are going to run into. There is a settlement about 40 or 50 miles East of here called Fort Dade. Between here and there you will find good farm land and lots of timber. If you go past Fort Dade, you will start getting into Indian Territory where they are having trouble with the Seminoles. After you settle your families in, we could use your help. All of you are wrong if you think you can stay out of this war. Sooner or later you're going to have to fight to stay here."

Facing Captain McKay, Jessie said, "When we get our families settled and if the war keeps coming this way, then I'll be back to fight; we have nowhere else to go."

One by one each of the other men spoke up, "So will I!"

As she watched the wagon and riders leaving, Belle walked up to Jessie and took his arm. "What was that all about; can we get some supplies here?" Speaking where all the wives could hear, Jessie answered the questions all of them waited to hear.

"The war has already reached here and there are no supplies to be had." Looking at the other men he said, "I think we had better move on tomorrow before we get caught up in the fighting going on here." He watched the other men as they all nodded their heads in agreement.

They left Brooksville the next morning and headed east and south for more than a week until they reached open country with lakes and valleys. John sat next to Myra on the wagon seat, looking at the strand of pine forest, with a twenty foot wide creek that flowed along its edge. The other wagons had come to a halt, and everyone watched John step down from his wagon and with his oldest boy Frank, walk along the bank of the creek talking and pointing. They all knew when Frank helped Myra down from the wagon that John had found his new homestead and a place to set up his saw mill. John smiled and walked over where the others were waiting, sitting on their wagons.

"I don't think I'm going to find a better place for what we are going to need. There is plenty of water for my steam engine to run my saw and enough timber here to keep this mill in business for years to come."

Looking out across the rolling hills, Dave said, "With this rich soil, I won't be far away."

The others followed the spring fed creek further south for another half mile past the pine forest, into a valley of knee high grass land. Dave Kersey pulled his wagon under a small stand of live oak where he and his wife Bonnie would build their new home and farm the rich soil of the bottom land. The three men stood under the shade of the oak branches.

"There is enough bottom land here for all of us to farm; there is plenty of water and the soil here is rich," Dave said as he reached and picked up a handful of black dirt.

"He's right," Bill agreed, pointing in the distance. "I am going further down the creek to that stand of red gum trees."

Standing under the shade discussing their future, Dave and Bill watched as Jessie turned his two wagons and headed east, away from the southbound stream. Not wanting to move too far from the others, he traveled no more than a mile further, when he came to another valley and stopped. Looking down from the ridge, he and his family sat on their wagons staring in awe at the two hundred acre lake, surrounded by several oak stands and cypress.

"Oh Jessie, I have never seen a place so beautiful; can we stop here?"

Jessie felt the burden of doubt he had brought all the way from Georgia lifted from his shoulders as he listened to Belle's words.

"Where would you like for me to build your new home?" Jessie's heart was racing as he looked at the smile on her face.

"There!" she said, pointing to a stand of huge water oaks, large enough to build their house under, a hundred yards from the water's edge.

For the next three months, all the men worked together getting John's saw mill ready. After cutting enough timber for John, Frank and Ed started sawing trees into lumber for houses. The other men continued to cut the tall straight slash pine trees while Jessie's youngest son, Horace and John's younger boys used the two oxen and two sets of John's mules to pull the logs to the mill. Each evening the cut lumber would be loaded onto the wagons until there was enough to build each of them a house.

Jessie and Ed were putting the last poles together to keep the milk cow and the oxen secure at night, when they saw a rider coming toward them from the ridge above the lake. As the rider came closer, Jessie saw that he was one of the men they had met in Brooksville.

"You're Jessie Tucker?"

"Yes I am, and you're Captain McKay if I remember right."

McKay stepped down from his horse and shook Jessie's hand, then turning to Ed, he held out his hand saying, "You're Ed"?

"Yes I am," Ed said, proud to be recognized as he shook McKay's hand.

Looking around, McKay spoke to Jessie. "You and the others have found a fine place to farm, but you may not have it long if we can't stop those Yankees from taking over Florida."

"You have talked to the others?" Jessie asked. As he spoke, he realized that McKay must have talked to the others because he didn't remember giving him their names.

"Yes I have. Actually, I am here on official business. You are officially recruited into the army. You and the other men have one week to prepare, and then you are to be in Brooksville. If you don't show up Mr. Tucker, you will be listed as a deserter."

"I knew this day was coming, but I was hoping I had more time."

"There is no more time," McKay said, as he mounted his horse. "If we don't stop them now, this war will be lost within a year."

Ed and Jessie watched until the captain was out of sight and without a word spoken, they both started toward the house where they saw Belle waiting.

Six

As Jessie, Bill, Dave, and John reached Brooksville, they rode into what looked like the center of town and stopped a man walking with a bad limp, leaning on a crutch. "Where can we find Captain McKay?" Jessie asked.

"Captain McKay is out with his cowmen, rounding up scrub cows to feed a starving army. If you're looking for the army office, it's just down the street on the right at the end of the next block, the second door from the end."

"Thanks," Bill said as they started on down the street.

Stepping into the dimly lit room, they paused a few seconds to let their eyes adjust. Jessie saw Captain Albritton sitting at a desk talking to a soldier. Walking across the room, he and the others stood behind the soldier until he had finished talking. Dismissing the soldier, the captain looked up and recognizing the four men, he stood and came around his desk to shake hands.

"I am glad to see you men; the others are already here."

"OK, listen up everyone." Sergeant Hannah spoke to the eleven men sitting on their horses, waiting to find out where they were headed. "My name is Sergeant Hannah. I have been sent here to bring as many men as possible back to Fort Myers where you will be part of the 2nd Cavalry Company B. We have to stop the supplies that the Union Army is sending from the east coast through the Everglades. If we can't stop them, we will lose this coast too, and if that happens, the war is lost." Sergeant Hannah turned his horse and headed south. Their nightmare was about to begin.

It had been five months since Jessie had ridden to Fort Myers to join the Confederate's fight. He and the other men had been given rifles and ammunition and little else. They had endured five months of fighting swamps, heat, bugs, and the Union supply lines. Their leader, Sergeant Hannah, was a local man who had been raised in the small trading post of Miami, on the east coast. The swamp was his back yard. Jessie knew they were lucky to have the sergeant to lead them in the Everglades.

Only once in the five months of fighting, did Jessie and his friends get a chance to return home and see their families. A storm had passed over and flooded the area, leaving four inches of rainwater. The men had nothing to do, and Hannah sent them home until the waters receded. It had taken four long days of riding to get home; Jessie was exhausted. Stopping his horse as he came to the edge of the valley, he looked down across the lake and saw his two small ones playing out by the barn. Their older brother was repairing a wooden fence rail, where they kept oxen and the cow at night. Looking out over his homestead, his heart swelled with pride. He knew that they had made the right decision to fight and protect their new life. Suddenly his exhaustion was gone. Watching his children playing by the barn, Jessie rode his horse around to the front of the house and tied it up. He wanted to surprise his Belle.

Belle heard the sounds of horse's hooves and looked out her kitchen window. Seeing her husband dismounting his horse, her heart leaped into her throat. He was standing in the doorway before she could straighten her hair.

"Jessie," she sobbed, "I thought I would never see you again." Grabbing Belle around the waist Jessie kissed her hard, letting her know just how much he had missed her. Knowing the children would be occupied outside and wanting to make up for the months apart, Jessie untied Belle's apron strings as she led him to the bedroom. As they closed the door, Jessie knew he was home at last.

Two weeks flew by as Jessie, Belle, and the children worked the farm and enjoyed just being together. Belle's joy lasted until the night she felt Jessie tossing and turning every ten minutes. She got up, started a fire in the stove and put coffee on. Jessie savored the aroma wafting through the bedroom, and he felt relieved that the night was over but also dreaded what he had to tell his family today. He felt almost as bad now as when he told his family that they had to leave Georgia. Belle was already sitting at the table sipping her cup of coffee; his cup sat opposite her. She watched him sit down as if he had lead in his pants and saw the look on his face that said I don't want to tell you this.

Before he could speak, Belle said, "Did you think that I didn't know this day was coming? I have tried to put the thought of this day as far away as possible, but after watching you toss and turn all night like the devil was after you, I know that day is here. I would beg you to stay if I thought it would stop you from going back, but I know it won't. We can tell the children tonight at supper. Let's try to enjoy every minute of today. Stop worrying now, I will make sure you sleep better tonight," she said smiling, with promise in her voice.

"I love you Belle Tucker." Jessie reached across the table for her hand. "I will speak to Ed later."

Jessie felt terrible that day. He had explained to Ed about having to go back to his outfit as they finished fixing a piece of equipment in the barn. "Edward," Jessie said with a choked voice, "you have taken on the burden of a grown man, I am so proud of you. I know it is hard, but take care of you mother, brother, and sister just like you have been doing. I will be home soon as I can."

"Pa," Ed said proudly, "I am a man now; you go do what you have to do, and I'll take care of things here." Jessie looked at his son and realized how much it was like looking into a mirror. Edward, at 6'1", stood even with him and looked out with the same crystal blue Scots-Irish eyes. Not knowing what else to say, Jessie stepped forward and hugged his son.

"Pa, I'm not a kid anymore; you can't be hugging me like that." He was secretly pleased at the affection from his pa, but it didn't seem right. He looked awkwardly at his father as Jessie turned and walked away. Edward's vision blurred as he followed.

The day had come. Jessie stood with both hands on Horace's sholders. Looking down, he saw the fear and uncertainty in his son's eyes as he spoke to him. "Your ma is going to need your help keeping firewood for the stove and water in the bucket, and Ed will need help from you to take the cows and horses to the lake to feed every day."

"I will Pa, I promise!" Horace answered back.

Kneeling down, taking Jenny into his arms, he saw the tears well up in her eyes.

"I don't want you to go, Pa," she said in that tiny voice about to crack.

Struggling to control his voice as he hugged her close, Jessie told her, "I will be back as soon as I can, but until I get back, your ma will need your help too, OK?"

"OK," Jenny said stepping back as the tear she could no longer hold back slid down her cheek.

Standing, he turned to Ed and watched the mixed emotions in his son's eyes as he held out his hand. Jessie smiled to himself as he watched Ed draw himself to his full height as he reached for his father's hand.

Belle stood waiting in front of their cabin, holding a cloth bag full of smoked wild hog and fresh biscuits for the trip. There would be no more tears shed in front of Jessie. She had cried herself to sleep last night in his arms, knowing he was doing what he thought was right; she wouldn't make him feel any worse. Jessie mounted his horse, placing the sack of food on the saddle horn as Belle handed up his saddle bags. Their hands held on to each other for a few long seconds, their eyes meeting. Jessie turned his horse and rode away. He didn't look back; he knew that if he did, the look in Belle's eyes might just make him stay.

Seven

This was the second tortuous trip for Lieutenant Knowles, moving supplies for the Union Army from the east coast through the Everglades to the west coast. He knew he was over qualified as a soldier, not meant to be here in this God forsaken country in the middle of nowhere, the heat so unbearably hot that his shirt glued to his body as if someone had poured water over him. Turning in his saddle to look back at his troops, he could see their fear; eyes shifting from side to side, faces intense, swatting at flies and mosquitoes, bugs that tormented them day and night. He looked ahead at his two Seminole guides, who also looked nervously from side to side, watching for the third scout who was due back. Where is he? Knowles wondered; he was getting a bit nervous himself. The scout should have been back by now. The Lieutenant knew they had every right to be nervous, having been attacked several times in the last few months by Rebel raiding parties. The Rebels were a small band made up of fifteen to twenty soldiers that could strike, kill and disappear back into the Everglades like panthers on the hunt.

A loud shot rang out from the oak strand. Long Bird, the missing Seminole Indian scout, let out a war cry that stopped the Lieutenant in his tracks. The soldiers sprang off their skittish horses and pulled them into the brush, waiting for the ambush fire that never came. Bravely, Lieutenant Knowles pulled his revolver from the holster, mounted his horse and rode into the oak strand where the war cry seemed to come from. A fallen Confederate soldier's scalp was cut most of the way across his forehead, before the lieutenant recognized his third scout, Long Bird.

"Stop right now!"

Long Bird looked up defiantly and said, "This scalp is mine, I killed him."

"You will not scalp a white man while under my command," the Lieutenant said, staring down at the scout. "You need to back track this soldier and find out where the rest of his group is. Do your job!"

The Indian rose from his grisly task and glared back at Knowles. Turning, he set off on foot into the brush and disappeared. Knowles hated dealing with these savages, but he must. They had saved the army time and lives in the past. No one knew these woods like the Indians.

As the Sergeant rode up with the other two scouts, he looked at the man on the ground and said, "Lieutenant, you should have let him have his scalp. The man is already dead and that's the main reason they work for us, scalps and the liquor." The lieutenant, an educated man from Ohio, hated the thought of scalping, especially white people; why the very thought of it made his skin crawl. "Do you want this man buried?" inquired the Sergeant. "I can get a couple of men to do it."

The Lieutenant took one more look at the dead man and said, "We don't have time for that Sergeant. It will be dark before we get through that swamp in front of us, and I don't want to get ambushed by the rest of his patrol. They could have heard that shot." He whirled his horse to head back to his troops who were still hiding in the bush. "Bring that man's horse and get the troops moving Sarge, and tell those scouts to keep a close lookout. I don't want to end up like that man back there."

As the Sergeant followed behind, he spoke to the two remaining scouts, "Don't think I don't know that devil is going to be back for his scalp; just don't let on to the Lieutenant. He is right squeamish."

Long Bird had only back tracked the soldier a half mile, before trotting back into the oak strand to claim his prize. The soldier was stupid; he did not understand that the scalp of his enemy showed his cunning and courage. He had other scalps hanging in his lodge from Creeks he had killed, they showed his bravery, but this scalp of the white man with its red color hair would show his cunning. Long Bird knelt over the body and once again grabbed the red hair of the white man, and as his knife flashed, an arrow went through his throat cutting his windpipe. Before he could react, two more arrows pierced his back into his lungs. He fell across the body and before he died, he heard the almost silent footsteps behind him. He knew then that he had not been so cunning.

Eight

Red Sun, Big Cypress, and Silent Stalker were returning from a trip east into the edge of the Everglades. They had been visiting what was left of their small tribe of Creeks. These Creeks had stayed behind when Red Sun and their band had moved west, far away from the warring tribes of Miccosukee and Seminoles, to follow Two Worlds and his vision. Red Sun had made several trips east and each time had been saddened by the continued losses of their braves. The urging of the Creek tribe members to fight the white man with them fell on deaf ears; Red Sun knew Two Worlds was right.

The three men hid in the outer edge of the oak strand, silently watching the white man. His hat was pulled down low over his eyes, covering his long hair, the color of the setting sun. Red Sun didn't know much about the white race and had never seen hair like this; was it magic? They saw the man stop his horse and stand up in the saddle, to look out through the end of the strand. The man looked up as he heard the screech and watched the osprey circling above. The three braves watched and waited in silence until the soldier turned and started out of the hammock. Red Sun also heard the noise of the other soldiers, but they were used to waiting for danger to pass by, so they patiently watched and waited.

Red Sun, feeling a nudge on his shoulder, turned to follow Silent Stalker's gaze. He noticed the Seminole, hiding between the oak trees until the white soldier was within fifty feet. The Seminole aimed his musket and fired. The white man never knew what happened to him.

The musket ball caught him on the side of the head, knocking him from his horse. Yelling his war cry, the Seminole Indian ran through the woods, jumping on the white man. His knife flashed across the man's forehead, red hair in hand, when suddenly a soldier rode into the oak strand, his pistol drawn and yelling something they couldn't hear. Grudgingly, the Seminole stopped scalping and listened to the white soldier. Wiping his knife and glaring at the mounted soldier, the scout turned and faded into the brush. The Creek Indians watched until the soldiers and the two Semimole guides left, leaving the partially scalped white man for the animals to eat.

After the last soldier was at a safe distance, Big Cypress whispered to Red Sun, "We should leave."

"Silent," Red Sun whispered. "The white man with hair of the setting sun might still be alive."

He waited to see what happened next; the spirits would show him the right way. They had waited only a short time before Long Bird came back into the oak strand to claim his prize. As he walked over and knelt down to finish scalping the man, a screech was heard. Looking up into the sky, they saw a lone osprey circle the oak strand, dipping up and down with the air current. Red Sun caught his breath; he knew the osprey was the spirit sign of his father, Two Worlds. Red Sun released his arrow first, the others followed with their arrows. Big Cypress and Silent Stalker did not know why they were protecting the red haired white man, but their leader Red Sun seemed to know, and they trusted his wisdom.

Walking to where the soldier lay, Big Cypress rolled Long Bird from the body and began to pull the arrows from the Seminole scout. Silent Stalker pulled his knife and grabbed the hair of Long Bird. Before he went any further, the tone in Red Sun's voice let him know that he was on the verge of making a grave mistake.

Red Sun asked with a face of stone, "Who will you say killed him? Remember, our people have never believed we need the scalps of other men to show our bravery." Silent Stalker knew the truth of the words that Red Sun spoke and felt ashamed.

All three heads turned when they heard a soft moan coming from the soldier. As another moan came from the injured man, Red Sun knelt and put his ear to the man's chest and felt the weak beating of his heart. "He is not dead; we must move him to water, if we are to keep life in him." Red Sun did not know why, but he felt that this was part of why Two Worlds had led them to their new village.

No one questioned Red Sun's decision. They cut two saplings about 8 feet long, then bound shorter pieces of wood across the long pieces to form a travois. They then lifted the man and placed him on the travois. Red Sun lifted one end of the sapling at the man's head and Big Cypress the end at his feet, raising it until the travois rested with the poles on their shoulders. Silent Stalker removed the knife from Long Bird's hand, picked up the rifle and followed.

Nine

Jessie opened his eyes and saw the old Indian looking down at him with his wise, ancient eyes. For a moment he thought he recognized the eyes from somewhere in time. Sensing he had seen them before in the same ancient face, he drifted into darkness, feeling only confusion. He heard chanting and felt heat as he opened his eyes, this time to total darkness. Sweat ran down his forehead and stung his eyes. He felt as if his body floated in space somewhere in hell, and he moved his hand to see if he could feel his body. A tremor ran through him, and he floated back down to that same distant space. The chanting seemed far off, but it kept pulling him back into the heat and darkness.

A cool trickle of water spread across his forehead and washed the stinging from his eyes. He heard the voice telling him he was alive. As he listened to the voice, the pain in his head drove him once again into confusion and darkness. The chanting drifted farther off and then faded.

The deerskin door of the medicine lodge opened and a sharp beam of light crossed the body of Jessie Tucker. Red Sun entered and quickly let the skin close over the entrance. As he felt his way along the wall across from where he had seen his grandfather sitting next to the pale body, he sat down and began to adjust to the heat.

"Grandfather, will the white man live?"

Two Worlds' words came slowly. "Yes, my son, he will live because he is important to our future."

Red Sun asked with surprise in his voice, "How can a white man be of any importance to our future? White men are the reason we are no longer a nation and live here in the Everglades, in slowly disappearing, small bands." Red Sun listened to the hiss of the steam as the old man poured more water on the hot rocks. He waited for Two Worlds to explain what he meant. As he waited, he felt the steam surround his body, the freely pouring sweat cleansing body and mind. He began to see the image of his grandfather in his mind, when he heard the words come slowly through the darkness.

"He is the beginning of the vision." After waiting awhile without further talk, Red Sun knew he would get no more answers, and so gave himself to the heat and released his spirit to soar.

Jessie heard the sound of voices, but could not understand what was being said. Slowly he opened his eyes to dim light and the inside of a room, filled with strange smells. He wondered again if he was alive or had passed on into another world. As he slowly turned his head, the dull ache started again. Lying there, he tried to remember what had happened. He had no recollection of anything, except the face and eyes of an old Indian somewhere in the past. The face of a young girl startled him as she looked down from above and smiled.

"Grandfather said you would wake up soon, and I am to go let him know when you do."

Jessie spoke in a pained voice. "Wait, am I on earth, or is this another world?"

She smiled again and said, "You ask funny questions. You are at my Grandfather, Two Worlds', village, and I must go now."

Waiting for answers, he slowly raised his hand and touched his forehead, feeling the bandage with his fingers. This was very painful, and again he wondered where he was and how he got here.

Two Worlds returned, his powerful presence drawing Jessie out of his dream state. "The wound will heal, but it will take time and then you can return to your own world," the old man said as if reading his mind.

"You are the face I keep seeing in a dream that comes and goes in my head."

"I am Two Worlds. My son, Red Sun, and two other braves of the village found you and brought you here. You were wounded in the head and your scalp almost removed. Your people thought you were dead and left you to feed the wild animals."

Jessie was confused. "What do you mean my people? Who am I that you say my people left me for dead?"

Looking at the man lying on the furs, Two Worlds realized that the wound to his head had removed his memory. Two Worlds had seen this happen to other men who had been injured in this way. Some had lived in a world with no past for the remainder of their lives. Knowing the value of hope to the spirit, Two Worlds told him, "Your memory has also been injured inside your mind, but it will heal with the wound."

"How long have I been here?"

"You have slept half of a moon cycle, but you will start to grow stronger now. Waiting Owl and her daughters, Little Moon and Little Otter, will take good care of you and make you strong again. They will see to it that someone is here with you at all times. So rest now and I will speak with you again when you are stronger." Two Worlds rose and left the room. Jessie lay still and wondered what the old man who called himself Two Worlds meant when he said your people, and why he didn't understand.

Ten

Bill Walsh rode his horse out of the pines and saw the rough board house with its open breeze way in the center. On one side of the breezeway was the kitchen, followed by the bedroom of Belle and Jessie. The other side had two bedrooms and the living room. The house was low and flat, with little pitch to the roof. Sitting under the giant live oaks with their limbs covering it, the house stayed shaded and cool, even in the summer. The outhouse was a hundred and fifty feet from the main house, and an open-sided barn stood between the main house and the lake. The home sat at the bottom of a sloping valley, covering most of 200 acres. Fed by springs, the water was clear and the lake was full of largemouth bass and bream.

Cattails grew along its edge halfway around the lake, and a few small cypresses were trying to grow along the edge of the farside. A small creek flowing from the south end, wound its way through a field of wild flowers that eventually fed into the Little Withlacoochee River. Because they threatened his children and what livestock he had brought with him from Georgia, Jessie had killed four alligators that inhabited the lake. The livestock included his riding horse, two hunting dogs, two work horses, two oxen, two good milk cows, one rooster and four laying hens, that were there due to the insistence of his wife. Bill saw the two milk cows grazing down by the lake where they were allowed to wander during the day. At night, they were brought back to the barn for milking and put in a small fenced pen next to it. The two blue tick hounds, whose bloodlines went back to Tennessee, saw him as he started to round the garden that Jessie's son had so proudly planted and maintained.

As the two dogs began to bark, Belle, Ed, Horace, and little Jenny waited for the rider to come closer. Jessie's two boys and Jenny, aged nine, looking like a smaller version of Belle with auburn hair and dark brown eyes, were all excited to see a visitor. Bill thought to himself again that there was nothing in those Everglades swamps that could make him feel this bad. He approached the yard and Jessie's family. They didn't recognize him until he was almost in front of the house. He was 15 pounds lighter and his face was drawn up from the long months in the Everglades. Ed suddenly recognized Bill's horse and trailing behind on a lead line, his pa's horse.

"Ma, it's Mr. Walsh," he shouted.

Belle's smile faded as Bill came closer to her. Easing back on the reins, Bill stopped his horse in front of her, ignoring the kids around him. He removed his hat and she saw the news in his face. Her knees went weak, but she had to make herself stand where she was, until she heard what she already knew was coming. Ed, Horace, and little Jenny were next to his horse, all asking about their pa. Was he coming home soon and was the war over? In their excitement, they had not yet recognized their pa's horse.

Ed glanced at his mother and suddenly froze, "Horace, Jenny, quiet!" The quiet became intense as the children realized something was wrong. Then Ed spoke to Bill. "Mr. Walsh, you better get down and come sit a spell. Horace, take the horses down to the lake and let them drink. Take Jenny with you."

"Can I ride on the horse?" Jenny asked.

"Sure you can," Bill said, as he swung down from the saddle and lifted Jenny onto the horse's back. He handed the reins to Horace, who started for the lake. Ed took his Ma by the arm and gently urged her toward the porch. Belle sat down on the edge of the porch, which was raised about two feet above the ground. Ed remained standing at her side, holding her arm, while Belle's eyes stayed fixed on Bill's face.

"I wish to God I didn't have to tell you this ... Jessie left camp to scout for Union supply lines and he never came back. We looked for him for over a week but never found a sign of him. That was over a month ago. We figure he might have been captured by the Union soldiers, which I doubt because Jessie would have known they were in the area long before they could have spotted him. He must have been ambushed by some of the Indians in the Everglades who were scouting for the Union. I'm sorry, Belle. I would trade places with him, if I didn't have to stand here and tell you this."

"You don't know for sure that Jessie's dead then, do you Bill?" Belle asked.

"No Ma'am, I don't. But if he were alive, we would know by now, unless the Union has him, and I just don't think they do."

"I understand how you feel Bill, but I'll just wait till the Lord tells me that Jessie's not coming home. Until then, we'll just keep the farm going. Ed's doing a fine job keeping everything up with Horace's help, so come inside and eat something. We were just finishing supper and the food is still warm." Belle slid from the porch and walked toward the steps. Bill looked at Ed, not knowing what to say next.

Ed looked him in the eyes and said, "I trust Ma and the Lord, and if she says Pa ain't dead yet, then I believe her."

"I haven't eaten since last night and that was a rabbit I killed and roasted over a fire, but I can only stay long enough to eat a bite."

Belle went inside to fix Bill a plate, and Ed turned to Bill and asked, "How come you got Pa's horse?"

"The army gave us a different kind of horse that was better suited for riding in the Everglades, and they don't have any need for our horses, so I brought Jessie's home with me."

Bill ate in silence, sitting at the table alone, while Belle and Ed busied themselves with clean up chores. They talked to Bill at the same time, telling him about all the things the family had done to the farm since Jessie had left to go fight in the war. Then they continued to speak about all the things they were going to do when

Jessie came home, as if the earlier conversation about him had never happened.

Ed sat down at the table opposite Bill. "Mrs. Walsh and your girls, Lily and Sharon, are doing fine. Horace and I have kept firewood cut for the stove, and Ma sends smoked hog, eggs, and some vegetables whenever we have extra. Mr. Campbell's sons have done the same thing, and they also helped your family put in a garden that gives them fresh vegetables, which helps. We all take care of Mrs. Kersey, but she stays a lot with Mrs. Campbell."

"I owe you and the other families a great debt for looking out for my family while I was away, but Dave and John both are on their way home now, so if you and your ma need anything, you let one of us know."

Ed answered awkwardly. "It's us and the other families who thank you. We thank you, Pa, and the others who fought to keep us all safe, and who made it so we would not have to move again."

Ed slid his chair back, stood up and walked through the front door, as Bill was finishing the last of the gravy with his biscuit. He yelled from the porch steps to Horace, to bring Mr. Walsh's horse. He walked on down the steps and started around the house to the garden, where his mother had begun pulling ears of corn and dropping them into the apron she held, folded up with one hand. Ed pulled his pocket knife from the pocket of his coveralls and began cutting okra from stalks taller than he was.

Bill came down the back steps, and Belle said, "While Ed is cutting you some okra, pick yourself a mess of those snap peas."

As Bill began to fill his pockets and stuff the inside of his shirt with peas he said to Ed, "It's been three months now since I've been home, and I know Martha and the girls are wondering if I'm still alive, but I won't be going back to the army now that the war is almost over. They sent everyone in our group home that wanted to go. So like I said before if you and your Ma need anything, you let one of us know."

Horace came walking up with Jenny in the saddle of Bill's horse, Jenny with a smile that melted hearts. Bill stepped up to his horse, removed a cloth sack from behind his saddle and lifted Jenny to the ground. He turned to Horace and said, "I really appreciate you giving Abe a drink of water. He needed it."

"Abe really liked the grass around the edge of the lake, Mr. Walsh," Horace said while he held onto the bridle. Bill emptied the peas from his shirt and pants pockets into the bag, and then as he held it open wide, Belle placed the dozen ears of corn inside. Ed cleaned his pockets of okra and added them to the bag. Bill swung up into his saddle after securing the bag of vegetables and handed the lead rope of Jessie's horse to Horace.

He looked down at Ed and Belle and said, "Martha and I and the girls will enjoy the fresh vegetables." Not knowing what else to say, he tipped his hat to Belle and turned for home.

Horace turned to Ed and asked, "Why did Mr. Walsh bring Pa's horse home, and where is Pa?"

Ed saw questions and fear in Horace's eyes, but he hurried him on saying, "Just take Pa's horse to the barn and put him away. Then come in the house and I'll explain." As Horace turned toward the barn, Ed saw the worry working its way into his walk.

Eleven

It had been over a month since Bill Walsh had come by on his way home, when thunder off in the distance woke Ed. He lay listening to the still of the night, waiting for the next clap of thunder, to determine how far away the approaching storm was. Then he heard another sound drifting across the breezeway into his room. As a cloud drifted away from the moon, its glow lit the room with soft light. Ed slipped into his pants and walked softly into the breezeway that separated the kitchen and living room. The living room was separated from the bedrooms by a big rock fireplace. He stood beside the fireplace, smelling the wind, looking and listening. As the lightning flashed off in the distance, he counted the seconds before the rumbling sound of thunder reached him again. He knew that a strong summer lightning storm was moving their way.

As Ed started to the barn to check on the animals, he heard a sound as soft as a whip-poor-will cry. He crossed the breezeway to the open door of Belle's room and looked in. Hearing the soft sob as it came again, he saw his mother sitting in a chair next to the open window with her back to him. He thought she had spoken to him, and he started through the door to go to her when he realized she wasn't speaking to him at all. What he had heard was a prayer to her Lord to please look over her Jessie and not to let him be suffering, whereever he was keeping him for now. Ed turned on the balls of his feet and quietly slipped off the porch and down the steps toward the barn, to check the gates before the storm reached the animals. As he heard the soft sound of a sob again, he knew that she had waited until she thought there was no one to hear her anguish, after the terrible agony of Bill Walsh's dreaded words. She had been afraid for Jessie from the moment he rode out of sight three months earlier.

The two dogs slipped out from under the porch where they slept. As they trotted alongside Ed, they reached up and touched his hand with their moist noses. Ed patted both of them on the head. "Well Dixie and Rebel, it looks like we have a storm coming." As he patted the dogs, he felt their nervousness and heard the horses stamping their feet in the barn. When he looked over at the chicken roost under the lean-to, he was surprised to see that the chickens were missing. Once again the clouds covered the moon and everything went dark. Ed stood still while trying to adjust his eyes to the dark, and then the lightning flashed and hung across the sky, sending streaks though the darkness like a spider web of fire.

For a split second, he saw the huge, black thunderheads as the lightning exploded; then they disappeared. Ed felt the first pangs of fear in his chest as the wind began to increase and he tasted the dust, swirling around his feet. Opening the barn door, he felt along the wooden wall to his right until he touched the lantern, hanging on a nail. Reaching into the bib pocket of his overalls, he pulled a match and raked the red head across the wall, raised the glass and touched the flame to the kerosene soaked wick. In the dim light, he saw the two work horses milling around in circles in their stalls. Holding the lantern up and away from his body, he softly approached the back of the barn calling to the horses in an attempt to calm them.

His nerves were suddenly jarred by the fluttering of wings, and he looked up to see the chickens sitting on the pole rail of the loft. "You girls having a night out?" he said, trying to chuckle and overcome the dread building up inside his chest. Ed had seen what lightning storms could cause when he lived in Georgia; hundreds of acres of woods burned and fields of crops washed away by the floods that sometimes followed the storms. He walked through the barn slowly, continuing out the back door to check the two oxen and milk cows. They were backed up under the lean-to, which was built against the side of the barn and covered the pen. As the lightning flashed and seemed to hang there in the sky, Ed saw the oxen moving about bumping against the barn wall, and then he heard another boom of the thunder no more than a mile off.

The sound of one of the horses kicking the stall sent him running back into the barn, to find both work horses running around in their stalls kicking and whinnying, fear reflected in their eyes. Jessie's horse was moving too, but seemed calmer somehow. Ed wanted to run for the house to wake Horace, but he knew if he left now, the horses would panic before he could get back. They would hurt themselves badly, and he couldn't let that happen. Fighting his own rising fear, he set the lantern on a shelf and eased open the first stall, talking slowly to the big mare, ready to jump back if she rushed him. She was the quiet one of the two; if he could get her to calm down it would have a reassuring effect on Preacher, the big 17½ hand stud. As Dolly backed her big frame into the corner of the stall, she seemed to settle some as Ed forced the panic from his voice. Talking calmly, he slowly approached until his hand gently touched her cheek.

"Dolly you have to help me now, because I don't know if I can handle Preacher by myself." He stroked her neck until he felt her quivering stop, letting her lids close over her large brown eyes as he removed the fear she had felt. Ed felt Dolly's 1300 pound frame slow down to a nervous pace, as he slipped his hand under her halter and walked her to the stall door, where a heavy rope hung from a roof beam. Ropes were placed each side of the door on all the stalls and were used to hold horses in place while they were being treated or shod. He slipped the end of first one rope and then the other, through the halter ring and adjusted the lengths so she could only move her head, no more than a foot either way. Then he closed the door locking her in tightly. Still talking as much to calm himself as the animals, he opened the door to Preacher's stall. Preacher ran around the stall once and then backed into the corner with his head thrown back, his eyes still wide with fear. His nostrils flared and his skin quivered, as an invisible river of energy rushed through his body like the open gates of a damn, releasing its pent up energy.

"Preacher, there's a bad thing out there coming our way, and I can't stay here with you for long." As Ed was fighting his own alarm, the lightning struck the ground no more than 100 feet away, exploding and sending its shock wave through the barn, causing his hair to stand up and freezing him in place. In that split second, Preacher's 1500 pounds of muscle exploded toward the open door, his shoulder hitting Ed in the chest like a sledge hammer. The powerful horse slammed Ed's body against the wall, leaving him with little air in his lungs. The last thing he heard as he fought blackness closing over him was the panicked winny as Dolly fought against her ropes.

Twelve

Belle heard the squeak of the steps as Ed descended into the yard, and her heart swelled as she was reassured that whatever happened, she could rely on Ed to take care of it. Looking up in gratitude, Belle prayed, "Thank you Lord for Ed, and since you have made a man out of my boy before his time, give him the strength of his determination."

Feeling the change in the air, Belle knew that Ed would be out checking on the animals by now, and she went into the kitchen to add wood to the banked coals in the stove. As she felt for the lantern sitting on a shelf next to the stove, she saw the lightning light up the sky no more than two or three miles away. Then Belle saw the sky full of thunder heads. Starting to feel anxious, she waited for enough heat from the coals to ignite the wood and went to wake Horace up, to help Ed prepare for the coming storm. Shaking him gently by the shoulder, she spoke as calmly as she could manage. "Horace wake, up now, you have to go help your brother in the barn with the animals."

As Horace woke in the dark, she knew that he heard the urgency in his ma's voice. She saw the concern in his young face when the lighting struck less than a mile away, lighting up the room in its eerie glow. "Something's wrong Ma, what is it?"

"Nothing's wrong Horace." She reached to touch his forehead; the image of her son lying there from the flash of light still frozen in her mind. "Light the lamp now and get dressed; don't wake your sister."

Belle walked back into the kitchen to heat the food, watching through the open window at the impending ferocity of the storm. The lightning lit the sky with a brilliant flash vanishing as fast as it appeared, followed closely by the clap of thunder, drowning out all sound but its own. For a moment she stood frozen in time, the storm unlocking memories of hair-raising thunder which would awaken them in the night. She would move into Jessie's strong arms while the storm passed over, their bodies absorbing the energy together. Later without a word, she would turn on her back, never leaving his arms. Belle stumbled back when the lightning bolt exploded as it struck the ground between the barn and the house, shocking her back to reality. She ran toward the door screaming, "Ed! Ed, oh my God where are you?"

She was coming down the front steps when she saw Preacher bolt across the yard in a wild fear. Turning towards the house she hollered back at Horace to put on a pot of water. Fear gripped her chest as she ran across the yard, stumbling and blinded by the heavy rain being whipped up by the wind. She tried desperately to see the small ray of light coming from the barn, and caught a glimpse of the barn as lightning flashed and disappeared in an instant. She fought her way through the wind and rain into the barn, fighting the paralyzing dread that threatened to buckle her knees. Using all the will power she possessed, clinging to the door frame, her wet night gown glued to her, she held down the fear and called out again.

"Ed, where are you?" All she heard was the panicked whinny of Dolly, fighting the harness ropes holding her in place. Gathering her strength, Belle walked past Dolly's stall to the open and empty stall of Preacher. She saw Ed lying dazed on the floor, curled on his side moaning and gasping for breath.

"Thank you Lord!" Belle cried. Taking Ed by the shoulders she struggled to turn him on his back.

Ed gave out a painful moan as his eyes came open, "No! No! Don't touch me, aahhh my ribs, I can't move!" Ed's breathing was labored;

he struggled with short breaths, bringing moans of pain. Belle used a piece of her wet night gown and wiped his head.

"Ed can you hear me?"

"Yes Ma, but you can't touch me, my ribs must be broken, and I'm having a tough time breathing."

"Ed honey, I can see you are hurt real bad, but I can't just leave you here in this stall. Lord I don't know how, but I got to get you in the house."

"I think I can help you with that," a voice spoke out of the dark.

Belle looked up as she felt his hand on her shoulder and sat down on her rear end when she saw Jessie's face looking down at her. Jessie slipped his hands under her arms, and lifted her up into his arms. She wrapped her arms around his neck and he held her that way, until the tears stopped. "You'll have to tell me where the Lord has been keeping you."

"I will after we get Ed in the house." Jessie turned toward the door and said, "Red Sun, I am going to need your help." As Belle turned, she stared in shock. She had never seen an Indian before, and she looked with wonder and fascination at their rain soaked clothes. Red Sun and Little Otter started forward, and Belle stood in awed silence looking between Ed and the young Indian girl, who could be no more than 15 or 16 years old.

Jessie pulled a wool horse blanket from the tack room and kneeling down, he spoke calmly to Ed. "Son we are going to have to lift you onto this blanket, and I know it's going to hurt some, but we have to get you into the house." Unable even to speak without pain, Ed only stared up at his pa and the Indians standing behind him and nodded his head slightly. "Belle, I'm going to need you and Little Otter to slip the blanket under him when we lift him." Ed moaned with pain, as Jessie slipped his hands under his shoulders, Red Sun lifted his hips and legs. With the blanket pulled under him Jessie said "It will be easier if we each take a corner and lift. Belle, you and Little Otter take the end at his feet. Me and Red Sun will carry this end at his head."

As they stepped through the open door of the barn, they were met with sheets of drenching rain. The lightning lit the sky further off to the west, and Jessie could see that the storm was passing. They made their way slowly through the slippery mud, trying to keep from sliding and losing Ed. Inside, they slowly lowered him to the floor next to his bed, where they could remove his rain soaked clothes before putting him in the bed. Then they would wrap his ribs tight with a torn bed sheet.

Horace stood next to the stove, still frightened by the alarm in his mother's voice when she ran out in the storm, calling Ed's name. When the door opened, he watched his rain soaked ma and pa coming in with strangers the likes of which he had never seen before. It made him wonder if this was a dream, and he only thought he was awake. Horace stood in shocked silence as they took Ed into the bedroom and laid him down on the floor. He watched in awe at the tall red man who slipped outside, closing the door, leaving him staring at this strange looking girl who stood looking back at him in her own confusion. He saw her shiver from the cold in her rain soaked dress, a dress like he had never seen before. "It is warm by the stove," Horace said, as he stepped away offering her his place next to the heat.

While Jessie was helping Belle wrap Ed's ribs and making him as comfortable as possible, he saw Red Sun slip back outside where the rain was already beginning to let up. Red Sun untied their horses from the split rail fence and led them into the barn, removed their bridles and left them there. Taking the lantern from the shelf, he closed the door and made his way back to the house where they were almost finished wrapping up Ed's ribs. Lying on his back and trying not to moan, Ed was fighting the pain. He was able to slowly straighten his legs which helped a little. Looking at Jessie with questioning eyes, he slowly said with shallow breaths.

"Ma said the Lord was looking out for you somewhere, and I always believed her Pa."

"Lie still now," Jessie said softly, "your ma is getting you something to help with the pain and it will help you sleep too. I will explain everything to you later."

Stepping back into the kitchen, Jessie saw the confusion on Horace's face as he stared between his pa, Red Sun and Little Otter. Walking over and kneeling down on one knee, he smiled at his frightened son.

"Is it really you, Pa?"

"It's really me," he said as he pulled his frightened son into his arms.

"I missed you Pa," he said as he choked back a tear that he didn't want the strange girl to see.

"I've missed you too, Son," Jessie murmured, waiting until he felt Horace's grip loosen around his neck. Then he stood up. Holding his confused son by the shoulders he said, "I will explain everything to you tomorrow, but I need you to go on back to bed now, we have things to do, and your ma and me are real busy right now." As he steered his son toward his bedroom, he said, "I will come in later and check on you."

"OK Pa," he said, as he crossed the breeze way, looking back at the two strangers one more time.

Later as everyone was sitting around the table, Belle brought the pot of hot coffee and poured Jessie a cup. She asked Red Sun and Little Otter if they wanted some, or could she fix them something else, not having any idea what that might be.

"I would be pleased to have a cup. It has been a long time since I have tasted some of the white man's drink."

As Belle filled a cup for Red Sun, she looked over at Little Otter, noticing for the first time, the wet clothes that still clung to her. She also saw that the girl was well on her way to becoming a woman. Belle set the coffee pot back on the stove and walked over to where Little Otter sat, arms folded across her stomach, trying to absorb all the strange things going on around her. This was nothing like what she had expected, when she had talked her father into letting her come with them.

Turning to Little Otter, Belle said, "You poor child, you must be freezing in those wet clothes."

"I'm OK, I will dry soon," she said as a shiver went through her.

"Nonsense," Belle said as she gently took the girl by the arm. Rising, Little Otter let Belle lead her out of the kitchen into their bedroom. Belle opened her drawer to her small dresser, that she had insisted Jessie bring with them from Georgia, and removed a soft worn cotton dress with flower prints. "It will be a little big on you, but we'll dry your dress by the stove. It won't take long; meanwhile I will heat up some fresh milk to warm you up." Belle hung the wet dress across the back of a chair by the stove, and she felt the softness of the hides and elaborate decorations of beads. She had never seen a more beautiful dress. After heating some milk for Little Otter, she poured herself a cup of hot coffee, adding sugar, the only way she liked it and sat down at the table across from Jessie. Jessie, seeing the questions in her eyes, looked at Red Sun and taking a sip of hot coffee, he started his strange tale.

Thirteen

As Jessie sat back against the hides and animal fur that supported him, he ate from the bowl of food and tried to remember where he was. Slowly looking around, he recognized the skins of the deer and furs of fox, wildcat, wolf, and otter. The smell of ashes from a small fire pit in the center of the lodge was at the edge of his memory as he struggled to find his place in this strange world he found himself in. As the light filtered into the lodge from the opening at the top of the lodge poles, covered with deer hides, he saw the sleeping furs where someone else slept. A bow hung by its string from one of the lodge poles. On another pole hung a war shield, made with thick hide stretched across a round wooden hoop. The hide was painted with scenes of past battles, and feathers from different birds hung by thin leather strips around the wooden hoop. Above the bow hung a quiver, made from the same thick hide as the war shield. The dirt floor was packed hard by the coming and going of many feet.

Jessie finished his food and feeling stronger, stood and walked around the lodge, looking at all the strange objects hanging from the lodge poles. He felt a bit sturdier now, this being the third day since he had slowly risen from his sleeping furs and fighting dizziness, had walked once around the lodge before collapsing back onto the bed of furs. He had lain there for a while, willing himself from the blackness he had fought for the last two weeks. Recognizing the dyed cotton shirt hanging above his bed of furs, he removed it from the pole and slipped it on. Looking down he saw his worn brogans with a pair of moccasins sitting across the toes. He removed the moccasins and studying the boots, he felt an urge to step into them, but could not understand why. He knew they were something he knew about, but could not place them in the present. Feeling that the moccasins were left for him, he slowly bent down, feeling the softness as he slipped one on each foot. Again he walked the length of the lodge circle, and when he came to the lodge entrance, he bent forward, raised the strip of deer hide and stepped into a totally unfamiliar world.

The bright rays of the sun blinded him. Bursts of light exploded behind his eyes, causing him to squeeze his lids tight and losing his balance, he fell back into the lodge poles. Stumbling sideways, his mind in a panic, he went down on one knee. Slowly he steadied himself, remaining on his knee until the star bursts of light stopped and then carefully, he opened his eyes under the shade of his hand. Rising slowly, he stood still, observing his surroundings from under his hand and feeling totally out of control of his life.

The lodges stood in a large circle. Small fires cooked the contents of iron pots, suspended on green limbs and placed between forked sticks, which were driven into the ground on either side of the fire. Women sat beside the fires, scraping flesh from hides that stretched between small tree limbs. As his eyes wandered past the hides, he saw a group of several women and young girls sitting on logs that were cut flat on top. They were under a shade built of small poles with a roof made of palm fronds, placed so tightly together, not a drop of rain could penetrate to the dry ground below. The women and girls were sewing clothing from soft hides and brightly colored cloth, and stringing beads received in trades with the white man.

Jessie began to walk across the center of the village, not knowing where he was headed but needing to feel the sun and the breeze on his body. He had taken only a few steps forward when four young boys came around the lodge, racing hoops pushed along with a stick. Seeing Jessie, whom they had never seen, but they had heard the rumors of a white man living in the old chief's lodge, they stopped so suddenly that their hoops kept rolling. Their mouths dropped open, their eyes not believing what they saw, and they stood frozen and stared. Reaching out and catching a hoop coming at him, he rolled it back towards the boys, who turned and ran as if they had just seen a ghost from one of the legends told in stories around the night fire.

Red Sun had seen Jessie come out of the lodge and stagger to his knees, blinded by the glare of the sun. He walked quickly to catch up and laughed at the fright of the young boys.

"I am glad to see you have strength again, we have waited for you."

"Who are you and where am I?" asked Jessie.

"I am Red Sun and you are in the village of my father, Two Worlds. Silent Stalker, Big Cypress, and I found you after your people left you for dead."

"Why do you say my people? Who am I?"

"I will take you to find your answers," Red Sun replied

As Jessie walked through the village following Red Sun, trying to understand how he fit into this world around him, he became even more confused as he watched the Indians living their lives in the village. Jessie observed the women wading in the shallows at the mouth of the cut. They were working together pulling a seine, which was handmade from small vines woven together. The women formed a large arc, starting in neck deep water and moving in unison to bring trapped fish onto the beach. It was low tide and men waded out to large oyster bars to load their baskets. Later, the people of the village would feast on oysters, which had been placed in boiling water until the shells opened, and on fresh fish, cooked on green branches over hot coals.

Red Sun led Jessie to a huge live oak and told him to wait under the shade of the outer branches. He watched this man who had saved his life approach the old man, who was sitting on a log with a flat top. Jessie noticed the ease with which Red Sun squatted on his heels and the respect he showed, as he bowed his head. Having left the lodge less than a half an hour ago and encountering the village for the first time, not knowing where he was or where he would go, Jessie watched anxiously and waited for answers. Then Red Sun looked back at him and motioned with his hand for Jessie to come and sit. Jessie squatted next to Red Sun and bowed his head. As he raised his head and looked into the wisdom in Two Worlds' eyes, he froze. A sense of knowing came over him like a gentle wave. Underlying this feeling of recognition was his anxiety and confusion. He spoke slowly as he tried to understand.

"You are the only memory of this life you have given me. All else is hidden. Why have you brought me here and given me this life? I see in your eyes that you have answers. Please tell me how I know you and why I am here?"

Two Worlds studied the man squatting before him, and hearing the confusion in his voice, told him the only thing he knew for sure. "Only time will reveal why you were sent to us; you must be patient and let your wounds heal. When you are ready, the answers you seek will come."

Fourteen

The sun had already passed overhead and was heading for the horizon on the Gulf of Mexico as Two Worlds relaxed on his log under the shade of the large oak tree. Hearing horses, he turned and watched as Red Sun, Silent Stalker, and Jessie rode into camp, returning from their hunt. Two Worlds' attention was immediately drawn to the deer lying across the saddle in front of Jessie. He could see the smile on Jessie's face and knew he had killed the deer with his own bow. The smile replaced the frustration and awkwardness of learning the art of shooting a bow, and his three weeks of practice had paid off. Red Sun also had a deer across his horse and Silent Stalker had two turkeys draped across his saddle, their legs tied together with leather straps. Several women met them and were given the deer and turkeys to be cleaned and readied for the cook fires. Later the hides would be stretched across racks to be cleaned and dried. One of the young boys took the reins of the horses and led them to the small pasture, where they were hobbled and left to graze.

Red Sun, Jessie and Silent Stalker made their way to the fresh water stream, where they waded out knee deep and began to wash the blood from their legs and clothes. Jessie now wore only a breach cloth and leggings, made for him by the women of the tribe. As he bent forward and splashed the cool, clear water over his face and head, the sun reflected the light of his golden red hair that now fell to his shoulders. He shook the water from his hair, feeling the drops run down his shoulders and back that were now almost as brown as those of his new family. It had been six weeks since Jessie staggered outside into the sun and into another world. He felt strong now and the wound had healed, leaving a scar across most of his forehead. The pain in his head came less frequently, but the confusion about who he was and how he came to be with these people was always present.

The glow of the cook fires was replacing the light of the sun as it set over the gulf, painting the huge, puffy white clouds a brilliant red and orange. As dusk approached, the sky was clothed in soft pink before the sun surrendered its last light to the fires. Jessie sat cross legged, leaning against the fur covered back rest in Two Worlds' lodge. He was enjoying a bowl of roasted venison, which had been cooked all afternoon in a large black kettle, simmering in gravy made with coontie flour. Jessie had been fascinated, watching the women of the tribe pounding the roots of the coontie plants, then drying the paste into flour. The venison was followed by turkey meat, which had been stuffed with wild herbs and slow roasted over the hot coals. The last light was fading through the opening of the lodge as Two Worlds finished his food and quietly waited for Jessie to finish his. After a few moments of silence he spoke.

"You should eat all you can, because after tonight there will be no more food for the next three days. Tomorrow, we will begin cleansing our bodies and preparing for the journey into the other world, where you will find your past."

Jessie slowly set the bowl down and looked into the old man's eyes, feeling dread and excitement warring in his chest. On an earlier hunting trip, Red Sun had explained to him why the old man was called Two Worlds. He explained to Jessie how with his powerful medicine, Two Worlds could travel into the realm of his ancestors, where he could see not only the past, but bring back visions of the future.

Two Worlds slowly rose and left the lodge, making his way to the warmth of the fire as the village was gathering for the evening discussions. Bending slowly, he eased himself into a seat and backrest that Woman of the Wind had prepared for him. Woman of the Wind was the last wife of Two Worlds and the mother of Red Sun. A few years before, Woman of the Wind had moved in with Red Sun's family, leaving Two Worlds to live alone in his medicine lodge. He belonged to the village now and she shared him with the others, out of her deep love for him and respect for the tribe. Her love could be seen in the way she cared for his every need. Woman of the Wind, Red Sun's wife Waiting Owl, and their twin daughters Little Moon and Little Otter, gathered herbs and roots to make medicines. They could be ground into a powder to make a healing paste or a tea and used for the relief of pain from wounds.

Jessie usually sat just outside the small circle, listening as they discussed their everyday lives. However this night they had made a place for him in their circle of trust. He could feel his spirit soaring and truly felt he was part of the tribe, listening as they spoke about the planting of the garden, how the corn and pumpkins were growing and whether they should plant more or move the garden. They talked about the amount of game in the area and how the grass for the small herd of horses was holding up.

Sometimes they gave a special gift they had made for someone, like the breech cloth and leggings they had surprised him with, or the mixture of oil and herb powder, to cover his pale skin so the sun didn't burn him. Now he only needed to cover his face on the hottest days. When the discussion of their daily needs was over, everyone grew quiet as they waited for Two Worlds to begin another story of their past. Jessie listened intently trying to understand as Two Worlds told of the legends of their forefathers and where they came from, the invasion of the white man who brought disease and of the soldiers who took the lands. Two Worlds spoke of the efforts of the brave warriors who tried to keep the tribe together as the people scattered to different parts of the earth. They learned about how the people of their tribe fought to hold on to their traditions as the white man pressed his way of living on their people.

Two Worlds lived as close as he could to the ways of his ancestors, using furs for clothing, building skin lodges instead of platforms and rolling the hides up the lodge poles in the summer so the breeze could flow through. They stayed away from the white man as much as possible. When the story ended and the fire burned down to glowing coals, most of the people wandered off to their lodges. A few sat and talked a while longer, discussing a hunt or maybe a trip to visit the people that had stayed behind and not followed Two Worlds. As the last of the stragglers returned to their lodges, Jessie, who was tired and happy about his acceptance as part of the tribe, lay down on his deer skin bed across from Two Worlds and wondered about the coming days.

Jessie sat on the bed of furs inside the sweat lodge, feeling light headed. He knew it was the effect of the small bowl of liquid, made by Woman of the Wind from the roots and herbs she had gathered and left in the sweat lodge. There was one bowl for him and one for Two Worlds. Even in the glow of the hot coals, Jessie could barely make out Two Worlds who was sitting across from him. They had been sitting in the medicine lodge since the sun had started to set, on the third day of their fast. He heard the hiss of water being poured over the hot coals.

As the wave of heat given off by the steam reached his body, more sweat poured down soaking the already wet furs. His mind began to keep time with the drums and the high pitched sounds of chanting. Outside, as the men beat the large circle drum, the women chanted, dancing in rhythm around the fire that lit up the camp. Jesse had no idea how long he had been sitting in the darkness of the sweat lodge. His body began to rock gently, in time with the chanting of Two Worlds, and soon he found himself repeating the sacred song over and over until he was in unison with the old man. Softly, the strong thin hands of Two Worlds covered his own hands, and he didn't notice when it happened, but Jessie realized that he was no longer in his body. He was floating somewhere in space.

Two ospreys circled high above the soldiers as they worked their way through the Everglades. They observed the single rider sitting inside the cypress hammock waiting. They watched as the Indian scout fired his rifle at the single horseman. The ospreys saw a bullet tear a path along the head of the rider, knocking him from his horse. Circling, they paid close attention, watching as the soldiers rode off and left the body. Then they witnessed the three braves kill the scout and take the body of the rider with them.

Jesse found himself flying with the ospreys as they rose up on the thermal currents until they were barely visible to anyone on the ground. Together they soared across the land, following the rivers and the spring fed lakes that dotted the landscape. Soon they could see the waters of the great Okeechobee. They viewed the cattle left there by the Spanish, which were now as wild as the land itself and multiplied by the thousands as they roamed the woods, foraging for food. They saw small farms and settlements, land where the timber had been removed and left behind to be over grown with brush.

Recognition swept over Jessie as he looked down and saw the small house and barn, sitting back from the lake under the giant oaks. Then, as he looked around, he realized he was alone; the house and barn were gone. He panicked and wanted to go back. He knew he belonged there. As memory began to overwhelm him, he squeezed his eyes tighter, trying to will himself back. Sounds disrupted his thoughts, the sounds of people talking. For a moment he thought it was the sounds of his family and he was late getting up, but he knew that it wasn't right, and as he began to focus on the sounds, he recognized where he was.

Jessie sat up and realized he was back in Two Worlds lodge, at the beginning of the day. As he rose to dress, he felt dizzy and light headed. Looking around, he saw his old clothes folded and lying across his brogans and wondered for a moment if they had always been there, and he hadn't noticed. He slipped on his pants and cotton shirt. As he pulled on his boots they felt stiff, and after a moment's thought he removed them and walked around the sleeping furs to find his moccasins. He wanted to talk to Two Worlds about going home now. He was anxious as he realized that his family would be worried, wondering what had happened to him and probably thinking him dead by now.

Fifteen

The people of the village watched him as he came out of the lodge, wearing his white man's clothes. As he looked about, he realised they could see he was upset and knew that something had changed. He was no longer one of them, and they all felt some sadness for their loss. They observed as Jessie spotted Two Worlds, who was sitting in the fresh water stream. He was bent forward, pouring water over his head with a gourd and letting the water run down his back.

"Two Worlds I need to talk to you, I remember who I am."

"Yes I know." The old man poured another gourd of water over his head. "Come sit here and let the water cleanse your body and clear your mind. Then we will eat; we have a lot to talk about."

Jessie removed his moccasins and shirt and started to wade in when Two Worlds said, "You can remove your pants, no one will notice."

Looking around and seeing no one watching, Jessie removed his pants, quickly waded in and sat next to Two Worlds. Two Worlds handed Jessie the gourd, but instead Jessie pushed himself forward under the water and swam against the current for as long as he could hold his breath, letting the cool fresh water cleanse his body of the sweat from the night before. Floating back with the current, he took another deep breath and put his face in the clear water. He saw his house and barn again, and his only thoughts were of going home.

As Two Worlds and Jessie made their way to the seats under the great oak, Rainbow, the wife of Eagle Hunter, and White Sun, the wife of Four Bears, were waiting for them with bowls of fresh cooked vegetables and bread made of coontie flour. Next to the bowls was a gourd of energy drink that Woman of the Wind had prepared. The women set the food and drink on the bench between them and went back to their morning cook fires. The smells reminded Jessie of his three days without food, and as he ate the vegetables with a carved out wooden spoon, he thought of nothing else until the bowl was empty and the bread was gone. Two Worlds ate slowly, relishing the taste as he knew his stomach could not accept much food at one time.

"Would you like more? They will bring you all you want."

"I don't think so," replied Jessie. "I'm afraid I am going pay later for eating this much so fast."

Jessie sat silently, collecting his thoughts while waiting for Two Worlds to finish. The images jumped about in his head, scenes of the present and of the past. He saw Belle standing in the yard watching him leave. He saw the men he had fought with in the Everglades. He saw himself turning his horse to leave the hammock where he had been watching the soldiers. He remembered the different faces that had come and gone in his dreams, the heat and smells of the medicine lodge. He remembered stepping out of the lodge, being blinded by the sun and staggering into this world of now. Slowly, as he put his thoughts in order he began to speak.

"I know I am alive today because Red Sun saved me from having my scalp removed and from being left behind to be eaten by wild animals. When I was brought here, I would have died even then, had it not been for your medicines. I have felt the people of your tribe accepting me as one of them. I have felt a sense of freedom here, gathering food from the waters and hunting meat with a bow along with the other braves, although I had my doubts in the beginning."

Two Worlds nodded his head slowly, smiling. He too had had doubts, but was pleased when Jessie had come back with his deer draped across his horse.

"I know I can never give back what you and the people of this tribe have given me, and I feel inside that there is more to what has happened here than I can understand."

Two Worlds sat his bowl on the bench between them. "Sometimes our ancestors send us messages in strange ways. I was sent a message by my ancestors that told of a change coming, a change that would affect the way we live as we know it today. With that message a messenger came, one who would lead us to that new world. Perhaps you don't understand your part in this yet, but it will come about and you will know then. Today, we will prepare for your journey home tomorrow. Eagle Hunter and Red Sun will go with you; he knows the way to the river that flows from the great waters of the Okeechobee."

"The Caloosahatchee; I know that river, and if I can get there, I know the way home."

Jessie spent the rest of the day talking to each one in the tribe and thanking them. Darting Bird gave him a new pair of moccasins decorated with a beautiful pattern of beads and shells. Little Wolf, Eagle Hunter's six year old son, gave Jessie his favorite hoop stick. Jessie took an osprey feather from his leather head band and with a narrow leather strip; he tied the feather to the back of Little Wolf's head. Jessie turned him around and swatted him on the butt. "Go be a brave now; you have just earned your first feather."

There was a sad quietness that evening as Jessie sat around the cook fire, eating his last meal with the people who had become his family. He felt torn between missing his own family and leaving the people who had brought him back from death and given him this new life. They had made him a member of their family with no reservation. He had come to love their simplicity and their commitment to each other. When Two Worlds sat down next to Jessie, he handed him a bow and quiver filled with arrows.

"I have no more need for these, for I am too old to hunt, and I have no more enemies to fight. This will provide you with food and protection on your journey back to your world where your family is waiting."

Jessie recognized the bow and quiver he had seen hanging from the lodge poles, where he had been sleeping for two months. He could feel the history that they carried, the moment he touched the bow and quiver. "Two Worlds," he said, "I am not worthy to be the keeper of this great history of your life and this tribe."

Two worlds looked into Jessie's eyes and said, "I trust you will keep it well, and it will always remind you that you have two families in your life. I will always know that I have another son and Red Sun has a brother from another world. It has been foretold that we will share our lives together again."

"I too feel that, but how will that be?"

"Only our ancestors who live in the next world know that, and they have chosen not to show me yet."

"Then I will keep this gift, and I will treasure it always."

Red Sun rose from across the fire and stood in front of Jessie. From his waist, he pulled a hunting knife with a beautiful bone handle, in a decorated sheath and presented it to Jessie.

"This came from a brave brother of mine who died in a battle and lives now in the world of our ancestors. He would want my new brother to carry it and protect his family as he did."

Jessie sat alone late into the night adding wood to the fire and trying to make sense of how he got here. He wondered if his family was safe and what was going on with the war. He continued to think about the war and when should he report back to his outfit. Would they send him back into the Everglades? Tired and without answers, he rose from the dying fire, went to lie down in his bed of furs and slept.

Sixteen

Jessie lay still on his bed of furs, listening to the sound of chanting being carried by the wind as it blew through the lodge poles. Gathering his thoughts, he wondered how long the trip home would take, but since he didn't know where he was, he couldn't begin to guess. Jessie was curious about the chanting; he knew it had to be Two Worlds, but he had never heard him do that in the morning. Maybe it had to do with him leaving, and Two Worlds was praying for a safe journey.

He rose and slipped into his pants and cotton shirt. As he reached for his boots he paused, then chose the moccasins for the journey home. He knew that once he was back home, he would be using the boots to work in. As Jessie stepped out of the lodge, he noticed that the wind was picking up and there was enough light to see the tree tops swaying. Two Worlds was standing at the shore line. Waves of water were breaking at his feet, and he was staring at the sky with his arms raised above his head. Jessie felt a prickling of fear working its way up his spine as he slowly walked down to the beach to stand next to Two Worlds. As the chanting went on for another minute, Jessie stood rooted to the ground, frozen in time. Two Worlds suddenly stopped and turning to Jessie, he spoke as if he were in another world.

"The vision has begun now." He turned and started for the lodge saying, "we must pack quickly."

Jessie followed Two Worlds as he conveyed the message to his people. Everyone started removing hides from the lodge poles. Braves retrieved the poles and began to make litters. Walking quickly to keep up with Two Worlds, Jessie asked, "What is happening here?"

"We must leave here quickly now, for the great winds are coming and will destroy everything in their path. The oceans will wash away all that you see here. We have very little time now, so pack only what you can carry. We will move our belongings on litters, and the women and children will travel on the horses."

At the entrance to the lodge Two Worlds stopped. Turning, he looked Jessie in the eyes, speaking as if he had suddenly remembered something. He spoke the words that would cause him sorrow for many years.

"Not all of the people will survive this. The great winds will carry some of them into the next world to be with their ancestors. This is why you were sent to us; your part will start soon."

"What part?"

"I cannot tell you that. You will know when it is time. We must hurry now." Turning and entering the lodge, Two Worlds began to pack the things he wanted to save. First he picked the tribe's most precious relic, wrapped in ancient hide. Then he placed his belongings in furs and deer skins, tying the bundles with strips of sinew. He would carry the valuable relic himself and put the other bundles on the litter.

He then moved outside saying, "I will go now to find Woman of The Wind; when you are ready you can help the others."

Jessie didn't have much to pack, and soon he had finished tying his bundle, which contained his boots, extra moccasins, his hoop stick and the powder that Woman of the Wind had given him for his recurring headaches. As he stepped outside, the wind was blowing harder and he saw Red Sun coming into camp with two horses. He went to meet him and asked, "What I can do to help?"

"Bring in the other horses and help with tying the litters; then put the women and children on the horses," Red Sun replied.

Galvanized into action by his fear, Jessie shouldered his bundle, grabbed the bow and quiver and ran to the hobbled horses. They were rearing and staggering in a panic, trying to break away and flee the oncoming storm. He knew that he had to get control of the horses or lose them. Walking slowly and controlling his own panic, he carefully pulled his knife from its sheath. Reaching up and grabbing the braided halter, he held the horse in place and talked to him until he settled down. Then he reached down and cut the hobble, freeing the horse to walk. As the first horse calmed even more, Jessie did the same with the other, and then with one horse on each side of him, he started back.

Trotting into the village, he saw Eagle Hunter wave to him, and he headed to where they were loading bundles and securing them to the litters with strips of hides. Eagle Hunter said, "I will take one of the horses and Four Bears will need the other one."

As Eagle Hunter took the halter of one, Jessie trotted across to where Four Bears and his sixteen year old son were assembling their litter. Jessie held the horse still as Four Bears and his son attached the litter to the horse. "Do you need my help anymore?"

"No, we are OK now," Four Bears answered.

The wind was beginning to howl through the tree tops, the beach was submerged, and waves were breaking over the tree roots. The sun had given way to an eerie light as dark clouds raced by. Warm rains whipped the lodge poles, which were being twisted by the wind and crashing to the ground. Jessie observed all of this as he walked slowly, letting the others pass by until he was the last one. He heard the increasing howl of the wind and watched as it began to scatter the remains of the small village. With a cold chill gripping his chest, he turned and began to follow Eagle Hunter, who was leading the people north, hoping to reach a large cypress hammock, where they could find the best shelter among the thick trees. He prayed that they would be far enough away from the ocean that the waves could not find them.

Jessie soon caught up with Two Worlds who was riding one of the Marsh Tackie horses. Star Dancer, who was the four year old daughter of Big Cypress, rode in front of him, being protected from the gale.

"Where is Eagle Hunter leading us?" Jessie asked.

As Two Worlds explained, Jessie remembered the hammock he was talking about, as he had been there on hunting trips. He knew it was still several miles away. Pushing against the increasing wind and rain and realizing how far they had to go, he felt the dread tightening its hold on his chest. Between where they were and the hammock, there was nothing but open scrub and small wooded areas, offering no protection. As the hours passed and the storm escalated, the women and children struggled to stay on their horses. It was getting harder for the group to stay together and the visibility was barely 50 feet.

The men were holding on tightly to the halters and were still having a hard time keeping control of the horses. Jessie saw that some of them were covering the heads of their horses with skins and it was helping to keep them calmer. He dropped back to the litter, removed a deer hide and walked back up to the head of the horse Two Worlds was riding. Placing the hide around the horse's head, he tucked the ends tightly through the halter, and then taking the halter he began to lead the horse. Two Worlds dropped the reins across the small horse's neck and pulled the protective deer hide cape further forward over his head to cover the child he protected, leaning as far forward as he could. Then he began a soft chant.

They were no more than half a mile inside the hammock, when Jessie realized that they hadn't seen anyone else for over an hour. He had fought the horse, hanging on to the halter with both hands and all of his weight for the last half hour in the blinding rain, to keep it from rearing up and throwing Two Worlds and the child. He was becoming exhausted, and the mare had started to calm as the trees slowed the wind, when without warning the storm hit with its full fury. Tree tops snapped, branches were being hurtled through the trees, when a branch hit the horse across the front leg. Rearing in panic, it threw Jessie several feet sideways. As he was trying to recover his breath, the stump of a tree just missed his head. Crawling through cypress roots, some protruding over three feet, he made his way to a large fallen cypress tree, its roots having given way to earlier storm winds. Jessie crawled around behind the roots and tucking himself as far under the protective trunk as he could push, he closed his eyes and began his own prayer.

Seventeen

Jessie had been curled up under the cypress trunk, shaking from the fury of the constant rain for at least an hour when the wind paused and the world around him became eerily quiet. He could hardly believe he had survived the fallen trees and torn branches. Crawling slowly to his feet, he felt wobbly and holding onto the cypress root, he gained some control of his legs. Surveying the wreckage, he wondered if anyone else had survived. Suddenly remembering Two Worlds and the child he was holding, Jessie looked around in a panic. Staggering back in the direction he had last seen Two Worlds, he got no more than fifty feet, when he heard the roar of the wind. Looking up, he saw tree branches being torn loose and thrown through the trees from the other end of the hammock. Running as fast as his wobbly legs would carry him, he headed for the back side of the fallen tree.

Jessie dove under the trunk as the eye of the storm passed over and the full fury of the storm's back side hit. He felt his legs being lifted up from the ground and was afraid he was going to be hurtled through the trees like a broken branch. Crawling further into the roots, he braced himself and held on until he heard the winds letting up. Limbs were no longer being thrown through the trees. The storm and its fury progressed inland, leaving a steady down pour of rain. Slowly moving his legs, Jessie worked his way out of the roots and rolling himself out from under the trunk, tried to stand up. Reaching up from his knees he grabbed part of a root and struggled to his feet. Leaning against the trunk, he made his way toward the smaller end until he could sit with his feet touching the ground. Sitting in shock, Jessie tried to gather his thoughts enough to comprehend what had happened and what he needed to do next. Suddenly realizing that his throat was dry, he wondered how that could be. Tilting his head back he closed his eyes and let the rain drops slide down his throat, swallowing the water as it filled his throat until his thirst was satisfied.

Looking around, it was hard to comprehend what he was seeing. The first thing that registered as Jessie was recovering his senses was water. The hammock was flooded, and the water was rising. Looking around he realized he was sitting on a mound of high ground, and it was hard to tell how far it reached with the fallen trees in the way. He could not see water ahead of him and maybe two hundred yards behind him, and he calculated that he had a hundred yards on one side and two hundred yards on the other. Jessie knew he would have to walk through the water to get out of the hammock. Remembering the hammock from recent hunts, he slowly began to put together a picture in his mind of where he had entered and how far he had made it into the hammock, before the storm's fury hit, and he had wound up under the roots of a fallen cypress.

The next image yanked him out of his shock and brought him to his feet. Panic rose up from the pit of his stomach, sticking in his throat and choking him. Running up the trunk to the roots of the fallen tree trying to see further, Jessie cupped his hands together, calling out at the top of his lungs, "Two Worlds, Two Worlds!"

Realizing that his words could reach no more than fifty feet through the rain, Jessie stumbled down the roots and began making his way back through the fallen tree tops to where the horse had thrown him. He climbed his way around, through, and over branches and tree trunks to the edge of the rising waters. Jessie looked up at the sky and saw that the light in the hammock would be gone within two hours. He knew that Two Worlds and the child he was holding could not have been thrown that far before their bodies would be stopped by a fallen tree. Finding his way back to where he had been thrown, he made his way north on the high ground, traveling in the storm's path. He had walked no more than fifty feet when he saw bundles wrapped in deer hides, tied to a broken piece of a litter and wedged between a downed tree trunk and several small branches.

Cutting his way through the branches, he was able to pull the broken piece of litter and bundles into the clear. Jessie saw that the bundles were part of the litter that had been attached to the horse that Two Worlds had been riding. He could see that one of the bundles consisted of skins used to cover the lodge poles, and the other was the one he had seen Two Worlds packing at the lodge. Untying the bundle of lodge skins, he pulled out a large section of deer hides sewn together. This was big enough to cut a hole in the center and slip over his head, to stop the rain and wind from chilling his body. Jessie pulled a thick piece of hide from the stack and removing his knife from the sheath, he cut two strips two inches wide and three feet long. Putting back the rest of the hide he rolled them tightly and tied them together at each end leaving a loop. Tying Two Worlds' roll of hides to the skins, he put a loop over each shoulder, letting the skins rest against his back. He knew he would need the hides later for shelter.

As he climbed over the tangle of roots and tree limbs to the area where he had been thrown, Jessie saw the tip of the bow sticking through fallen branches. He couldn't tell if it was broken until he had laid the rolls of hides down and clawed his way through the branches. He saw the rest of the bow wrapped in the strap of the quiver. Some of the arrows were gone and two were broken. Backing out of the branches he checked the bow for breaks or cracks but saw none. Checking the arrows, he removed the two broken ones which left seven he could use. It was becoming difficult for Jessie to make his way through the fallen trees and twisted off tree tops, carrying the hides on his back with the bow and quiver across his shoulder. He knew that at the speed with which he was able to get through the obstacles, he would never make his way out of the hammock before dark. All he could do was to try to find higher ground, if there was any.

The sight of the small leg of a child sticking though the branches stopped him in his tracks. He wanted to look away and not see it, but his mind wouldn't let him. He stood there telling himself that there was nothing he could do for her now; she was gone. He must leave her and keep moving. He had to make his way out of the hammock, but as the sob caught in his throat, he began working his way toward her, knowing he could not leave her to the animals. The top of a cypress had been torn off by the winds, and it looked as if she had been caught under it as it crashed to the ground. Pulling back the debris, he saw the arm wrapped around her waist. It looked broken as he pushed one branch out of the way, and pulling back another branch with his arm, Jessie saw the lifeless body of the old man with the child pulled tightly against his chest. With his knife, Jessie began to cut away what branches he could, and breaking the bigger ones, he threw them aside making a path clear enough to remove the old man and child.

As Jessie gripped the arm to pull it away from the child's body, he thought he felt the arm tighten slightly! Snatching his arm back, his breath stopped short in his chest. He stared at the old man and again the body looked lifeless. Reaching once more, he gripped the arm and tried to lift it from the body. Again he felt the arm tighten. Holding on to the arm, he reached to feel Two World's forehead. As his hand touched the skin, he felt it quiver in response. He moved his hand away from the forehead and saw the eye lids flutter. The eyelids opened and Two Worlds looked into Jessie's eyes.

Straining, the old man said, "There are more that have survived. Some are injured; some have passed on into the world of their ancestors. You must find them. They are lost now and will be looking for you." Stunned Jessie could only stare and try to understand what had just happened here.

As the realization dawned on him, Jessie spoke, "You have been away, and I saw your spirit enter your body as you returned."

"Yes and I have seen the others scattered with the wind. You must continue to the end of the hammock and build a great fire, to send a signal to the ones who can make their way to you. Then you must send out some men to find the broken ones. It will be hard, many will not make the trip," Two Worlds said.

"There is not enough time to reach the end before dark," Jessie replied. "We have maybe an hour left."

It took Jessie a moment to realize that something had changed. Looking around, he saw that the rain had stopped, and streaks of sun light were finding their way through the broken and twisted branches to the water soaked earth.

"The water will stop rising now," he told Two Worlds. "We will be safe here and I will use this time to make you a comfortable place with shelter, until I can find a way to get you out of here. I will not leave you here and you are going to have to let me take the child now, there is nothing we can do but send her body to her ancestors."

Jessie felt the broken arm give way and he laid it gently along Two World's body. Extracting the small body he heard a sob escape the old man's lips. "I am sorry this old body could not protect you. Go and be with the one who brought you here."

Jessie knew that Two Worlds had seen the death of the child's mother. Looking down at the lifeless body, he saw the small broken neck and the gash on the side of her head. It looked as though the base of a broken tree top had caught her on the head as it crashed to the ground. She never knew what hit her. Jessie made a bed upon a stack of palm fronds that he cut with his knife. He covered her body with more palm fronds.

After Jessie cut and broke away more limbs, he had a path wide enough to carry Two Worlds to the bed he had made from the bundle of lodge skins. Realizing that Two Worlds could not help, Jessie knelt and reaching his arms under the old man's body, he leaned back rolling the body into his arms against his chest. He was surprised at how light Two Worlds felt. He barely heard the moan as the body went limp. Standing slowly, he backed his way out of the branches, and carried Two Worlds to the furs. Again he knelt and laying him down gently, he slipped his arms from under his body. Going back to the place from which he had removed Two Worlds, he retrieved the cape from the tree limbs and carried it back, laying it over the old man.

It was getting harder to see as the shadows withdrew taking the light with them. Jessie laid the last of the palm fronds he had prepared, so he could sleep above the rain soaked earth. Checking Two Worlds once more before lying down to rest, he placed the old man's bundle next to the bed of skins. Looking down at the seemingly lifeless body, he knew that Two Worlds was not there. He was once again searching for his people. Jessie collapsed on the palm fronds, letting exhaustion finally over take him.

Jessie woke slowly. He had slept fitfully through the night, disturbed by sounds. Some noises were close enough that he could hear the soft rustle of animals working their way through the broken limbs, searching for their lost ones. He was awakened once by the scream of a panther further off. He lay listening for an answering call that never came.

Straining to see though the blackness, he could see nothing past his arm's length but a few stars poking through the tree tops. What little light came from a sliver of the moon was absorbed before it could reach the hammock floor. Standing, his body felt bruised all over. Jessie could barely move his arms and legs as he stumbled to where Two Worlds lay as still as death. Trying not to panic, he knelt down and softly shook Two Worlds' shoulder. Moaning at the touch, the old man opened his eyes.

With a lot of effort, he spoke slowly. "My spirit is here, but my body can barely contain it. Your task is great; you will leave me here and go now. You must find the ones that have survived and take them to safety."

Jessie was deeply distressed. "I cannot leave you here, I owe you my life." He wasn't sure he could do what was being asked, but Two Worlds had saved his life and was asking. He knew he had to try even as he feared for his friends' life. "You cannot survive if I leave you here without food and you cannot drink the water; it will be spoiled now."

With difficulty the old man spoke to Jessie. "You must go now and find your way to the end of the hammock. It will be difficult, but the land will be dry until you reach the end. There will be many animals, but they will not harm you. Beware of the snakes; they will also be seeking dry land. When you reach the end of the hammock, you must build the fire we spoke of. The survivors will need a signal."

"The wood is still wet and I have no flint to start a fire," said Jessie.

Slowly with great effort, Two Worlds turned his head and looked at the bundle that Jessie had placed by his side. Pausing to catch his breath, he said, "Open my skins and inside you will find a small gourd filled with powder that I have saved for the rifles when we need them."

Jessie untied the straps and unrolling the deer skin hide, began looking through the contents. He spotted a carved gourd about the size of his fist and removed it. Holding it, he pulled the stopper and poured a small amount of gun powder into his hand. The gourd had kept it dry.

"There are cloth patches in the small otter fur pouch, and with that you can start the fire," Two Worlds said. Then he closed his eyes.

With a feeling of dread, Jessie pulled his knife from its sheath and cut a four inch strip from the bottom of his cotton shirt. Searching the area, he found several tree stumps and limbs with shallow depressions, still full of rain water. Laying the strip of his shirt in the water, he waited and let the cotton material soak it up. Tilting his head back, he squeezed the water from the cloth and drank his fill. Then he soaked the piece of shirt once more until it was dripping. Walking back to where Two Worlds lay, he let the water drip across the old man's lips. Two Worlds opened his mouth, letting the drops trickle down his throat. After Jessie had squeezed out most of the water, he laid the strip of cloth across the old man's forehead.

Two Worlds spoke without opening his eyes. "You must leave me; I am in the hands of the Great Spirit now, and there is no more you can do for me."

Jessie placed the gourd and fur pouch inside the quiver with the arrows, then rolled and tied the skins that he had used to protect him from the rain. Dropping the strap over his shoulder, he looked once more at Two Worlds and left. It was past noon when Jessie saw the open space beyond the hammock. His clothes were soaked with sweat, and hunger gnawed at his stomach. He watched the animals slip away as he struggled over, around, and through the tangled tree tops and torn limbs until he was exhausted and stopped to rest. Using a large leaf, he scooped water from a broken stump to satisfy his thirst.

As he looked up at the sun to guess what time of day it was, he saw that there were no leaves left on the trees. It was another hour of struggling through the debris before he reached the end of the hammock. As he stepped out into the full sun, he was blinded by the light which reflected off the water that covered the open land. Stepping back into the hammock to get out of the sun's glare, he stared at the open space littered with broken trees. As far as he could see, nothing was standing between him and the scattered oak and palm strands. Half a mile away, he saw the remains of what had been a pine strand the day before. The brittle wood of the trees had snapped like match sticks from the full force of the wind.

Searching along the high ground of the hammock, Jessie found dry palm fronds and gathering several, he carried them to the outer edge. Crumbling the dried fronds into a small pile, he then placed several cotton patches from the fur pouch into the center of the fronds. Next, removing the stopper from the small gourd, he sprinkled a thick layer of gun powder over the cotton patches. Removing the belt from his pants and slipping the knife from its sheath, he held the end of the metal buckle in the powder and raked the back of the knife blade up and down the buckle's edge.

The sparks from the pieces of metal ignited the powder, catching two of the cotton patches on fire. Bending down with his face close to the small flames, he gently blew into the fire until the palm fronds suddenly exploded into life. Quickly, he added larger pieces of the palm fronds and other broken branches and waited until he was sure they were burning. Looking around, Jessie found pieces of dry cypress limbs and began building a bonfire. As these limbs were consumed, creating a bed of hot coals, he added bigger pieces of wood until the blaze reached higher than his head

He didn't have to go far to find green branches torn from the trees. Dragging the ones he could find with the leaves still attached, he threw them across the flames. Clouds of black smoke rose high into the sky. Adding more dry branches to keep the flames going, he threw on more of the green tree tops until he had piled the branches as high as he could throw. Exhausted, he found a fallen tree and unrolled the deer hide, making himself a place to sit and sank to the ground, leaning back against the trunk. His body hurt everywhere. Ignoring the pain, he rested his head against his chest and slept.

Eighteen

Jessie came awake slowly, wondering what sound woke him up, and then he heard it again, the sound of voices. Rising slowly to give his muscles time to stretch, he walked out to the edge of the woods and saw a group of people, some walking and some on horseback. He walked out to meet them and as he got closer, he recognized Red Sun leading one horse with Woman of the Wind on its back. The horse was pulling a travois containing several bundles tied with strips of hide. Jessie's chest tightened when he saw two bodies draped across the horse that Waiting Owl and Little Otter were leading.

"We saw the smoke from the fire. Are there more here with you?" Red Sun called out.

"No, you are the first that I have seen." As the straggling group came closer, he recognized the bodies of Four Bears and his wife White Sun.

"Where are Grandfather and Star Dancer?" Little Otter asked. She lowered her head and cried as Jessie explained what had happened to Two Worlds and the four year old child.

As Jessie led the group back to the fire, he realized that Little Moon was missing. Speaking to Red Sun he asked, "Where is Little Moon?"

"She was with Eagle Hunter and his wife Rainbow; Spirit Dancer, their two year old daughter; and Little Wolf, their six year old son. We were separated before we reached the forest of trees on the other side of the hammock." Red Sun explained. "I managed to tie the horses' heads tight to a tree and we found some shelter in a clump of large cypress trees. We came upon Four Bears and White Sun on the outer edge of the trees. It looked as if they never made it into the forest. I saw what looked like one of the horses off in the distance but no other people."

When they reached the fire, Jessie helped unload a bundle of lodge cover hides and made a resting place for Woman of the Wind. Then he helped Red Sun lead the horses out of sight of the others, and they removed the bodies of Four Bears and White Sun. After tying the two horses to a tree, they walked back to the fire.

"There is no more than two hours of sunlight left," Jessie said to Red Sun. "I will help you build the fire back up to keep the smoke going for others to see, and then I have to go back and find Two Worlds. I don't know if he can make it another night. He is hurt pretty bad. I also have to bring the child out. I cannot leave her there for the animals."

"I can take care of the fire," answered Red Sun, "but you cannot make it back though the forest of broken limbs and tree tops before dark."

"I will take one of the horses and stay on the outside where we can make faster time. I have to try."

"But you can't bring both of them out alone. I will go with you."

"No!" Jessie insisted. "I will go back in the morning for the child. She will be alright until then." Mounting one of the horses Red Sun had brought in, Jessie urged the horse into a trot and gave him the reins. The little Marsh Tackie was suited for this type of land, and Jessie let him work his way around the broken branches and twisted tree tops. It had been over an hour when Jessie thought he was close to where he should cut into the hammock. He heard the screech of the osprey and looking up, he saw it circle just ahead of him, and then it turned and flew across the tree tops.

Jessie rode to where he thought the osprey had turned and entered the hammock. He let the horse work his way around and over the debris and got down to move branches when the horse could go no further. Making a trail deeper into the hammock, he finally saw the area he had cleared for Two Worlds. Seeing the spot where he had left Two Worlds, he stood rooted to the ground, and his heart pounded as he watched a huge panther rise up and limp away. Panic clenched his stomach as he franticly made his way to the cleared spot where he found the old man sitting against a broken tree trunk. A piece of hide was wrapped around his broken arm to relieve some of the pain.

Jessie knew that he had just witnessed something of the power of the old man that was far beyond his understanding. Squatting in front of Two Worlds he said, "We have to hurry to get you out of these woods before dark."

"There is plenty of time, and it is good to see you; rest for a while and we will leave," Two Worlds responded.

"It is good to see you too, Two Worlds, but I am fine." Lifting the old man up from the ground to sit him on the back of the small horse, he reflected once again on how light and fragile he felt.

After putting the roll of lodge skins in front of Two Worlds and placing his fur cape over the thin shoulders, Jessie led the horse and started back. The sun had almost dropped down below the tree tops as they made their way out of the woods and into the open plain, littered with tree branches. Jumping up on the horse's back, he put his arm around the fragile body and pulled the old man against his chest. Jessie once again gave the horse the lead, and they started the slow trek back. They had been riding quietly for an hour before they saw the glow of the fire. It was another hour before they reached the end of the hammock and turned towards the flames. The smoke was no longer visible in the dark. As Jessie and Two Worlds got closer to the fire, he could see that there were more people who had found their way to the smoke.

Red Sun saw the horse and riders and met them at the edge of the fire light. Reaching up, he took Two Worlds from Jessie's arms and carried him to where Woman of the Wind lay, placing the old man next to her on the skins. With tears running down her cheeks, she gently ran her small wrinkled hand over his face. With her heart smiling, she removed broken twigs from his hair. Two Worlds watched Woman of the Wind's expression of concern for him.

"Were you afraid I would not come back?"

"No. I knew you were alive; I saw you circling above us when you were showing us the way here. I was only concerned of how bad you were hurt. There are a lot of the people missing and I fear for them now."

"The worst is not over, and we must rest and prepare ourselves for what is to come," Two Worlds told her.

Woman of the Wind rose from the hides. "I will go and make what medicines I can to help the injured. I will prepare the wood strips and we will have to straighten your arm so it will heal right."

When Woman of the Wind came to Little Otter, she said, "I am going to need you to feed your Grandfather. Shred some meat from the breast of the great crane we have cooked, and take a piece of the coontie bread and a gourd of fresh water, and tell him if he does not eat, I will come feed him."

Little Otter saw the cuts and bruises on her Grandmother and saw she was in pain; she also knew that she would be up most of the night helping the injured people, not only with their wounds, but also their sorrow over their lost ones. Jessie also knew she would put aside her own pain and be up most of the night. Watching, he saw her going to where the bundles had been put to be sorted out in the day light. Woman of the Wind knelt and began to look for her healing bundle. He saw her give a sigh of relief as she pulled her bundle out, and in the light of the fire, she unwrapped the fur hide and began sorting her medicines.

Jessie walked around the large fire and over to a smaller fire where Big Cypress sat with his two boys, eight year old Little Feather and ten year old White Eagle. They had arrived just before dark. Jessie sat down cross legged in front of Big Cypress. "In my heart I have terrible news I bring to you."

"I know," Big Cypress said, "Red Sun told me about my daughter. Her mother is dead also. Tomorrow I will go with you to bring her back to her mother."

Jessie's head was throbbing as he cut strips of the roasted venison and tore away a piece of coontie bread. Finding a small drinking gourd, he filled it from the fresh water bag. Carrying his food, Jessie walked to join Red Sun and his wife Waiting Owl. Little Otter was sitting cross legged with her back to her mother, wincing as her mother tried to comb the tangles from her long black hair. Jessie sat on the ground between Red Sun and Two Worlds, who was sitting up and leaning against a fur, covered back rest. Before biting into a strip of venison, he asked. "Two Worlds, what should we do?"

"We must wait; there are more survivors coming. Keep the fire going through the night to light the way; it can be seen from a great distance. The smoke will guide them during the day."

After Jessie ate as much food as he could manage, he found a bundle of sleeping furs and made himself a bed. Lying on the furs, and feeling the throbbing pain in his head that had returned, he wasn't sure how much longer he could hold out. Waiting Owl startled him by touching him on the shoulder. He turned to face her and she handed him a drinking gourd with a small amount of liquid in it.

"Woman of the Wind said that this will stop the hurt in your head." Thanking her, he swallowed the liquid and handed the gourd back to her. As the pain eased, Jessie wondered once again how he got here. Did the old man know this was going to happen? Was everything already planned? If so, why didn't he know? Or were the predictions just a good guess? He didn't think it was that easy. He felt the relief you get when pain goes away, and he slept.

It was after midnight when Jessie awoke. Looking at the fire, he saw that the wood was burning down, and he rose from his fur mat. He began adding limbs that they had gathered earlier, throwing the branches as high as he could without letting them topple over. Watching the flames build up, Jessie first heard the sounds of an animal moving though the water. The sound got louder as the animal came closer. He thought it must be a bear smelling the cooked meat or wild hogs that roamed the Everglades.

The last thing Jessie expected was to see Silent Stalker step into the edge of the light, leading the horse by the halter. Then Jessie recognized his wife Raven, slumped forward and behind her his nine year old son Snake Handler. Walking toward them, he looked for the younger son Cripple Hawk, and his stomach began to knot when he could not see him. Not another child missing, he thought. As Silent Stalker came closer into the light, he saw the young boy wrapped in furs and tied to the litter behind the horse. He knew that the boy was either dead or badly hurt by the way he was bound to the litter.

"I have been traveling to the light since it was dark. We were heading back to the camp hoping that whoever survived would go there, but I saw the smoke in the afternoon and so we turned back this way. Is everyone else here and safe?"

"No, but some have made their way here; some are still missing and some are dead."

As Jessie walked into the camp with Silent Stalker, others were coming awake and gathering to see who else had found their way to the light. Red Sun and Waiting Owl met them at the fire, and Woman of the Wind followed them with her bundle under her arm. Red Sun reached up and helped Snake Handler down from the horse.

"Be gentle with Raven, she has broken ribs and her shoulder is also injured," Silent Stalker said. Reaching up, Red Sun let Raven slip from the horse into his arms, hearing her moan with pain. Waiting Owl hurried and spread first hides and then furs, close enough to the fire to make a comfortable place to lay her down. As Red Sun knelt and carefully laid Raven on the furs, Woman of the Wind knelt down beside her. Tenderly lifting her head, she helped Raven drink the medicine from the small gourd to stop the pain and ease her into sleep.

Jessie saw that everyone was awake by the time Woman of the Wind finished checking to see how badly Raven had been injured. Wrapping strips of hides around her ribcage as tight as Raven would allow, gave her some relief. By the time she finished, the medicine had begun to work and Raven was almost asleep. Jessie reached down and helped Woman of the Wind to her feet as she rose to go check on Silent Stalker's youngest son Cripple Hawk. Holding on to Jessie's arm, she slowly walked to where they had moved his small broken and bruised body next to Waiting Owls' sleeping furs, so she could watch over him through the night while his mother slept.

Jessie watched Woman of the Wind kneel next to the small body and open the furs. Deep bruises covered his small chest. Laying her ear softly against his discolored skin, she could barely hear the soft beat of his heart. After checking the gash across the side of his head, she covered him with the furs and rose slowly to her feet. Jessie heard her moan softly as her own body told her that she too was bruised and hurt.

"Grandmother," Jessie said with concern, "you too must rest." Woman of the Wind spoke with hurt in her eyes as she promised him that she would rest soon, but now she needed to make a healing paste to cover the head wound. Woman of the Wind would do her best to heal the child, even though in her heart she knew that his spirit was more in the next world than in this world and would not be coming back. Knowing their pain, her heart cried for Silent Stalker and Raven, and for Snake Handler, who would no longer have a brother.

Jessie didn't sleep the remainder of the night. He had stayed up for a while, talking to Two Worlds, asking the question that had concerned him all that day. "What are we going to do about the dead?"

Then Two Worlds spoke. "Go in the morning and get the child, and when you are back we will talk further."

Big Cypress explained to his two sons where he was going and that they were to remain there and help wherever they could. He was mounted when Jessie rode up on one of the Marsh Tackies with his pack resting on his back. In it were strips of venison, coontie bread and a small drinking gourd. They nudged the two Marsh Tackies forward and gave them the reins, letting them work their way through the broken trees and branches.

It was shortly before noon when Jessie and Big Cypress rode their horses into the make shift camp. Big Cypress was carrying the small child held tightly against his chest. He swung his leg across the horse's back and still holding his child, he slid to the ground. Carrying his daughter to her mother, he knelt and laid the child next to her, and then he began a far away chant.

Jessie turned as he heard the moaning and wailing of another mother who had lost a loved one. He saw Raven leaning over her son Cripple Hawk, whose spirit had made its final choice. Silent Stalker knelt behind her with his arms around her chest to keep her from falling, and chanted though his tears. Snake Handler sat back in the roots of a fallen tree, silently watching his family though his tears and not able to understand any of the things that were happening around him.

After Jessie had ridden out with Big Cypress to bring his daughter back, Red Sun sat cross legged in front of Two Worlds, who was leaning against his fur covered back rest. They were discussing the search for Little Moon, Four Bears' son Spirit Snake, also Eagle Hunter and his family.

"You will need to take the extra horses. Go east around the other side of the hammock. They are still there and waiting on you. I will help you find them," Two Worlds said.

The hammock was more than two miles long and a mile wide. Red Sun had followed the osprey more than a mile along the east side, letting the horses make their way through the debris, when he saw the osprey turn and fly inland across the tree tops. Turning, he started working his way into the hammock, but the closer he got to the edge of the trees, the thicker the debris became. Tying the lead lines of the three horses to a branch, he started forward on foot. He spent two hours pulling small branches aside and working his way around the larger fallen trees. Red Sun was frustrated with the slow progress and angry that it was keeping him from his daughter. Little Moon was the gentle one, like her mother. Hearing the almost constant screech above him, he wanted to scream as he put all of his strength into clearing branches out of his path.

He had to stop for a second time to listen, before he heard the yell. Letting out a loud whoop, he waited for the reply. He couldn't see anyone, but he knew it was coming from his left. Looking around, he realized that he had drifted away from the direction he had been going in when he started into the hammock. Now he understood what the screeching was about. Working feverishly, he proceeded in the direction that the yelling was coming from. He saw limbs moving, and then he saw Spirit Snake, pulling and throwing branches as he worked his way toward him.

Reaching Spirit Snake, he saw the bruises and cuts covering his face and arms. "Are you OK?" Red Sun asked.

"Yes," Spirit Snake answered. "A lot of the scratches are from pulling branches to make a trail, but I could not move enough to carry Little Moon or Eagle Hunters son and little girl."

"Where are Eagle Hunter and his wife Rainbow?" Red Sun asked quietly.

"They are dead," Spirit Snake answered. "I could not help them. We were separated when the big winds came and the horse bolted, carrying Spirit Dancer and Little Wolf. Little Moon and I were able to keep up until a tree fell across the horse killing him. Little Moon and I managed to take the little ones and crawl behind the tree that fell on the horse. We were able to get the furs and lodge hides and build a shelter, but yesterday when we were trying to find a way out, Little Moon slipped and fell. I think her foot is broken; it has gotten bigger and she cannot stand on it."

"Where are Little Moon and the small ones?" Red Sun asked.

"They are not far away," Spirit Snake answered. "This is as far as I could clear the limbs by myself."

Spirit Snake turned and led Red Sun no more than a hundred yards when he saw the skins stretched across branches making a shelter. He saw Little Moon lying on a bed of furs with a little one on each side of her. When she saw her father she called out, "I knew you would find us, Grandfather said he would guide you to us!"

"Your Grandfather was here?" Red sun asked confused.

"I saw him last night in my dreams. Oh Father, Spirit Snake says Eagle Hunter and Rainbow are dead."

Turning to Spirit Snake, he asked, "How do you know they are dead, did you see them?"

"Yes I went back to where we were when the horse bolted. They had followed for a ways, but I think they were in the open and were killed by falling trees. They are not very far from here," Spirit Snake replied.

Pulling the strap from over his shoulder Red Sun asked, "Have you had anything to eat, I have brought meat from the great bird's breast, bread and a bag of fresh water."

As Red Sun was removing the food and water from his roll, Spirit Snake said, "I have food and water from Eagle Hunter's travois, and there is a small spring flowing with fresh water."

Red Sun turned to face Spirit Snake. "Follow my trail back out to the edge of the hammock, and you will find where I tied the horses. Bring them here." Red Sun knelt down and gently lifted Little Moon's foot. "Move your toes." Little Moon winced as she slowly moved her toes up and down. "You have twisted your ankle, but it is not broken." Cutting a long strip of soft deer hide he wrapped the ankle as tightly as Little Moon would allow. "Are you hurt anywhere else?" he asked.

"I have bruises and scrapes, but I am OK," she smiled bravely.

Red Sun smiled at his daughter. "I am going to find Eagle Hunter and Rainbow, and when Spirit Snake comes back with the horses, tell him to bring two of them. I will make a path."

Red Sun found the two bodies under the branches of a fallen tree. He had removed Rainbow's broken body and was trying to move the heavy branch that was pinning Eagle Hunter's body to the ground. He could lift the branch, but he could not move the body at the same time. As Red sun was trying to figure out a solution, Spirit Snake arrived with the two horses. Spirit Snake pulled the body free when Red Sun lifted the heavy branch. Together they lifted the bodies up on the backs of the horses and led them back to where Little Moon was waiting. It took most of an hour searching though the tangle of limbs to find what bundles they could. Lifting Little Moon onto the last horse, they placed the two year old in front and her six year old brother behind her. They tied the bundles to the bodies on the other horses. No one spoke, and with heavy hearts they started out of the hammock and headed back to the other survivors.

It was late afternoon when Jessie spotted the small party still a quarter of a mile off. As the group got closer, he recognized Red Sun leading two of the horses and Spirit Snake leading the other horse with Little Moon and the two small children. Sadly, he looked back at the others and saw the grief on everyone's faces when they realized whose bodies were draped across the horses.

As Red Sun led the group into the waiting camp, he saw that the fire had been allowed to burn down to hot coals. A wild hog and more breast of the great bird were being cooked, and he realized that they no longer needed the smoke as a signal. He was surprised to see platforms being built high above the ground, and then he understood what they were going to do with the dead. Two Worlds had made his decision. Two Worlds knew they could not bury the bodies of the dead where the animals could dig them up, and time had run out. This was the third day, and the bodies were starting to decay. Scattered everywhere were dead animals left by the great winds of the storm. They were decaying too, and Two Worlds knew they could not stay here any longer. Jessie had worked with the other suvivors and by dark, all the platforms had been built and large dry branches were piled as thick as possible underneath. The bodies of the small children were placed with their mothers, wrapped in skins and placed above the platforms.

Jessie watched as the darkness closed in. With Red Sun on one side and Silent Stalker on the other, Two Worlds solemnly approached the platform. The young braves supported him as they walked down the line of platforms, and Two Worlds lit each fire with a flaming torch. Then the people circled the fires, chanting and wailing late into the night until the fires died, leaving only memories and grief in the ashes. Jessie lay awake on his sleeping furs as the sun rose bringing the light of a new day. He remained quiet as he watched the small group of survivors rise and begin packing what belongings they had left. The only sounds were the crying of the ones still grieving. Jessie knew that he would hear that sound for many days to come as he gathered his bow and quiver, along with the back pack containing his belongings. They were not the only weight he would carry on his shoulders.

Jessie helped to make two travois with beds of fur to carry Two Worlds and Raven. Then he loaded what belongings they had found onto the three other travois. Red Sun lifted Little Moon up on the Marsh Tackie's back and placed Spirit Dancer in front of her and Little Wolf behind her. She had not let them out of her sight since she had gathered them in her arms and kept them safe in the hammock. Spirit Snake offered to stay with them in case they needed something.

Jessie and Big Cypress lifted Woman of the Wind onto another horse. She had insisted on riding, instead of lying on a travois, so she could observe her patients. Big Cypress then lifted his two sons, Little Feathers and White Eagle, up on the back of the horse he would lead and waited for Silent Stalker. Silent Stalker placed his only remaining son on the horse that would carry him and Raven. Jessie watched as Silent Stalker led the horse to the front of the bereaved group of survivors, to lead them forward to the Caloosahatchee River. From there, Jessie would take over and lead the people to where their new life would begin.

Turning once again, Jessie looked back and saw the smoke still rising from the ashes from the night before. Suddenly, he felt the impact of what he had just witnessed and felt the pain of the people who had given up so much after giving him his life back. Jessie had fought men face to face, knowing it was kill or be killed. He had felt the pain when they had sent bodies home after a battle. Some of the soldiers he had gotten to know quite well, but he could never have imagined the sorrow he felt at this moment as he turned to catch up with the others.

Nineteen

It was three days before they reached the Caloosahatchee River. They could see the water marks high on the banks from the run off of the great waters of Lake Okeechobee. It had been six days since the storm had passed, and the great lake had emptied the storm waters out into the Gulf of Mexico. They had moved northwest away from the destruction of the storm and the stench of the dead animals and birds. It would be a long time before the smell would diminish. Arriving at the river when the sun was still high overhead, Red Sun sent Silent Stalker east and Big Cypress west, to find a place shallow enough to cross. Breaking out food, they found shelter from the sun and rested while they waited. They were beginning to heal from their injuries now, but the sadness still hung over all of them like a heavy fog. Very little conversation had taken place in the three days since they had left their loved ones at the hammock.

Jessie walked beside Two Worlds as they made their way slowly along the river bank, letting the old man exercise his legs. He was walking further each day now. Jessie was amazed at the strength that those small, ageless muscles possessed. "Two Worlds, I understand now that I play a part in what is happening here, but I still do not understand what I am to do. I know that you and the others who are now my people must come with me, but I have no idea what will happen when we reach my people."

"I am afraid the spirits of my ancestors have not told me either."

"Well, since your ancestors' spirits have brought us this far, I will trust they will eventually let us know. Until then we will find a safe place to rebuild your village and let the people heal."

Two hours later Big Cypress rode into camp. As he and Red Sun approached Two Worlds and Jessie, he said, "There is a place about a mile from here where there is a shoal in the river. The water is no more than knee deep to the horses and we can carry the travois across on our shoulders. If we leave now we can make the crossing before dark."

Two Worlds nodded his approval and Red Sun went to ready the others. They had just finishing getting everyone across the river and preparing the fires for the night when Silent Stalker returned. Riding his horse though the shallow water, he stopped in front of Red Sun and told him that after more than an hour's ride, he had seen no shallow place to cross. He was relieved that Big Cypress had found a place. Tying the horse for the night, he went to check on his wife and son. He saw that she was now able to stand and walk some; then they sat by the fire, eating and talking softly.

After everyone had eaten, some were sitting around their small fires; others were still exhausted and lay in their sleeping rolls. Red Sun tapped Waiting Owl on the shoulder and turning, he discreetly pointed to the river. Spirit Snake had his arm around Little Moon's shoulders and she had her arm around his waist. Jessie saw them moving slowly toward the river together as she hobbled on her swollen ankle. There they sat and talked. It was the first time that Little Moon had been away from the little ones, who were now sleeping.

As they sat listening to the night sounds of the river, Spirit Snake asked, "What are you going to do with Little Wolf and Spirit Dancer?"

"I will raise them myself; they are mine now."

"I will help you," Spirit Snake said. "We will raise them together."

"We are not old enough yet for my father to let me leave my family to become your wife, but I will be waiting for that day to come."

"My mother and father are gone, and I am a man now. When we arrive at our new place the white man is taking us, I will build my own lodge. I will build it big enough for our new family; big enough to add more when you are my wife."

Putting her arm through his, she leaned against his shoulder and quietly answered, "I know."

They traveled slowly to give everyone a chance to heal, stopping early each day to hunt fresh game and gather herbs and berries. On the sixth day, Jessie recognized the Withlacoochee River.

"I have been this way on my way to Fort Myers as a soldier; we will need to head east from here. We are no more than three or four days to my place." He could see the confusion in their faces, but he had no idea what to tell them because he still did not understand what was going to happen either.

They traveled for four more days, and as they were making their way by moon light, Jessie could sense where he was and knew he was close. He was anxious to be home, and his heart beat a little faster when he came to the back side of the lake. He led the small group down into the valley and further around the lake into a small strand of large live oaks. They were now close enough to see the outline of his house and barn, and he spoke loud enough for everyone to hear.

"We will build your new village here." Quietly they began to unload the travois. They removed the hides they had been able to save and started lighting fires. Watching the lighting in the far distance, he could see it was heading their way. Jessie worked quickly, helping the people make temporary shelters and get settled for the night.

Seeing that everyone had their shelter made, Jessie walked to where Two Worlds and Red Sun had made their shelters close together. "It will be easier to explain to my family what has happened if Red Sun would come with me."

"Everyone will be alright here tonight, and I will come with you," Red Sun answered.

"I will come with you too," Little Otter said, jumping up.

"No, you have no need to come."

"She is welcome to come," Jessie said. "I would like my wife to meet her."

As they started out around the lake, watching the lightning that was no more than a half a mile away, Jessie wondered if they could beat the summer storm, moving in their direction. About half way between the strand of live oaks and his house he urged his horse to a trot. The storm was coming on fast and he saw the full outline of the house and barn, when the lightning lit the sky for a brief moment. He heard the boom, as the lightning bolt struck the ground by the barn, and a minute later saw the big work horse in a panic as he galloped by. The rain was almost blinding as they came close enough to the barn to see the faint glow from the lantern.

Stepping down from their horses, they walked them into the doorway of the barn. Handing the reins to Red Sun, he made his way to the end of the stalls, where he saw Belle on her knees and heard the moans coming from his son. Reaching the stall, he heard Belle tell Ed she didn't know how, but she had to get him into the house somehow.

"Maybe I can help you with that," he said.

It was before dawn when Jessie awoke and felt Belle still cuddled in his arms. Breathing in the smell of her hair and remembering last night, he found himself in that world where time stands still and nothing exists except this moment. Belle, feeling Jessie's passion, smiled to herself and pulled him on top of her. They shared that moment together and made up for the heartache and lost time, until he was finally home to her.

Day light was breaking as Belle handed Jessie his cup of coffee and asked, "What are you going to do now?" She knew it was going to be a hard time for Jessie, but she would give him whatever help he needed.

"After I help get Two Worlds and … his people … started on building their new village, I am going to ride over to see Bill and let him know I'm back. Then in a few days I'm going to ride to Fort Myers and let the army know what happened and find out what's going to happen now." He realized he had almost said "my people" and felt momentarily disoriented.

"Bill said the war was almost over and was told to go home, and that has been two months now," Belle said as she poured her coffee and placed the pot back on the stove.

"I still need to notify the army that I am alive. They will have me listed as dead, and I don't want that."

"Yes," Belle said, "I don't want that written anywhere as long as I'm alive!" Belle took her cup of coffee and sat across the table from Jessie. "Are you saying that the Indians are going to live here from now on?"

"Yes, they are my people now also, and what happens to them happens to me."

"I owe them my future, because without you I would have no future," Belle said.

"There are things going on here that are beyond my understanding, but I know that all of our futures are tied together. Before I went off to fight, I had planned to clear as much land as we could and farm, but now I don't know," Jessie said to Belle as she refilled their cups with coffee. "I will talk further with Two Worlds and Red Sun to see if they have any idea of what might happen from here, but first I have to help them to relocate, and we'll go from there."

As Belle sat back down and handed Jessie his coffee, he took her hand in both of his and said, "Our world as we knew it, doesn't exist anymore for us or them. All of our lives will go in a new direction now, and none of us has ever been there. Our friends will want to share the world we are going to create, but not everyone is going to be happy about what is going to happen here. There are a lot of people who think all Indians should be eliminated or drove off. They could be in danger staying here."

"Surely, the Walsh's or Kersey's or the others wouldn't want to harm them?"

"No, but there are people in this country that have fought in the Seminole wars and had friends die at the hands of the Indians. They will always carry that anger. It doesn't matter if these Indians were never involved in that war. The people who lost friends and family to the Indians are very dangerous, but we will prevail."

Looking up at the sounds of feet shuffling across the breezeway, he saw Ed holding his ribs with one hand and the door frame with the other as he made it into the kitchen.

Belle rose from her chair and went to meet him. "You should not be out of bed yet."

As he put his arm around her shoulder, he said, "I heard you talking, and I just wanted to talk to Pa before anyone else gets up." He sat down very carefully in Belle's chair. She went to the stove to pour Ed a cup of coffee. He drank it black just like Jessie did. "I sure am glad to see you home Pa. I always believed Ma when she said you would be home one day."

"It's good to be home too, Son. I am very proud of the man you have become while I was away.

"We have all shared the load Pa, but we sure missed you. I am sorry I have hurt myself and can't help, now that you're back. I should have been more careful with Preacher; I know how spooked he gets. I should not have gone into the stall."

"You did what you had to do Son, and sometimes you just don't know when things are going to happen. You do like your ma says and get well; everything is going to be fine now. We'll find Preacher today. He won't go far. More than likely he's down by the lake having breakfast."

"Just like we're going to in a few minutes," Belle said. "It will be ready by the time you wake up the little ones, Jessie. Jenny hasn't seen you yet."

Jessie shook Horace gently, waking him first.

"Are you really back for good? I thought when I woke up this morning you would be gone again."

"Yes I'm back home," he said, reaching down and lifting Horace from the bed and standing him on his feet. "If you don't stop getting big, I won't be able to lift you off the floor."

"But I want to be bigger! I wish I was already as big as you. Then I could go whereever you go, and then you could never leave me again."

"I won't ever be leaving you that long again, and it won't be long before you are as big as me. Get dressed now; your mama is waiting on you with breakfast."

Jessie watched Horace buttoning his pants on the way to the kitchen, and then he sat on the edge of the bed, looking down at Jenny, a small version of her mama. He felt the pain of all the ones who had lost a child in the storm. Leaning down close to her ear he softly whispered, "Daddy loves you."

Her eyes came open and looking up, she asked, "Is this a dream?"

Leaning back down, he kissed her on the forehead and asked, "Did that feel like a dream?"

Jumping up, she wrapped both arms around Jessie's neck, and with her little feet bouncing up and down, she cried out, "Daddy's home, Daddy's home!"

Coming though the kitchen door still clinging to Jessie's neck, she looked at her mom first and then Ed and Horace. Smiling, she announced in her excited little voice, "Daddy's home!" Jenny sat on her daddy's knee and ate her breakfast while he explained to the boys what he had to do today. He made it clear that it was important they all do their jobs as usual. He would take over Ed's chores that Horace couldn't handle until Ed was better.

Jessie sat on the seat of the big work wagon, loaded with arm size poles, twelve to fifteen feet long. This was the third day that they had been cutting the poles from knee deep water in the cypress pond a mile away. He had offered to build houses for all of them, but he knew the answer before he asked. They had all declined; they would stay with their tradition.

Horace sat beside the man he couldn't get enough of since he had come home. Jessie watched with pride as his son handled the reins, urging the horses on with a gentle slap on their rumps. He had taken his turn on the long trip from Georgia and knew the temperament of the two big work horses. He had learned to handle Dolly and let her handle Preacher. Horace guided the big wagon under the big live oak where Big Cypress was waving at them and stopped. Hopping down, Jessie and Horace began helping unload the lodge poles, laying them in a circle. Later, when he would have help, they would stand the poles up, but first Big Cypress would help the others.

Having unloaded the last of the logs, Jessie turned to Horace and said, "Drive the wagon to the barn, and take Dolly and Preacher down to the lake to graze." As Horace started for the wagon, he saw the four boys: Snake Handler, Little Feathers, White Eagle, and six year old Little Wolf, standing next to them.

Turning back, he called to his pa, "Can they come with me?" He pointed to the four boys standing and watching with awe. Horace had learned about the tragedy that their families were dealing with, but had not known what to say to them.

"Yes," said Jessie, "and if they want to go, I will explain to their parents where they are. It will be alright."

Walking over to where the boys were watching him, Horace explained to them where he was going and invited them to come with him. The older boys didn't know Horace, but they had been watching him with curiosity for the past three days. They had been standing around and were bored with having to stay close to the women. They all nodded their heads at the same time.

"Let's go then, Pa will explain where we are going." After helping Little Wolf up and into the back of the wagon, they all sat with their legs dangling over the edge of the wagon bed. Holding on to Little Wolf in the middle, they began to giggle as the wagon started down the bumpy road to the barn. Snake Handler crawled back into the wagon, stood up and balancing himself, stepped over the wooden seat back. He sat down next to Horace in silence. It was five minutes before Snake Handler asked.

"Could you show me how to make the horses go where you want them to go?"

"Sure!" Horace answered and handing the reins to Snake Handler, he began to explain.

Twenty

Waiting for daylight to break, Jessie sat at the kitchen table drinking coffee. Everyone was up and waiting for the breakfast that Belle was starting to serve. Jenny carried her daddy's plate very carefully across the kitchen as they all held their breath, but she wouldn't let anyone else wait on her daddy. Setting the plate on the table, she crawled up on Jessie's knee and began to help her pa eat his breakfast.

"Horace, when it gets light enough, I need you to saddle my horse for me. I'm riding over to see Bill Walsh, Dave Kersey, and John Campbell this morning, to let them know I'm back. Then I'll be riding on over to FortMyers, and I should be back in a few days."

"I want to go with you Pa," Horace said with concern all over his face. "I'll ride Dolly, and I won't be any trouble. I can do it Pa!"

"I know you can, Son, and you wouldn't be any trouble to me at all, but I surely need you here to take care of things. Ed can only do light chores and someone has to take the animals out and bring them back every day. Maybe you can get your new friends to help you."

"OK Pa, but when I'm through with the chores, can I go down to the village and play?"

"Sure you can, but be sure and check with your ma first."

Jessie placed the sack with the fried bacon, smoked wild hog and a half dozen baked sweet potatoes in his saddle bag. Turning back to Belle he said, "Don't worry, I'll be fine. I just have to get this settled."

"I know, but my heart will go with you until you return safely; so go now and don't let them keep you."

Picking Jenny up, he lifted her above his head and as she squealed with delight, he told her, "Take care of your ma until I get back now, you hear?"

"I will, I'll take good care of Ma."

"I'll bet you will," Jessie said, as he stepped up in the stirrup, swung his leg over and sat in the saddle. He leaned down and looking Belle in the eyes, he said, "The devil himself couldn't keep me away now."

It took a little more than an hour of riding to reach Bills homestead, located under an oak stand on the Little Withlacoochee River. He noticed that Bill had about 10 acres cleared and plowed under, and was close to being able to plant. Swinging down from his horse, he wrapped the reins around a small tree in the yard. He heard talking as he headed toward the open barn. Stepping inside, he saw Bill, his wife Martha, and their two girls separating sacks of seed on a rough board table. Martha's breath caught in her throat as she put her hand over her mouth and stared. Turning around, Bill stopped short and stared. After several seconds of silence Bill said, "I must be looking at a ghost, 'cause that can't be you standing there. We looked for over a week, searching for a body, thinking an animal had dragged you off to some lair or gator hole."

Sitting on a chair on the front porch with a glass of water one of the girls had brought him, Jessie explained what had happened and described the journey back. When Jessie had finished, Bills first question was, "What are you going to do with them?"

"I don't know yet, but at this point, I do know that whatever is happening is bigger than me."

"Well, you know that if you ever need my help, all you have to do is ask, and I'm sure John and Dave will tell you the same. We have all been in this together since we decided to leave Georgia, and we fought together to keep our homesteads. We are going to keep clearing what land we can and will be planting tobacco and later on, corn. It seems that those are the two things people want most, and sometime in the future I'm going to build a grist mill over the stream. There are going to be more people moving down into this area, now that the war is over."

"Not too soon I hope," answered Jessie. "I would like some time to get settled, without having to deal with people and their problems that they will bring with them."

As Jessie rose to leave, Bill said, "I'm just guessing, but you know the war is probably over by now, and the Yankees have more than likely taken over Fort Myers and that whole area. They won't care if you're dead or alive. You're just going to be another rebel they will have to deal with. Maybe I should come with you. It's probably not real safe out there right now. There are going to be a lot of angry people out there, and they don't even know who they are angry at until they see you coming!"

"No, I have a double barrel, twelve gauge shotgun in my scabbard that will keep me safe, but I thank you for your offer anyway." As he mounted his horse he said, "I'll stop by on my way back and let you know what's going on." With that he turned his horse and headed to John Campbell's place, another half mile up the river.

Jessie followed the river bank, observing the bottom land, and he thought about how rich the soil was and how much cotton one could grow here. The land was covered with pickerel grass for a half of mile, which stopped at the beginning of a pine forest. The forest grew on each side of the river as far as the eye could see. Keeping to the river, he came to the end of the pine forest, and there stood the Georgia style, wood house, a couple of hundred feet from the stream. John had built the open breezeway house before he had gone to Fort Myers to fight, and Jessie noticed another section that he must have added after he came home.

Turning up from the creek, Jessie was surprised that John's pack of cur dogs had not met him before now. Jessie sometimes wondered why John had always kept at least six of the biggest, toughest dogs he had ever known, but he knew they matched his size and personality. At six foot four and at least two hundred and fifty pounds, John could be as tough as a bear yet would cry like a baby, listening to his wife give birth to another boy. Each time another boy was born, Jessie wondered if John was too big to have a girl, but he had seen John's wife Myra, who was close to six foot herself, up and about washing clothes the day after giving birth. They were tough, rugged people and well suited for this rough country.

Riding up to the front porch Jessie called out, "Hello, anybody home?"

Myra stepped through the door and stopped in her tracks. "If you're who I think you are, you're supposed to be dead."

"You know," he said, "I have thought the same thing several times myself."

"From the looks of that scar across your forehead, I would say whatever happened to you, it was bad. Why don't you get down and let me fix you something to eat. John and the boys will be back soon; they are down the hill there working at the saw mill."

"I'm OK for now, but thank you anyway. I'll just go on down and find John."

"OK, but tell him to send the boys on up to the house, that dinner is about ready."

As Jessie turned his horse, heading further down the creek, he laughed at Myra's forthright statement about his scar. She was the first person to mention it to him, but that's who Myra was. She said whatever came to mind and didn't give it another thought.

The dogs were the first ones to see Jessie coming and started howling. They took a stand between him and John and the four boys, showing their teeth and giving a low growl. Pulling up, he stopped his horse, knowing if he went any further, they would attack and defend their territory.

Looking up, John shouted above the barking dogs, "If you're a ghost, I'm going to let them dogs eat your horse out from under you!"

"I ain't no ghost, so call them puny dogs off, before I have to eat one for supper!" Jessie shouted back.

"If you ain't no ghost, you have to be one lucky son of a bitch. Frank! Call them dogs to you while I go squeeze that rag on that horse to be sure it's real." Reaching Jessie as he stepped down from the saddle, John grabbed him and pinned his arms against his sides, crushing him to his huge chest and lifting him off the ground.

"If you don't let me down, I'm going to have to kick your big ass!" Jessie bellowed.

Laughing that rumbling laugh of his, John said, "That's what I've always loved about you Jessie, you never think it's your ass getting kicked."

Giving him a big ole smack on his forehead and setting him down on his feet, John looked at Jessie's scar with concern and said, "That looks like an interesting story. Come sit and tell me why you ain't no ghost."

"Myra said to tell you to bring the boys, that dinner is ready." Jessie replied.

"Alright, you can tell me after we eat. How is your family? I haven't had time to check on them since I've been back."

"They're fine," answered Jessie, and he explained what happened to Ed as they walked back to the house.

John held their three year old on his big knee, feeding him gravy and stew from a wooden bowl that Myra was filling from a large cast iron pot which hung from an iron rod in the fire place. Tasting the bowl of stew that Myra had placed in front of him, Jessie realized he was eating beef.

"Did you kill your milk cow?"

"No. This is one of the scrub cows that roam these woods."

"I've seen them," Jessie replied, "but they were always spooked and ran away from me. They looked pretty scrawny."

"I know, but I get tired of eating wild hogs and venison, and Myra either grinds the meat in the sausage grinder or cooks it in a stew for hours until its tender. Then it's not bad."

"It's really good!" Jessie said. "I'll remember this. How did you get close enough to kill it?"

"Just turn them cur dogs loose, and they will have one on the ground before you can bat an eye. That's what they were bred for. I just never used them for that in Georgia, but if you want to round up cows you can't beat a good cur dog for that. How are those Tennessee blood hounds of yours?"

"Fine, the bitch is about to have pups."

"Well if you ever want to trade for a good catch dog, just let me know," John replied.

After everyone had finished eating, John put the three year old down and told the other boys, "Take the little one and y'all go play awhile before we go back to work." Pushing and shoving each other, the boys started for the creek to play, all except the oldest boy Frank, who was Ed's age and looked as if he was going to be as big as his pa.

"Hold it, hold it!" His booming voice stopped them in their tracks. "Get back here and take the little one with you." Mark, the fourteen year old, who already stood almost six feet tall, waited as the three year old ran to him. Grabbing him, he swung him up and onto his neck, and ducking his head low to miss the door way, he took off running and jumping and playing horse. You could hear the screaming and laughter half way to the creek.

Myra stepped into the open doorway and called after them, "One of you bring me up a bucket of water from the creek." Shaking her head, she turned back to the table and started removing the dishes.

John pulled his pipe from the pocket in his overalls and began loading it with tobacco as he listened to Jessie explain what had happened in the Everglades. Jessie told John and Myra about how Two Worlds and his people had given him his life back and accepted him as one of their own, while they waited for his memory to return. He described the devastation of the storm and told them about the survivors and their grief and the journey home.

When Jessie finished, John stood up and walked to the fire place. Knocking the ashes from his pipe, he turned and asked, "What are you going to do with them?"

Jessie gave him the same answer he had given to Bill and Martha. "I'll have to wait and see."

John walked back to the table and stood behind Myra, covering her shoulders with his big hands. "Me and the boys have the saw mill running if you need lumber for houses, and Frank here is already a hell of a carpenter."

"That's right Mr. Tucker, and I'll be glad to help. It sounds like you're going to need it," Frank added.

"I still have bolts of cotton I brought with me from Georgia," Myra said, "and my sewing machine still works if you need clothes."

"I thank all of you for your generosity, but they are already putting up their lodges. They will keep their traditions, and they are very good providers. My biggest worry is how people are gonna react when they find out there are Indians living here."

Getting red in the face John said, "We'll put the word out that we are dammed good at hunting people down, and if anybody harms one of those people, we'll hunt them down and string them up, no matter how many of them there are!"

"I hope it never comes to that," Jessie said. Standing up, he thanked them both for their kindness and explained that he had to go.

As Jessie was mounting his horse, John said, "If you can find Captain Parker, he may be able to help you with this problem. He did live there around Fort Myers, but who knows where he is by now. If you do find him, tell him hello for me. I always liked him; he was straightforward with us. And tell him I can still carry one of those little horses under each arm," he laughed.

Smiling, Jessie turned his horse and headed for Dave Kersey's place.

"Tell Dave and Betty hello for us," Myra called after him. Not looking back, he raised his hand above his shoulders and gave a wave.

Crossing the shallow stream of the Little Withlacoochee, Jessie headed south and found himself once again in the open grass lands, stretching as far as he could see. He had ridden no more than a half mile, when he saw Dave Kersey's place, two hundred yards downstream. The house sat about seventy five feet from the fresh flowing water and was built in the shadow of two oaks that had to be a thousand years old.

Jessie watched as Dave gripped the plow handles and guided the mule, turning the soft rich soil into rows as straight as arrows. Only a man who had spent years behind a plow could make rows like that. As he proceeded down the slope, he had to admire the land that Dave had picked to settle down on and farm. Dave was one of the best farmers Jessie had ever known. When they had lived in Georgia, he had a couple of families that sharecropped and helped with the farm. Dave and his wife Bonnie never could have kids, but that wasn't stopping either one of them from building their farm. It was hard work, but they didn't mind; they had worked just as hard on their farm in Georgia. It would just take a little longer here, that's all.

Dave brought the mule to a halt and stood watching the rider coming down the slope. Reaching between the plow handles, he lifted the shotgun he carried and placed it across the top of the handles. He didn't trust anyone these days with ex-soldiers wandering the country side and stealing what they could. He had heard about a couple of families being robbed at gun point and he wasn't taking any chances.

"I'll be dammed and gone to hell if it ain't Jessie Tucker!" Dave hollered. Walking toward the rider, he reached up and took the reins and with a look of amazement he asked, "Is it really you?"

"It's me."

"Well by God! You are the last person on this earth I expected to see; we left you for dead after searching those swamps for over a week."

"I know," said Jessie, swinging down from the saddle and taking Dave's big rough hand.

Still shaking his hand, Dave asked, "Have you been home yet?"

"I've been home for more than two weeks, and now I'm on my way to Fort Myers to let them know I'm alive."

"But the war is over, and Captain Parker sent our whole group home. Ain't nobody gonna care now if you're dead or alive. I heard there ain't anybody there now but the Yankees," Dave said.

"Then I'll let the Yankees know I'm alive and to take me off their list of dead. If they have Captain Parker's records, I'll be listed as dead, and I don't want my name on that list!"

"Well it doesn't make sense to me, but you never did let that stop you. Why don't you stay overnight and I'll have Bonnie start some supper. You can't get very far today before dark," Dave insisted.

"No, I appreciate the offer, but I'm in kind of a hurry to get this over with, so I'm going to get as far as I can today."

"Lord, Lord!" Bonnie exclaimed, as she got closer to Jessie and recognized who Dave was talking to. Reaching up and wrapping her arms around his neck, she gave him a warm hug. Then she stepped back and said, "I know Belle must be a happy woman. I can't even imagine thinking Dave was never coming back. Poor thing; how is she?"

"She's fine; we're both fine now."

"Well come on to the house and let me fix you something to eat."

"Thank you Bonnie for the offer, but I'm OK. I've got food in my saddle bags and I need to make as much time as I can today," he explained again. "I'll stop again on my way back when I have more time."

"Good," said Dave. "I want to hear what happened out there."

Looking back from the top of the valley, he saw Dave and Bonnie still watching. Giving a last wave he rode south, glad he didn't have to tell the story one more time today. He would stop on his way back, but he just couldn't do it again today. It was taking too much out of him, every time he had to relive the painful memory.

Twenty-One

It was on the fourth day of riding from early morning until almost dark, when Jessie reached the Caloosahatchee River. He decided to stop while he still had enough light to gather fire wood for the night. The next morning at daylight, he sat waiting for his cup of coffee to cool down enough to drink without burning his mouth. The sun was just peeking over the horizon when he mounted his horse and turned west, toward the bridge that would take him to the south side of the river and into Fort Myers. It was past noon when he rode up from the river bank to the road and crossed the bridge. Riding into the overcrowded settlement, he saw Union soldiers everywhere. He wondered why there were still so many soldiers here if the war was over. As he rode down the main street, he saw bars everywhere and heard the loud fake laughter of the whores as the soldiers bought them drinks while bartering for their wares.

When Jessie stopped in the middle of the street to try to get his bearings, a drunk solider came out of the bar and yelled at him, "The Rebel bar is at the east end of town! What's left of you anyway," he laughed as he staggered down the dusty street to another bar. Jessie rode on down the street to the east/west intersection and turned east. He was at the edge of town when he spotted the recruiting building, but all he saw was two bored Union soldiers with rifles, lingering outside. Stepping down from the saddle, he wrapped the reins around a broken hitching post next to a few other horses. The two soldiers met him at the door, and one of them began to question him.

"I've never seen you here before, were you one of the rebel soldiers?"

"We were all one of the soldiers at one time," Jessie answered.

"Well the war is over now, and as long as you behave yourself you can go on in and drink with your buddies, but don't come out drunk and causing trouble, or you will wind up in the brig with the others who wouldn't listen to my advice." With that he moved away from the door.

Jessie stepped through the doorway into the dimly lit room and stopped, giving his eyes a minute to adjust. He could barely see that there were a couple of men standing at a rough, wooden plank bar with a shelf built on the wall behind it. On the shelf were what looked like jars of homemade, rot gut whiskey and moonshine, the kind that can take you two days to get over a drunk or kill you. As his eyes adjusted to the light he saw three more men sitting around a table with their own bottle.

Jessie crossed the rough wooden floor to where the three men sat and asked, "Mind if I sit down?"

"That depends on what you want," said one of the hardest looking men he had ever seen. He knew the tough lines of the man's gaze came from hard fought battles, fought face to face with men trying to kill you before you killed them. "If you're looking for a free drink or sympathy, you're in the wrong place Mister, there ain't nothing free here and no one gives a damn what you been through. We all have been there."

Keeping his eyes locked on the other man's eyes, Jessie said, "I buy my own when I want a drink, and I don't need no sympathy; I got a wife for that. What I do need, is some answers to a few questions."

"I don't know if anybody here has the answers you're looking for, but sit down and ask your questions," the tough man said.

Looking at the other two men at the table, Jessie saw the same hardness in their eyes, and he knew these men were taking their losses hard. As one of the men poured himself a shot of whiskey in his glass, Jessie told the men about being shot and saved by a small group of

Indians in the Everglades. He went on to explain that he was just getting back and wanted to find out what was happening. The man he had first spoken to was looking at the scar across his forehead.

"Damn! You're one of Captain Parker's swamp fighters!"

"Yes, I was."

"Well y'all didn't stop enough of them; the sons of bitches still took over the town," one of the men across the table said. "But then I guess none of us stopped enough," the man added and took another drink from his glass.

"Well most of those boys are gone on back home," the first man said. "A couple of them that live close by are still hanging around until the captain gets over his wound he got in the last battle, when the Yankees were taking over Fort Myers. He was shot in the leg and can't get around very well yet. He lives a little ways on out of town, not far from here. It's easy to find. Just keep heading east for about a mile and you will see a road turning north. He's at the end of that road on the river."

Jessie stood to leave and stretched his arm across the table to shake hands. All three men stood up, and the hard eye'd man reached for Jessie's hand.

"I'm Sam Walker and I apologize for my rudeness, but there are too many men walking around feeling sorry for themselves and wanting somebody to buy them a drink."

Jessie shook hands with the other two and said, "My name is Jessie Tucker and if you ever hear that I'm dead, don't believe them," he laughed. "What's with the two Union soldiers outside?" Jessie asked, as he started to leave.

"They have a law now, that if a rebel is drunk on the street, it's a two dollar fine or a week in jail. There's been some trouble with drunken rebels getting into fights with the Yankee soldiers," Sam answered. "As a matter of fact, one of the captain's men has been in their brig for a couple of days now. He left here drunk, and them two soldier boys outside arrested him. That's why they stand outside the bar, so they can arrest you when you come out."

"Well I saw bars full of drunken Union soldiers when I came down the main street, some of them could hardly walk," Jessie remarked.

"Yeah we know, but they're in charge now." Sam said.

While untying his horse, Jessie asked the soldier who had questioned him and given him the rules, how he could find their lock up.

"That's not hard to find," the soldier smirked, "just go back to the main street and go left and it's a couple of blocks down on the left, you can't miss it. It's the old jail. You will see a couple of soldiers on guard outside. Lieutenant Berkley is in charge, and if you're wanting to get somebody out, you're going to need cash and not rebel money either."

Jessie nodded at the soldier, mounted his horse and turned toward Main Street. At the crossroads, he turned left and rode the two blocks. Tying his horse to the hitching rail, he started toward the door when the two soldiers stepped in front of him.

"What do you want here?" a heavy set soldier asked.

"I'm here to see a Lieutenant Berkley."

"What you want him for?"

"If you will get out of my way, I'll tell the lieutenant that," Jessie said, trying to keep control of his patience.

"You dammed rebels are all the same. I don't know what you got to be cocky about."

"Looking at you, I know you will never know; now are you going to move or do I need to call the lieutenant out here!" Jessie replied. Moving out of the way, he let Jessie pass.

Inside, the lieutenant was seated behind the old desk that the sheriff had used before he lost his town to the Union army. "What can I do for you?" he asked as Jessie approached his desk.

"You have a man in here you brought in for being drunk a couple of days ago, I want to get him out."

"Hell there's a half dozen men back there for being drunk on the street. We're not going to tolerate drunks fighting with our soldiers.

Which one do you want to get out, and unless you have two dollars they all stay here," the lieutenant said.

Jessie reached inside his pants pocket, took out two silver dollars and laid them on the desk.

"You never did tell me his name," the lieutenant said.

"I don't know his name; I'll know him when I see him."

"Sergeant," he called to the man across the room, who was sitting and leaning his chair back against the wall. "Take him back there and let him pick himself out a drunk," he laughed.

Jessie almost threw up when the sergeant opened the cell where five men sat or lay in their own vomit. Pulling his shirt tail over his nose and mouth, he stepped inside the cell, and looking around, he spotted Sergeant Hannah from the settlement on the east coast, called Miami. This was the man he had followed all over the Everglades. Squatting down in front of Hannah, Jessie held his shirt tail over his nose with one hand and shook Hannah's shoulder with the other.

"Get up! I'm taking you out of here."

Looking up, Hannah asked, "Who the hell are you and what do you want?"

Moving the shirt aside he looked at Hannah and said, "I'm going to get you out of here, so get up and come with me." Then he put the shirt back over his mouth and nose to keep from gagging.

With fear in his eyes, Hannah pushed himself away. "You're dead; why are you here haunting me now? I searched half of them Everglades for over a week looking for you, and I would have looked longer, but the other boys made me quit so they could go home. Please leave me alone. I tried," he whimpered.

Dropping the shirt from his face, he took Hannah by both shoulders and pulled him close. "Look at me now, I'm no ghost; I'm alive and as real as you are and I'm taking you out of here." Jessie saw the dried blood covering the gash on the side of his head and asked, "Can you walk? If you can't, I'll carry you out, but you're coming with me."

Hannah reached up, putting his arm around Jessie's shoulder and tried get up. Jessie put his arm around Hannah's waist and lifted him to his feet. Looking around at the filth and the other four men watching, he wondered if any one of them had eaten since they had been in here.

As Jessie walked from the back carrying Hannah around the waist, the lieutenant and the sergeant held their noses and the lieutenant said, "If you got some more of those silver dollars you can take them all," he laughed.

"Where can I find some water?" Jessie asked, ignoring the man's remarks.

"There's a water trough out back by the corral where the horses are kept, and take that little thing he calls a horse with him," laughed the sergeant.

"I know it's not very clean," Jessie said, as he lifted Hannah and sat him in the trough half full of water, "but it will take some of the stink off you." Walking to the end of the trough, he took the drinking cup hanging from the pump and filled it with water. He poured the water down the pump while he pumped the handle, until it was primed and the water started to flow from the lip, filling the trough with more water. When the trough was almost full, he told Hannah to keep washing until he got back.

Jessie walked back around to the front of the building where his horse was still tied and opened the saddle bag that held his shotgun shells. Reaching to the bottom past the shells, he pulled out a small leather bag. He turned to go back inside and after taking one look at Jessie's face, the overweight guard moved away from the door. Dumping the coins from the pouch on the desk in front of the lieutenant he said, "You will find enough there, I want those other men out of that filth."

"I don't know why, they'll be back in there within a week," the lieutenant remarked.

"I want those men out of there now!" Jessie said, with controlled anger.

"Sergeant, get those two guards outside to help you and take those men out back, he can have them all!" the lieutenant laughed, as he counted the coins.

It took over an hour and two more troughs of water before Jessie got them all cleaned up as much as he could. He had threatened to stick their heads under the water until they drowned if they didn't get in the trough, clothes and all. Jessie watched as two of them wandered off down the street looking for another drink.

The other two mounted their skinny, half-starved horses and riding by Jessie, one of them said, "I sure do appreciate you getting me out of that mess. You wouldn't happen to have another one of those silver dollars? I sure could use a drink about now."

"No," said Jessie. As he turned to help Hannah mount his horse, he thought that the lieutenant was probably right; they'd all be back in there within a week. Heading east, Hannah led them to the turn off, and turning north they headed for the river to find Captain Parker.

"I thought you lived over on the east coast," Jessie said to Hannah.

"I do,' replied Hannah, "but the captain got shot in the leg about six weeks ago, in the last scrimmage before the Yankees took over Fort Myers. I'm hanging around until he's better. He's already getting around with a cane, so I shouldn't be here much longer. I can't wait to get out of this mess here. You saw what it was like back there. It gets to you after a while, that's why I wound up getting drunk and ending up in their jail. I really appreciate you getting me out, but you really gave me a scare back there. You were the last person I ever expected see again. I really thought you were a ghost!" Hannah chuckled and paused for a few seconds. "I really did look for you as long as they would let me. I just want you to know that."

"I know; I wouldn't have expected any less from any of you."

You couldn't see Parker's place until you rode into the yard. Built low a hundred feet off the road, it almost disappeared in the thicket of cabbage palms. Beyond, there was a fifty foot path from the house to the river. Dismounting and leading the horses up to the house, Hannah called out, "Don't shoot Captain! It's me, and you ain't gonna believe who I've drug along!"

Walking their horses on around to the back of the house, Jessie saw the captain sitting in a wicker chair with his leg up on a stool. On a small table next to his chair was a jug of moonshine. Seeing Jessie, Parker grabbed his cane and came up out of the chair staring with his mouth dropped open.

"Well damn me to hell!" Parker said, waiting for Jessie to come closer. Shaking Jessie's hand he asked, "Where in the world did he find you? I heard he had gotten drunk and thrown in that jail."

"Well I'm afraid he found me," Hannah replied, "and yes I was in jail and would still be there, if this ghost hadn't come along and gotten us all out."

"Sit down and have a drink of real moonshine that won't burn your guts out, and tell me where in the hell did you get that scar across your forehead. It looks like you were almost scalped by some Indian!" Parker exclaimed.

"It's a long story," Jessie said, as he took the bottle and waved the captain back to his chair.

"I got time," Parker said, "so pull up a chair and tell me about it."

Jessie and Hannah each pulled a cane back chair up in front of Parker's stool. Sitting down, Jessie took the lid off and drank a long pull of smooth shine, and passing the jar on to Hannah, he gave them a short version of what had happened. Parker took another pull on the jar and passed it to Jessie, who passed it on to Hannah, saying, "No more for me thanks, I've got a long way to go to get back home."

Wiping his mouth with the back of his hand, Parker looked at Jessie and said, "What are you gonna do with them?"

Lowering his head, Jessie smiled to himself and thought, if one more person asks me that I'm going to shoot him. Looking up he answered, "I don't know, but they are with me now, and we are just going to take it from there."

Parker spoke seriously now. "The Indians I have known were dammed good with cattle; almost all of them have cows. That's why they use those little Marsh Tackie horses; there's nothing better in the brush as you very well know. There are thousands of wild Spanish cows all over this country."

"What in the world would I do with a bunch of wild cows even if I could catch them?"

"You could drive them over to Punta Rassa or even to the Port of Tampa, which is even closer to where you are. They are paying ten to twelve dollars a head in gold coin and shipping them to Cuba." Hannah replied.

"I don't know," Jessie said, "I don't know anything about driving cows."

"I do," said Hannah. "If you could use my help, I really don't have a good reason to get stuck back in that little settlement called Miami. That place is never gonna get anywhere. There's nothing but mosquitoes and sand gnats there."

"I don't have money to pay anybody anything," Jessie said.

"You don't have to pay me nothing. If you can feed me, you can pay me when we sell some cows. I'd be willing to go back with you and talk to your Indians and see if they know anything about cattle. If they don't, I'll just make my way on over to the east coast and head home. But I sure would like to try."

"I suppose it wouldn't hurt to talk to the Indians, and I wouldn't mind the company riding back, but I can't promise you anything."

"Take him with you and get him out of my hair. He's driving me crazy, babying me around like I'm senile or something!" Parker said, taking another pull from the bottle. "If you're going to try this cattle business, there are three of those Marsh Tackies left from when I sent everyone home. Only a few of the boys kept theirs, and the Yankees don't know I have any animals or supplies left. Parker looked at Jessie's horse. "I see you got your horse from Bill."

"Yes, he dropped him off on the way home."

"That's not all I got, them Yankees don't know about. Come on out back with me." Rising from his chair and balancing himself with his cane, he led them to another building behind the corral, where he kept his horses and the three Marsh Tackies.

Jessie guessed the building to be about ten by twenty feet. It was hidden from view by scrub oak, and you could have walked within twenty feet of it and never noticed it. Hobbling around to the back and grinning, Parker showed Jessie a moon shine still. "They would really like to find this," Parker laughed, "but this is not what I brought you out here for." He led them back around to the front and pulling a key from his pocket, he opened a large lock hanging from the steel latch.

Reaching inside, he took a lantern from a shelf, and bringing it outside, he struck a match and lit the wick, keeping the flame low. "You want to be real careful in there with fire unless you're ready to go to hell fast." Laughing, he stepped through the door, being careful not to stumble and drop the lantern. Following Parker inside and letting his eyes adjust to the dim light, Jessie saw some barrels of what he thought might be gun powder. Stacked in one corner were several muzzle loading rifles, and Jessie recognized a crate that contained bayonets. Next he saw several heavy bags, containing lead shot.

"What are you doing with all this?" Jessie asked.

"I'm just keeping it from those dammed Yankees. Most of this is left over from those supply lines we raided, and I stored it in case my men needed it. If you wait until tonight, we'll load those Marsh Tackies with everything you can carry. Then if you follow the river further east a couple of miles to where you can make a crossing, them Yankees will never know you been here."

"Well I could certainly use a bit of that powder and lead shot; I don't know anywhere else to get any of this, now that the Yankees are in charge of everything in this country. They aren't about to sell us guns and powder. You don't happen to have any shotgun shells left do you?"

"I do at that!" The captain grinned and pulled back a burlap bag uncovering a short wooden box. Painted on the lid were the letters, 12 Ga.00 Buckshot.

"Damn! Now there's something I can really use!"

"Take the whole case; I'll never use them, and I got a half of a case of No.4 turkey shot. Hannah, see that box under that shelf by your right leg? Lift it up on this counter. With a big smile on his face, Parker moved to the counter and pulled the lid off. Then he stepped back so Jessie could see. "Go on!" Parker said, nodding to Jessie. Jessie reached inside and lifted a heavy object wrapped in oilcloth. He removed the cloth and stared at an officer's Remington .44 caliber pistol in its leather holster. Amazed, Jessie looked at Parker. "The finest the Union makes," Parker grinned. "Better yet," Parker said, "there are two cases of 16 shot .44 caliber Henry Repeating Arms rifles against that wall behind you and four cases of ammo for them and the pistols."

Over whelmed by all of it, Jessie almost forgot why he came here. Looking at Captain Parker he said, "Captain, there's one more thing that's more important than all of this. It's why I came here to start with."

Puzzled as he heard the seriousness in Jessie's voice, Parker asked, "What in the world could be that serious?"

"I want my name taken off that dead list of yours! Have you turned it over to the Yankee's yet?"

"Damn! You are the only dammed person in the world I know who would come this far just for that, but it don't surprise me none. No, I haven't turned over anything to those bastards yet, and I might just have a big bonfire one night. All the paper work is inside my house. Now, let's put together what you and Hannah are going to take with you. I'll be glad to get rid of some of this stuff."

By the time Jessie and Hannah brought the three loaded horses around front and prepared to leave, the moon was well up in the sky, giving them enough light to find their way east along the river.

"You boys know that if them Yankees catch you with those guns and ammo, they will probably shoot you on the spot," Parker reminded them.

"We know," said Jessie, "but there ain't no reason for any Yankees to be where we're going. I'm more worried about roving gangs of rebel deserters than any Yankees. Captain, there will be a lot of grateful people for what we are bringing back with us. I wish we could have known each other under better circumstances. If you ever need to be somewhere else, just head to Fort Dade and ask around and you will find me. If these Yankees find out what you're hiding out here, they'll be wanting to string you up."

"I know, but I'm hoping that most of these soldiers will be going back home soon, and they will forget about me out here."

"What will you do?" Hannah asked.

"Maybe I'll put together an outfit and round up some of those wild cows and take them down to Punta Rassa, I don't really know yet, but I'll be fine," Parker replied.

Twenty-Two

With the three loaded horses in toe, Hannah led the way east along the river bank for the next three miles, until they came to a shallow crossing in the river. Reaching the bank on the other side and a safe distance from the Union soldiers, Jessie took the lead. They traveled north east for another three hours before they stopped. Then they hobbled the horses, laid out their bedding and slept.

It was just daybreak when Jessie filled their cups with boiling hot coffee. As they sat and blew into their cups, waiting for the hot, black liquid to cool enough to drink, Jessie turned to Hannah and said, "I know it's none of my business, but if you wouldn't mind telling me, I'd like to know why you're not going back home. Don't you have family there?"

Hannah blew into his cup for a few more seconds and said, "No, I don't have any family left." He paused for a moment, before continuing. "My name is Justin Hannah, and I was eleven years old when my father brought my mother and me from Savanna, Georgia, to a small settlement called Miami and set up a trading post. A schooner brought supplies to Miami every six to eight weeks. We did a lot of trading with the Creeks and Seminoles. My father was honest and well respected by the Indians and they brought hides and furs to trade.

"When I was twenty, I fell in love with the most beautiful Indian girl I had ever seen. I earned her father's respect, and along with two rifles, powder, and rifle balls, she became my wife. A year later she gave me a son. I had never been so happy. I left the fort and went to live with her family. For the next few years, I followed the tribe, moving to wherever it was safe and traveled back every so often to get supplies and see my parents. They loved their grandson and always spoiled him with love and gifts. The last time we went back to visit, we found them dying with the black fever. Two days after we buried my parents, we closed the store and headed back to the tribe. My wife and son came down with the fever and died on the trail.

"I didn't go back to the tribe for over a year, for fear I would infect the rest of them. I worked my way over to Lake Okeechobee and then worked for a man named Noah Dunkin out of Texas, building a ranch on the east side of the lake. A year later, I finally went back to the tribe, found my wife's father and told him what had happened. He told me that within a month after I buried my wife and son, one of the braves brought the fever back from a trading trip and they lost almost half of the village. I even went back to Savanna, Georgia and found my mother and fathers people. They were small cotton farmers in the delta.

"When the war came, I wandered back south ending up in Fort Myers where I got a job on a schooner, running supplies from Texas to Mississippi, to Alabama and back to Fort Myers. I crewed on small supply boats, running Yankee barricades for a while, until the Union army started moving down into the west coast of Florida. There they set up the outpost and began moving supplies from the east coast to provide for their troupes. Then I heard about Captain Parker putting together a small raiding party to go in the Everglades, and I volunteered."

"What about the Indians we fought and killed with the Union soldiers?" Jessie asked.

"They were Rouge braves who fought mostly for whiskey and a chance to kill. The Seminoles are a peaceful people who only want to be left alone to live their lives as a free people."

"I'm sorry to hear about your family," Jessie said, knowing there was nothing he could say to ease the painful memories; so he finished his coffee and began to load the horses.

It was close to noon on the second day, and Jessie was heading north east toward the Withlacoochee River, when they saw five riders in the distance. He could tell by their clothes and the way they rode, that they were not Union soldiers. He had seen enough soldiers to know the difference. These men weren't constantly looking over their shoulders; they were riding with the confidence of men being in control of their surroundings. Their confidence came with fire power. These were ex-soldiers who had now become outlaws, raiding and killing to take what they wanted, and Jessie knew they were going to want what he was carrying. Easing his shotgun out of its scabbard and laying it across his lap he, spoke to Hannah.

"What do you think about those men?"

"I think they are going to kill us if we let them. We should head around that small stand of red gum trees and see where they go."

"I agree with you." They watched the riders split and send two men to block their path, in case they tried to turn back and make a run for it, and three turned to cut them off going forward.

"That's better," Jessie said, low enough for only Hannah to hear. Hannah had the new Union .44 out and held it in his right hand on his lap. He held the reins with his left hand, easing his horse about six feet away to Jessie's left. Still speaking low Jessie said, "When they get within twenty feet we attack, just as we did with those Union supply lines. I'll take the one in the middle and the one on the right with this 12 gauge, and we'll see if you're any good with that new pistol of yours."

Hannah smiled to himself; these men had no idea who they were up against. "I'll cover the other two while you reload," Hannah said, low under his breath. They rode on while watching the riders' every move. Twenty feet away, he saw the sneer on the leader's face that comes from the gang mentality that causes men to think they're invincible.

Dropping the lead line of the pack horse, Jessie raised his shotgun letting the reins fall across the horse's neck. He kicked his horse in the ribs and let out a screaming yell at the same time as Hannah, freezing the riders for that one second it took to lift and cock the .44. He heard the boom of the shotgun a second before the .44 exploded, sending a ball of lead though the rider's chest, followed by the boom of the second barrel which blew both riders out of their saddles, with chests full of buckshot.

Turning his horse as soon as he saw the other rider fall from his saddle, Hannah charged the remaining two riders who were attacking from behind and riding fast, firing their pistols as they charged. Dropping the reins from his left hand, he pulled the other .44 from his waist band and began firing both pistols while yelling at the top of his lungs. Grabbing the reins, Jessie turned his horse just a few feet away from the other panicked horses. He dropped the reins and thumbed the lever on the breech, flicking the barrels downward, popping the breech open and ejecting the spent shells. Without looking down, he loaded two more shells and flipped the breech closed all within four seconds, warning Hannah who was already thirty feet ahead of him to hold up as he saw both riders drop from their saddles.

Jessie pulled up when he reached the two men lying on the ground. One of the men had caught a ball in the throat and the other had been hit once in the shoulder and once in the upper chest. Both men were dead.

"Damn it!" Jessie said. "All they had to do was just let us mind our own business and continue on their way."

"This is not the last time this is going to happen," Hannah said. "There are a lot of angry men who have lost everything. Then there are a lot of men out there who are just bad men, and they don't care who they take from or how many they kill doing it. I don't see the Union being in any hurry to do anything about it. You make your own law out here. What do you want to do with them? If it was left up to me they would stay where they lay. The bastards don't deserve being buried, and we have no tools to dig with."

"I don't like it, but your right," Jessie said. "There's nothing we can do for them now. We need to round up all those horses before they scatter too far. I'll head south where the other horses are headed."

They were both back in less than an hour and began taking the saddle bags from the horses, dumping everything in a heap on the ground. Sifting through the mound of extra pistols and ammunition, they found a small money pouch in each saddlebag and dumped all of the coins in a pile.

Counting the gold coins Jessie said, "There is over two hundred dollars here. We will split it."

"No," said Hannah, "all I need is twenty dollars. You have a lot of people you're going to need that money for. I'll take that Morgan gelding there; they make good riding horses, and I can work cows with him. A man can always use an extra horse when he's working cows."

They removed the guns and belts from the five men and placed them in the saddle bags. Stringing the horses out with lead lines, they each led four horses. Jessie took a last look at the dead men and shook his head. "Dammit, what a shame!"

Jessie led them north east until he came to the Withlacoochee River and followed it east until he came to the Little Withlacoochee. There he turned north, and after another day of travel, he saw Dave Kersey's farmstead. It was late afternoon, and Jessie saw the rain clouds moving away in the distance when they rode down into the small valley. Stopping outside the house, he called out. Dave stepped out onto the porch shading his eyes as he looked into the sun. Seeing the two men on horses he could tell that it was Jessie and another man.

"Get down Jessie," Dave called out, "and bring your friend inside; we just started supper."

"I don't know about Jessie, but if he says anything about having to go on, I'll stay and eat his share," laughed Hannah.

"Sergeant Hannah?" Dave asked, in complete surprise. "Get down off that horse and bring Jessie with you. This just gets stranger and stranger all the time." Dave came off the porch to shake Hannah's hand as he dismounted. "I never thought I would ever see Jessie again, much less the two of you riding in here together. Both of you come on inside."

As Jessie approached the door where Bonnie stood in confusion, she said, "It is good to see you again."

Leaning down he gave her a hug. "Good to see you again too! I want you to meet the man Dave and I followed all over the Everglades. This is Sergeant Hannah."

Stepping forward, she took his hand.

"You can call me Justin; I'm not in the army now."

"I have heard about you; now come inside and let me feed you."

Taking the reins, Dave said, "I'll put the horses in the corral for now, and later after we eat something, you two can help me make sense of all of this."

It was early evening when Jessie and Justin rode down the sloping valley on the west side of the lake. Jessie led the way through another stand of huge live oaks and followed the water's edge. As they rode closer with their string of horses, Jessie saw Belle standing in the yard next to Ed; then he saw Horace and Jenny running from the barn to stand next to their mother.

Suddenly Horace and Jenny recognized their pa and started running toward them, both yelling "Pa, Pa, you're back!" When they reached him, he took his foot out of the stirrup and let Horace put his foot in. Bending down, he took him by the arm and lifted him up on the horse behind him. Then he reached down low, took Jenny under her arms and lifted her up in front of him. They were both beaming when he rode up to Belle and Ed.

"Well if you aren't becoming a surprise every time you go away and come back!" Belle said, laughing.

As Ed observed the stranger and the loaded horses he asked, "Where did you get all of this, Pa?"

"Let me get down first," Jessie said, putting Jenny back down while Horace slid off the back. Stepping down from the saddle, he met Belle and hugged her. Looking down at her smiling face, he said, "It's all done now, I'm back."

"Does this mean I don't have to say goodbye for a while?"

"I hope so for a really long time." Turning, he took Ed's out stretched hand and patting him on the shoulder, Jessie asked, "How are your ribs, Son?"

"Much better; I can lift some light things and I'm getting stronger every day."

"Good! I'm proud of you Son; you've become quite a man."

Turning, he said, "Everyone, I want you to meet the man you've all heard about." Looking up at Justin, he said, "Get down and let me introduce you to my family." Justin dismounted and Jessie said, "This is Sergeant Hannah, the man I rode with in the Everglades."

Walking over to Belle and Ed, he shook their hands. "You can call me Justin, and I'm glad to meet all of you."

"I know who you are," Ed said. "Pa talked a lot about you. He said you were raised in the Everglades. I sure would like to see it one day."

"I'm afraid it's going to take more than a day," Justin replied. "I've lived there most of my life, and I still haven't seen it all."

"Let's take these animals to the barn and get them unloaded," Jessie said, "and maybe I can explain what happened. Horace, why don't you take Jenny and see if you can pick enough berries for your ma to bake us a cobbler pie?"

"Be careful, watch out for snakes!" Belle yelled after the kids, already on the run to find a pail.

After they were done unloading the horses, Jessie explained what had happened in Fort Myers with Captain Parker, and how he gave them the supplies. Then Jessie told the others about the fight on the trail.

"There were five of them, and you and Mr. Hannah killed all of them?" Ed asked, in awe.

"Well, Justin killed most of them," answered Jessie.

"You could have been killed!" Belle said, looking in horror at Jessie. "There wasn't any way for you to have gotten away from them?"

"They didn't give us any choice," Justin answered. "They meant to kill us and take what we carried. Instead we killed them and took the horses and their supplies."

"It frightens me to think what could have happened to you out there," Belle answered. "Couldn't you have just given them what they wanted? We could get more supplies."

"They would have taken what we had and killed us like hogs just for the fun of it," Jessie answered. "These were bad men and they might have been back. They had to be stopped. Luckily Justin was with me, or I would probably be lying out there dead right now. Let's put all that behind us now. Things have changed and we have a lot to do."

Jessie and Justin spent all morning building a safe place to hide the weapons and ammunition in the back of the feed stall. When they had finished closing the new store room, Jessie said, "Later we will build a more secure place, but for now they will be safe and dry. As Belle joined them, Jessie said, "Tomorrow we will start building a larger corral for the horses. Meantime we'll take them to Two Worlds' camp and let the boys watch them. There is plenty of grass around the lake for them to feed on, they won't go far. Belle, I'm going to take Justin with me to see Two Worlds, and I'll be back by dark so go ahead and feed the kids. We'll eat something when we get back."

Twenty-Three

As they rode into Two Worlds' village, Jessie noticed the new lodges in place. Some of them were only partially covered with new skins, and Jessie realized that there weren't enough hides left after the storm, but he knew it was only a matter of time before the hunts would provide all the hides they needed. Jessie saw Two Worlds sitting on a log under the shade of one of the live oaks, talking with Red Sun, Silent Stalker, Big Cypress, and Spirit Snake. Jessie observed Spirit Snake sitting cross legged on the ground and realized that at sixteen years old, he was no longer a boy.

As Jessie and Justin rode up and dismounted, everyone but Two Worlds rose to their feet to greet Jessie.

"We have wondered when you would return," Red Sun said. "Spirit Snake said he saw you riding around the lake with a rider and several loaded horses yesterday."

"Yes," said Jessie. "I want to introduce to you a man who I fought with in the Everglades. He has become part of us now and he also saved my life on the way back here. He has some ideas about the cattle that roam these woods."

Justin nodded his head at everyone, keeping his eyes on Two Worlds. Then he walked over to the old man and squatted on his heels. Bowing his head, he said, "Grandfather of Grandfathers, I remember you from when I was a young boy and you and your people brought hides and furs to trade with my father, at the trading post at the Miami Fort."

"Yes, I remember you and your father and mother well. Your father was always fair with us, and he was the only trader who would trade with us for guns. I was sorry to hear about their death from the sickness. I also heard you had married a Seminole woman and lived with them until the sickness took your wife and son. I heard no more about you after that, but it is good to see you again," said Two Worlds.

"It is good to see you again, Grandfather." He rose and turned to the men still standing there, listening. "I do not remember your names, but I remember all of your faces," Justin said, looking at each of them.

"I am Big Cypress and I remember you. You were the same age as I."

"Yes, but you were already almost twice my size, and I see you didn't stop getting bigger." Justin said, laughing.

"I am Silent Stalker, and you used to shoot my bow. That was before you shot an arrow through your father's window, almost hitting a trader, who was inside talking with him."

"Oh yes," Justin laughed. "My father wore a switch out on my butt after everyone left."

"I am Red Sun, and I also remember your Father well."

"Yes, you did most of the bargaining with my father. It is good to see all of you. Jessie told me about you saving his life and your losses from the storm, but I had no idea he was speaking about this tribe. My heart goes out for your losses. I am aware of the pain of losing people you love, and I know how hard it is to get your life back again."

"I am Spirit Snake, the son of Four Bears. My father and mother were killed by the great winds of the storm. I am taking his place as a man in the tribe," he said, bringing his closed first across his chest covering his heart.

Seeing the fierceness in his face, Justin nodded his head in acknowledgment and said, "I can see that, and I will speak to you as a man and not as a boy."

"There are things that I would like for you to hear and think on as a tribe," Jessie said. "I will let Justin tell you what we have talked about and why he is here."

Jessie sat with the others while Justin spoke. "Before the war among our people, a few cattlemen were selling their cattle to be shipped to Cuba. Now that the war is over, they are trying to get more cattle to sell to Cuba, but most of the ranch cattle were either sold to or taken by the army. There are few ranches left in this country, but there are thousands of wild Spanish cows left here and they roam free, for anyone who wants to go to the trouble of rounding them up from the woods and putting their brand on them. The buyers will take anything they can get."

"I remember when I was a young boy," said Red Sun. "I worked with the cattle on the great Paynes Prairie owned by the Chief Micanopy before we were pushed south into the Everglades. That's where we got the small horses we call Marsh Tackies, the type Justin rides now. We had small herds of cattle for a lot of years before the white soldiers made war against us, and we had to kill them to feed our people. If we left them to graze, the soldiers took them or left them dead to rot, so we could not feed our people. The Marsh Tackies are the greatest of horses for hunting cattle in the thick brush."

"We brought back three more," said Justin. "It is what we rode when we were fighting in the Everglades. If this is to happen, it won't be easy. Those cows are as spooked of man as we are of ghosts. We will need more than horses to get them out of those thickets they like to hide in. When I worked the ranch over on the east side of Lake Okeechobee, we used short whips and cow dogs to round up the cattle. We have until the end of winter before there's any need to start rounding up any cows. Until then, we are going to need to search out and find good areas to build holding pens. This will keep them safe until we can put our brand on them, and we will need to build them a few miles apart. Jessie, you're going to have to come up with a brand between now and then. In the meantime, I will go into Tampa and find out where to drive the cattle to sell. I know that there is a commissary that has whips, and I'll see if I can find some cow dogs somewhere."

The light was beginning to fade when Jessie was ready to head home. "Justin, you are welcome to stay, and I know Belle has food for us."

"If it is OK with Two Worlds, I am going to set me up a place here."

"You are welcome to stay here as long as you would like," Two Worlds told him. "We will build you your own lodging."

"That doesn't surprise me," Jessie said. He turned and faced Two Worlds. "In two days I would like to bring my family here. I think it is time for everyone to meet."

"I agree," said Two Worlds. "We are ready now. Everyone is settled again, and it would be good to celebrate something new. It will help to start the healing."

Belle was up two hours before daylight, her stove ablaze and pots on every burner. She and Jenny had picked a large pot of snap peas, and Ed had cut another pot of okra. Belle was making cream corn from a half bushel that Horace had picked for her. She had everyone busy all day before milking, picking vegetables and stacking wood for the stove. She had sent Horace and Jenny down by the lake where the blue berries grew wild and had them pick almost a water bucket full for cobbler, which was cooking in a large pot on the stove. At dawn the day before, Jessie went to a small oak stand about a mile away, where he knew hogs were rooting up palmettos and feeding off acorns. He killed a young shoat and dragged him back to the skinning rack next to the smoke house. Then he cleaned him while Ed built a fire and started the smoke. Jessie figured it would be ready to eat by noon, and he wondered if he could slow Belle down a little bit. She would be ready and pacing by ten o'clock.

Jenny and her ma sat together in their best dresses while Horace drove the buckboard wagon. He rode proud in his new cotton pants and shirt. They followed Jessie and Ed, who had picked a big roan stud out of the horses that Jessie and Justin had brought back with them. Belle had made new outfits for Ed and Jessie, but she was waiting on a special occasion before letting either one wear them. Jessie watched with pride as Ed worked the spirited roan, calming him and teaching him to obey his commands. Ed knew that he must feel strange to the horse, as it became obvious that he had only had one trainer; but he knew that in time the horse would get used to him and calm down.

As they reached the village, Jessie saw the new poles for Justin's lodge. He was sitting under the lean to he had built for temporary shelter until he had enough hides. Justin would be comfortable for now, as it was late September, and it would be another month before it got cold. By then, he would bring the women of the tribe enough deer and cow hides to cover the lodge poles.

Jessie saw the young ones playing hoops down by the lake. The rest of the villagers were gathered in front of Two Worlds' lodge, where he was sitting on his fur covered backrest. He saw the pots hanging over fires and the small deer being slow roasted over hot coals. He was pretty sure that one of the pots was full of turkey, cooking in coontie gravy. The thought made his mouth water, and he smiled in anticipation.

Belle tapped Horace on the knee to get his attention away from the boys playing down by the lake and said, "If you stop this wagon before we go right past the village and help with the unloading, you can go play."

"Sorry Ma, that's my new friend Snake Handler."

Belle saw one of the boys waving and Horace waving back. "Lord knows I can only imagine how he got his name, but don't you go handling no snakes, they could be poison."

"OK Ma," he said, hardly able to contain his excitement. Stopping the wagon, he hopped down and asked, "What do you want first and where do you want it?"

"Never mind, I'm not ready yet. Go on and play with your friends."

"Thanks Ma!" he said over his shoulder as he ran.

Stepping down from his horse and dropping the reins to let them trail, Ed walked back to the buckboard to help his ma down. First he took Jenny under her arms, swinging her around once, making her giggle and put her on the ground. Turning back to his ma, he stepped closer and said in a low voice, "Ma, remember the girl that came to the house the night I got hurt and Pa came home?"

"Yes," she nodded.

"Well there's two of them!" he said confused. "Which one was it that came to the house?"

"I don't know; you'll just have to figure that out for yourself." She smiled at his confused look. "But help me down before everyone thinks I can't walk."

"Sorry Ma," he said, helping her to the ground.

Waiting Owl came forward to meet Belle, and taking her by the hand she said, "It is good to meet the wife of the man who has done so much for all of us. Please feel welcome by all of us here in our world."

Woman of the Wind, Raven, Little Otter and Little Moon came forward, touching her on the arm and shoulders as they introduced themselves.

"I am Belle, and it is I who will be forever grateful for saving not only my husband, but the father of my children. You will always be welcome here with us," she said, looking at each of them.

Taking Belle by the arm, Waiting Owl led her to join Two Worlds and the other men. Jessie had introduced Ed to Two Worlds, Red Sun, Silent Stalker, Big Cypress, and Spirit Snake. Ed liked Spirit Snake right away. He saw him standing tall and proud, and he understood that this boy had become a man while still young, just like he had.

"I remember you," Ed said to Red Sun. "You were with my father the night of the lightning storm, when I was hurt."

"Yes, I am glad you are better."

"My ribs are only a little sore now."

As Waiting Owl approached with Belle, she saw Little Moon walk over and stand next to Spirit Snake. She put her hand lightly on the back of his arm and smiled at him. Ed's disappointment showed until he turned and saw Little Otter smiling at him. His heart almost burst, and he could only stand and stare until she came closer.

"I am glad you are well now," she said, reaching and touching his ribs softly, letting her hand slide down his side.

"Yes," he managed to say as he choked. "I am fine now." The feel of her touch going all through his body made his knees go weak. Suddenly Ed became aware of everyone watching the two reacting to each other, and he blushed, but he couldn't take his eyes away from her until she turned and walked over to stand next to her mother. Belle looked at Woman of the Wind and they smiled, both aware of what had just taken place with that touch.

Everyone was feeling over stuffed from trying all the different foods, including the little ones, who had each eaten two helpings of the blueberry cobbler. The women were comparing the way they took care of their men and children, and Belle was looking forward to having female company for a change. She offered them the use of her sewing machine, if they would show her how they did such beautiful bead work.

Two Worlds had moved his resting seat away from where the women had gathered. Now he sat under the shade of a large oak limb, loading his ancient pipe with tobacco while everyone waited. When he finished tamping down the tobacco, he lit the pipe and drew a mouth full of smoke. Then he passed it to Red Sun, who passed it around the half circle of men, who were sitting cross legged on the ground. When the pipe reached Jessie, he drew a puff of the tobacco through the long decorated stem and turned to Ed and handed him the pipe. Feeling as much a man as he ever had, Ed took a long draw and held it in his mouth, trying not to choke on the strong pungent flavor. He passed it to Spirit Snake, who was also experiencing acceptance as a man in this discussion of their future.

As the pipe was being passed around, Two Worlds spoke. "Everyone here has experienced moving cattle through the brush in the past. We have the horses to do what you speak of and can gather the cows. My only concern is for the safety of our braves when they run into other white men, who do not like us being here in what they call their land. Every time we have had to fight the white man for our lives and the lives of our women and children, they have brought the soldiers to war on us."

Jessie spoke from where he sat. "You are all part of my family, as my family is of yours. I will fight any man who tries to harm anyone of my family!"

"That goes for me also!" Justin spoke up.

"Justin and I will be riding with you when we are rounding up cattle and pushing them to market. I don't expect trouble with us riding with you, but I have a double barrel shotgun for anyone who doesn't want to listen. We are the law out here and that is the first law," Jessie said with conviction.

The men spent the rest of the afternoon making plans to build holding pens this coming winter and talked about the round up and branding in the early spring. They would keep bringing the cattle in until there were enough cows to make it worth the drive to the shipping yard. One of the first things needed, was tools to build strong pens and also tools to work the ground so they could grow vegetables. After a long discussion, it was resolved that they would use Jessie's farm equipment to turn up five acres of good soil close to the lake and work the garden together to feed everyone. It would be a job to keep out deer and hogs, but they decided they could eat all of the different animals who wanted to feed on their garden.

It was agreed that Justin and Ed would take the work wagon and go to Tampa to get information. There, they would take the opportunity to buy tools and supplies for the village. While they were in Tampa, they would have some branding irons made. Before they left, Jessie would need to come up with a brand. It was late afternoon when they started for home, but it was Jessie who was driving the wagon. Ed told them he would bring Horace and Jenny home before dark and that the three of them wanted to stay a while longer.

"OK," Belle said, "but let Horace and Jenny ride on your daddy's horse. I don't trust that roan; he has too much energy for them."

"OK Ma."

On the way back, Belle slipped her arm through Jessie's and said, "Oh Jessie, I am so glad you brought them here. Are you sure you can protect them? They have lost so much; I am so worried."

"I know; I will do the best I can."

Squeezing his arm she said, "I know you will."

Part Three
The Crackers

The Double T Ranch

Twenty-Four

Ed and Justin were a half mile away from Tampa. Ed was driving the large work wagon, pulled by Molly and Preacher. Justin rode the big Morgan alongside as they followed the Hillsborough River west. The first pungent smell of the stock yards started overpowering everything else.

"Whew! What in the world is that smell?" Ed asked.

"That," Justin replied, "is the holding pens where we are going to drive the cattle to. They have made it easy for us, being on this side of the river. We won't have to drive them through town."

Approaching the cattle pens, they could see the docks jutting out into the river with two ships tied up, waiting to be loaded. There were at least a thousand head of cattle waiting in two different pens, and Justin and Ed noticed several brands. Trying to ignore the overpowering smell of cow manure, Ed guided the wagon up to what looked like the cattle office and stopped. Getting down, he joined Justin as he reached the open door of the office.

As they entered the dimly lit room, three men looked up as the man behind the desk asked, "Can I help you with something?"

"I'm looking for the cattle buyer," Justin said.

"That would be me, but neither one of you look like you have any cows to sell. What can I help you with?"

"Well you're right, we don't have any cows yet, but by this summer we intend to have that problem solved. What I need to know is; are you going to be buying cattle then, and what they are going to bring?"

Standing up and coming around the desk, he extended his hand first to Justin and then to Ed. "I'm Tom Marshal and I am the buyer, and yes I will be buying all the cattle you can bring in. The prices will depend on the shape of the cattle. Some fellows bring in cows that look like they were run all the way here and nothing left on their bones but hide. For them, they are only worth eight to ten dollars a head. If you slow them down and let them feed on the drive and put some meat on their bones they are worth twelve to fifteen dollars a head. Are you talking about ranch raised cattle, or are you planning on popping those Spanish scrub cows out of the bush?"

"They will be the wild Spanish cows," Ed replied. "How many can you take at one time?"

"I will buy all you can catch," laughed Tom.

One of the men sitting in a chair that was leaning against the wall laughed and asked Ed, "You ever rounded up any scrub cows, Son?"

"No Sir, but I'm going to learn," he said, drawing himself up to the full height of his pride.

"Well good luck," the man chuckled, "I'm sure you're going to give it one hell of a try."

"Well," Tom said, "however many you wind up with, just take it slow bringing them here, there's no time limit. Whenever I get enough for a full load, I ship them out."

"Where would I find a commissary that carries farm supplies?" Justin asked.

"Just follow the river for another half mile, and when you reach the bridge, you'll have to cross over to the main part of town. Three streets down, turn toward the Gulf, and you will find it about two blocks down on the right. You can't miss it," Tom replied.

"Thanks," said Justin, shaking Tom's hand as he started for the door.

"We are mighty grateful," Ed said, also reaching for Tom's hand.

"I hope to see you this summer," Tom said as he shook Ed's hand.

Bringing the wagon to a halt, Ed read the sign over the door: Wooten Hardware & Farm Supplies. After setting the brake on the wagon, he hopped down and started inside. Justin tied the reins to the back of the wagon and followed Ed into the long narrow building. Looking around, he saw the store was half empty and hoped that they were going to find the supplies they needed. An older, heavy set man came out of a small office and greeted them.

"Hello, I'm Ralph Wooten, and I only accept cash money and none of that worthless confederate paper. If you need anything they used for the war I probably won't have it."

"I'm looking mostly for farm equipment," Justin spoke up, "and I pay with gold."

"Well I might be able to help you there. Not much call for farming equipment these days since the war. Not too many men left to farm. What do you need?"

Ed pulled the list his ma had made from his pocket and began reading. "First we need a half dozen hoes, two shovels, four axes, two cross cut saws, three hand saws, a half dozen hammers. Then, a half of a keg of sixteen penny nails and a half keg of eight penny nails. Two turning plows with the collars and harnesses with the plows. Four number two wash tubs, three cast iron cooking pots and two posthole diggers should do us. How much of that do you think you have?"

"Well other than the nails, because I'm not sure of how many I have, I can fill your whole order. I can give you a good price on all that, since there's not much call for any of what you want, if you're sure you can pay for it all."

"Well just how much are you talking about?" Ed asked.

Wooten walked back to his office, got his pencil and paper and started adding numbers. Returning, he said, "It all comes to sixty three dollars, and I'll throw in what nails I have."

Ed walked over to where Justin was looking at the axes and saws. "What do you think? Does that sound like a fair price?"

"Give him sixty dollars. He'll take it."

Ed pulled out the small leather pouch and shook out three twenty dollar gold pieces. He walked back to the store owner, holding out the gold coins in his hand. "I got these three twenty dollar gold pieces; if you want them, we got a deal."

The owner's eyes got bigger when he saw the gold coins. "Since you're paying in gold, we got us a deal."

After loading the supplies into the wagon, Justin turned to Ralph and said, "I have one more question. Where would I find a place to buy some leather goods?"

"Well if anybody has, it would be Francis Shere who owns the stables and feed store. He has a black smith shop next door if you need your horses shod. Just follow this street another two blocks, turn right heading back toward the river, and you will find him at the end of the road on the water."

Ed saw the large stable barn and the wooden pole corral, ending at the river's edge so the horses could have access to water. Ed read the sign above the stable doors: TAMPA FEED & SEED and below that in smaller letters: Stables – Tack Supplies – Blacksmith. Ed slowed the wagon to a halt in front of the tack shop and set the brake. Dismounting, Justin walked up the steps where an old black man was sweeping the porch and asked, "Is the place open now?"

"Yas Sir," the old man replied. "Mr. Francis is inside and he can help you with anything you want."

"Thanks," Justin replied as he entered the store with Ed behind him. They walked over to where a man sat at a long work bench, underneath an open window, repairing the stirrup on a saddle.

Looking up as Justin and Ed approached, the man asked, "Can I help you fellers?"

"Well I hope so," Justin replied. "We need some rope, but what I really need is some cow whips and branding irons."

"Well, you have come to the right place. How much rope do you need? Show me the brand you want made and how many do you want?"

"I'll need six, thirty foot lengths of rope and six of these branding irons made up," Justin said, handing the man the paper showing the shape of the branding irons.

Ed broke into the conversation and asked, "Would you mind if I put my horses in your corral so they could get to the water?"

"Sure you can," the man answered.

"Jefferson!" he called.

The old black man came hurrying through the door. "Yas Sir, Mr. Francis?"

"Jefferson, unhitch those horses from their wagon and turn them loose in the corral."

"Yas Sir, Mr. Francis. I'll do it right now. Do you want me to give them some feed too?"

"No," Ed spoke up. "I will help you with the horses." He headed for the door with the old man following him.

"I'll have the blacksmith start on your branding irons, but it will take him until tomorrow afternoon to make them," the stable owner stated.

"Then I will wait on them," Justin answered. "Now how about those cow whips, do you have any made or do I need to wait on those too?"

"I have whips made up. What lengths do you need? I have eight footers, eleven footers and I also have a couple of eighteen footers. I make them all myself and they are the best you'll find anywhere," Mr. Francis said with pride.

"I'll take a half dozen eight footers and a couple of eleven footers. The eighteen footers are more than anybody can handle right now."

Taking Justin over to a wall where the whips were hanging on pegs, Francis pointed to the whips and said, "Why don't you try these out while I cut those ropes for you."

Taking down one of the eight footers, Justin gripped the smooth wooden handle covered with soft leather and uncoiled the tapered braided leather with the three foot popper at the end of the braid. Looking around to make sure he had room, he swung it over his head and then forward and when it reached the end, he flicked his wrist back and heard the crack of the whip, loud as a rifle. The movement of the braided leather was as smooth as soft butter. Justin smiled to himself and reaching for the eleven footer, again swinging it over his head and forward he felt the smoothness as his energy reached the end of the three foot popper and heard the rifle crack sound again. Knowing the eight footers would be best in the heavy brush and the eleven footers out on the open plains and marshes; Justin thought it would be easy to teach the others with these whips.

Picking out the whips he wanted, Justin carried them to the counter next to the work bench where the newly cut coils of rope lay. "I want to add a dozen saddle blankets to the list, and while we are here, I want to get the horses shod."

"That's not a problem," Francis answered. "I have a couple of horses I can loan you if you want to leave yours and the wagon here in the stables. Everything will be safe until you get back tomorrow afternoon."

"That would be fine. We have a few more things to do while we are here."

"There's a hotel back down town if you're looking for a place to stay."

"No thank you, we'll just find us a place outside of town. I don't particularly like the smell here with all of these Yankee soldiers around."

"I can't say I blame you," Francis agreed, "but I do some business with them and they pay American cash. I'll keep all of your supplies here until you come back tomorrow, and you can pay me then."

Justin leaned against the rail, waiting as Ed and Jefferson were walking back up from the river. When they got to the gate, Justin told Ed what was happening and asked him if he would pick them out a couple of horses and saddle them while he talked to Jefferson for a minute.

"Sure," Ed said, heading for the stables to get a rope.

When Ed walked away, Justin turned to the old man. "Mr. Jefferson, I need to find a black preacher."

"Well Mr. Justin, you'll have to go to the quarters to find him, but it's Reverend Ike who you be looking for."

"Where are the quarters?"

"You'll have to go back to the road going through the main part of town. Go south for about a mile, and you'll know it when you get there. Houses will be on both sides, you turn left almost to the end and you will see the church on the right. Reverend Ike lives in the house out back of the church."

Everyone stopped and stared as Ed and Justin rode their horses down the dirt road between the rows of small wooden unpainted shacks, the blacks called home. Old women were sitting in homemade rocking chairs; old men were tending small gardens out back. Two young boys were carrying buckets of water from a well to fill up the wash pots and tubs. They all stopped to stare as the white men rode past them. Justin could see the concern on some faces as they wondered what these two men could want here. They still lived in fear of the white man's motives. The new government had too many things to worry about. They didn't have time to be concerned with what was happening to the blacks. They all watched as the two men rode around back of the church and dismounted at the preacher's house. Speculation ran up and down the quarters as to what was going on, but they would wait for word to reach them later.

It had taken all Ed could do, to contain his curiosity when Justin told him he had one more thing to do before they left town for the night. Now he was more confused than ever as Justin walked up onto the porch and knocked. Getting down off his horse, he stood and waited. The Reverend's face showed his curiosity and concern as he stood in the open door way facing Justin.

"What can I do for you?"

"I don't mean to disturb you, but are you Reverend Ike?"

"Yes I am," the barrel chested man answered in his deep rumbling voice, a voice that could call God down at will, Justin thought. Just right for what I need, he thought to himself.

"I don't mean to bother you, but I need a few minutes of your time, if you could afford it."

Ed tied the horses to a small tree and followed Justin and the preacher to the rough wooden tables under the oaks. The preacher took a seat on a bench and invited the two men to have a seat on the other side of the table. Looking across the table he asked Justin, "Just what can I do for you?"

For the next fifteen minutes, Ed listened as Justin explained to the preacher about Jessie, the Indians and how the war had brought them all together. He told the preacher about their plans to round up the Spanish cattle and drive them here to sell. "We don't have quite enough help, and that's why I'm here."

"I'm afraid you have come to the wrong place. As far as I know there are no cow men here."

"I'm not looking for cow men. What I need is a trail cook, one that can be mobile while we are rounding up and branding cows at different holding pens. They will have to live mostly out of a cook wagon, but we will build them a house to live in when we are not doing cattle. I know there are a lot of displaced people since the war, and I was hoping you might help find someone who needs a place to be. They would be treated and paid fairly."

"Are you a Christian man, Mr. Justin?" Reverend Ike asked.

"I don't rightly know; I went to church before my father moved us from Savanna, Georgia, when I was seven years old, but there was no church where we settled in a small outpost here in Florida."

"I'm a Christian," Ed spoke up. "My ma took us with her every Sunday to church before the war came, and we had to leave and come here."

"You sound like you have a good Christian family," the Reverend said to Ed. "There is a couple that worked on one of the plantations before the war. It's gone now, but she was the cook for the field hands and he did carpentry and minor repairs on the plantation. He broke his leg in a fall, but he gets around just fine and could be a lot of help if he had the chance."

"Could I meet them?" Justin asked.

"Come with me." The Reverend rose from the table and led Justin and Ed around the back of his house. A woman, who was bent over a tub of hot water, washing clothes on a wash board, looked up and over to a man hoeing in a small garden.

"Franklin, Sara Mae, there is someone here I want you to meet. Why don't you hold off what you're doing for a few minutes and come sit with us and listen to what these gentlemen have to say."

Franklin limped slightly over next to his wife, looking unsure and said, "Sure Reverend, whatever you say." He and Sara Mae looked at one another in confusion and followed them back to the table under the trees.

When they sat down across the table with the Reverend, Justin explained what he had told the Reverend about his needs and asked them if they were interested. They both looked at the Reverend with questions in their eyes. The Reverend, seeing the doubt in their faces, said to them, "After talking with these men, I think it might be a good opportunity for a new life if you're up to it. If you don't want to go, you don't have to. You can stay here until we find you a place."

"I don't have any problem doing what you ask," Sara Mae said, "but what about my husband here; I can't leave him alone."

"It's going to take two people when we are branding cows, and then it will be weeks on the trail driving them here to be sold. We would need both of you if you would come. We will pay you both for your work," Justin answered.

Sara Mae looked at her husband Franklin, waiting for his answer. After studying the two men sitting across from him for several seconds, he spoke directly to Justin. "I won't have no man looking at me like I was some cripple to feel sorry for. If I can't do my job I'll leave. Anybody call me cripple names will have me to deal with. I won't never be somebody's slave ever again. If that's understood, just tell us when you wants us to go with you."

"That's understood," said Justin, amazed at the pride these people carried so soon out of slavery. "We will be back by here tomorrow afternoon with the supply wagon. Have all your things ready to go."

"Mr. Justin, that won't take but a few minutes for what we have, you looking at most of it right now," Franklin said.

The Reverend talked with Justin as he walked them to the front of the house where the horses were tied. Ed moved around his horse and opened his saddle bag. Reaching in, he removed the small leather bag and shook out two silver dollars. Walking to where the Reverend and Justin stood, he waited till Justin and the Reverend finished up by shaking hands as Justin thanked the minister for his help.

Ed then stepped up to the Reverend and said, "When Ma used to take us to church, she always put something in the collection basket. I won't be here when you pass your basket around, but I would like to give you this." He handed the Reverend the two silver dollars.

"Thank you Son, this will help put food on the tables for some children." Then he shook Ed's hand saying, "God bless you both."

Twenty-Five

Riding back into town, Justin asked Ed if he had ever seen the ocean.

"No."

"Well, we got a couple of hours. Let's take a ride; everybody should see the ocean. Maybe we can find a restaurant that has fresh oysters. You ever ate any oysters?"

"No I can't say that I have. What do they look like?"

Laughing, Justin said, "Well I think it is best that you wait and see."

It took another thirty minutes of riding before they made their way through town. When Ed saw the endless expanse of sparkling water, he stopped and stared. "How far does it go?"

"All the way to a country called Mexico."

When the road ended at the edge of the sand dunes, Justin turned toward a restaurant with a back deck, looking out over the beach. A group was sitting around several tables drinking beer, and the centers of the tables were heaped with oyster shells.

"This is the place," Justin said to Ed. Leaving their horses tied to a low tree branch, they headed for one of the empty tables. A middle aged waitress sauntered over with a slow smile on her face until she could determine who she was dealing with. If they were local water people, they would be relaxed and in no hurry. If they were from up north they would be impatient, demanding and complaining about the slow service down here. Like down south here was a foreign country, she thought.

Justin watched and smiled as the waitress sauntered across the floor. He loved the slow, easy way of the locals who lived their lives on or around the ocean. Wherever he had sailed into a port, it was the same; few ever left the water. They just couldn't think of a better place to be.

"Evening boys, what can I get for you?" she asked as she approached the table.

"Well my young friend here is from the middle of Georgia and has never eaten any seafood, much less good oysters," Justin answered.

"And you?" she asked with questions in her eyes.

"I sailed around the edge of this gulf for a couple of years before the war, crewing on cargo boats, and I have tried the best oysters they had to offer in every port. I've never had oysters from this area yet, but from the looks of those shells stacked up on those tables, I think I'm going to like them."

"Well we like to think that ours stack up with the best," she said as a smile reached her eyes. "Is that what ya'll are having?" she asked.

"Not me," said Ed, "I want to see one before I say I'm going to eat it."

"I think we had better start him off with some fried snapper and whatever else you have," Justin said, "but I'll start with two dozen oysters and go from there."

"We have snapper, grouper, trout and redfish; do you want to try some of all of them?"

"Yes," Justin replied, "I'll eat some with my oysters. How about beer; got any?"

"Yes we have beer; one for each of you?"

"I've never drank beer," Ed said, looking at Justin.

"Well it's time you did," Justin said. "So bring us two glasses of beer."

"Coming right up," she smiled, sauntering back inside.

The sky was just turning pink when the waitress brought the first platters of fried fish and a platter of oysters to the table. They drank two glasses of beer while they were waiting. Ed had taken to the taste right off and drank both of his before Justin finished. He was disappointed when Justin suggested he wait and eat some food before drinking any more.

"We'll have some more beer now," Ed said, before she could set the platters on the table.

"Well aren't you anxious for someone who wasn't sure if you would like beer!" she smiled as she set the platters on the table.

"Other than the beer, can I bring you something else?"

"Just keep the oysters coming," Justin smiled as she turned away.

Staring at Justin as he tilted the shell above open lips and let the oyster slide off into his mouth, Ed said, "You can eat all of those things you want, but I ain't putting one of those in my mouth. I'll just eat the fish; it's delicious."

An hour later, they finished their fourth beer while watching the rim of the sun touch the water of the Gulf of Mexico. They both sat in awe as the sun dropped below the horizon, painting the sky a brilliant red hue. The waitress smiled at the glow on Ed's face when she brought the change back from Justin's twenty dollar gold piece.

"That was wonderful," Ed said, smiling from ear to ear. "I've never eaten anything like that."

"You fellers be careful," the waitress said as Ed wobbled while getting up from the table.

"You have a name?" Justin asked the waitress.

"Julie," she smiled. "Thank you for asking."

Justin placed a silver dollar on the table and said, "Thank you Julie, my name is Justin."

"I hope to see ya'll again sometime soon," she responded with sincerity. Not many men around those parts knew about tipping a waitress. This one was not a rookie.

"You sure will," Justin spoke and turned to follow Ed.

"Where are we going to sleep?" Ed asked as they reached the horses.

"Well, you are going to experience something else new tonight. We're going to take a ride down the beach and find a place to sleep for the night." They rode in silence, both over whelmed by the beauty of the constantly changing colors, the sun's rays reflecting off the sky and floating clouds pushed by a gentle breeze. The sun was retreating, taking with it the last rays of light as the night pulled its blanket of darkness across the sky. Justin rode up to the edge of the sand dunes, away from the high tide line and into a small stand of coconut palms. There he dismounted. He opened his bundle of sleeping furs while Ed found himself a smooth area and unrolled his blanket. They sat in silence for an hour, taking in the night and the endless number of stars, watching the sliver of a moon rising in the night sky. Giving in to the sound of endless waves lapping at the shore, they slept.

It was well past noon when Justin and Ed rode up to the stables and dismounted. Francis Shere got up from his work bench when he saw the two men enter his store. Coming to meet them he said, "All your things are ready." Smiling proudly, he continued. "The branding irons are made and your horses are shod. If you are ready to leave, I'll have Jefferson hitch the horses to the wagon."

"I'll hitch them up," Ed said, "but I could use his help."

"Jefferson!" Shere shouted.

"No need to holler Mr. Shere. I will tell him on the way out," Ed said, heading for the door.

"Would you like to check the branding irons, just to make sure they're what you want?" Francis asked, heading for the counter where the irons lay.

Justin followed him to the counter where he picked up one of the irons and inspected it closely, twisting the letters and then banging it on the floor against the thick wooden boards. "Good and solid," Justin remarked, "they will do just fine. Do you have the bill?"

Francis reached over and pulled a piece of paper out from under one of the irons. He handed it to Justin and gave him a minute to look it over before asking, "Is everything alright?"

Justin looked at the list and studied the prices: 6 ropes, 30 ft @ .60 each, 6 cow whips, 8 ft @ 1.50 each, 2 cow whips, 11 ft @ 1.75 each, 12 saddle blankets @ .50 each and three horses shod @ 2.00 each. The total was $28.10. "It looks fair enough to me."

"Well everything is in the wagon except the branding irons," Francis stated.

While waiting for Ed to finish with the horses, bring the money bag and pay the bill, Justin walked around the store looking at the wares and spotted a small pile of rifle scabbards, stacked across a row of barrels. Picking up one, he checked the quality of the leather and hand stitching. "You make this yourself?" Justin asked, holding one up for Francis to see.

"Yes Sir, I make all my leather goods. I've been at it for over twenty years."

"I have to say, this is the best quality and workmanship I have seen in a long time. Add a half dozen of these to the list."

"Yes Sir, that will be an extra 2.00 each, and I'll just add an extra 12.00 to the total making it an even $40.00," he said, smiling.

Ed came through the door with his saddle bag over his shoulder. He put down the saddle bag, reached inside and brought out a small leather pouch. "Everything is ready. How much do we owe for the rest of the supplies?"

"Forty dollars," Francis answered. He smiled again when he saw the gold coins drop from the bag to Ed's hand.

Handing Francis the two twenty dollar gold coins, he said, "Thank you and tell the blacksmith he did a really good job on those horse shoes."

"I thank both of you," Francis said, watching as the two walked to the door. "By the way, if you need something I don't have, I can get it ordered and shipped in about six weeks."

In one smooth motion, Justin slipped his foot into the stirrup and swung up into the saddle. He nodded to Francis and said, "That's good to know."

Taking the reins, Ed gave the horses a gentle slap on their rumps and headed back toward Main Street and out of town in the direction of the quarters. At the turnoff for the church, Ed started down the dirt road through the quarters. Justin was riding along the side of the wagon, and he slowed his horse to a stop when he saw the ancient woman. She steadied herself with her cane as she stood and walked to the edge of the porch.

"Good afternoon Ma'am," Justin called as he removed his hat in respect for the woman's age.

She spoke in a low wavering voice, and Justin had to listen closely to hear. "This is a mighty fine thing you're doing for Franklin and Sara Mae, I've known them both since they were born and I can tell you right now they are both mighty fine folk. They will do you proud if you threats them right."

"Yes Ma'am," Justin said, "they will be treated with respect; I give you my word on that."

"God bless you both," she said, moving back to her rocking chair. Ed had removed his hat along with Justin and putting it back on, he flicked the reins across the horses' rumps and started the wagon on down the dirt road to the church. He nodded back as people smiled and stopped to wave.

When Ed stopped the wagon in front of the church, there was a small crowd of people milling around under the shade of the large oak, saying good bye to their friends and wishing them well. Sara Mae had a bundle, wrapped in what looked like an old worn sheet, and Franklin was standing next to a two foot by three foot wooden crate. In the crate, there were some small tools and a couple of cooking utensils. A large cooking pot sat next to it.

The Reverend came out of the church as Ed and Justin came to meet him. Shaking their hands, he said, "I want to send them off with a prayer and then they are in yours and God's hands."

Justin and Ed removed their hats and bowed their heads as they saw Franklin, Sara Mae, and their friends bow down on their knees.

Looking up at the heavens, the Reverend prayed in his booming voice, "Oh Almighty God, you have chosen yet another road for these children of yours to travel to reach your golden gates. Oh Lord, walk beside them to help keep them safe until it is time to call them home."

"Amen, Amen!" came the chorus from the small crowd as they rose from their knees and gave their final hugs.

Justin rode alongside the wagon, talking to Franklin and Sara Mae. "We have one more stop to make before we head back. Sara Mae, I want you to think about whatever you are going need to feed at least ten people on a cattle drive that will take six to eight weeks. We will kill what meat we need, but you'll need all the other fixin's. Franklin, I want you to think about any tools you will want to fix a broken wheel or axel. We are going to be turning this wagon into a cook wagon that can carry the supplies, and we want to make room for you and Sara Mae to sleep in."

Ed spoke up and reminded Justin that they had a lot of wood working tools at home.

"If Mr. Ed has tools at his place then I shouldn't need anything else. I'll use hard wood to make a frame for the wagon, but we will need good strong canvas for the wagon cover," Franklin replied.

"We have that too," Ed said. "We used it for shelter on the way here from Georgia."

"Then it sounds like I won't be needing anything else Mr. Ed," Franklin spoke quietly.

Franklin pointed the way through town to the Suwannee Store by the river. Pulling up to the front of the store, Ed brought the two horses to a halt. Jumping down from the seat, he helped Sara Mae to the ground and walked her through the door into the store. Franklin waited patiently on the wagon seat, watching the people pass by. He knew that they were wondering what he was doing, sitting there by himself.

Looking down from his ladder, where he was putting supplies on one of the higher shelves, the owner asked, "What can I do for you folks?" He started down the ladder with a puzzled look on his face.

"Miss Sara Mae here is going to tell you what she's going to need. Give her whatever she asks for," Ed said.

"Well just how are you going to pay for this?" the store keeper asked. "I don't take no confederate money; it's worthless now."

"You'll be paid in gold," Ed said.

"Yes Sir," the store keeper replied, and turning to Sara Mae, he said, "Just tell me what you need and I'll see if I have it."

"First thing I can think of will be four twenty five pound sacks of flour, five one gallon pails of lard, twenty pounds of coffee, fifteen pounds of sugar, two pounds of salt. Oh ... and two tins of baking powder. What kind of cooking utensils you carries, Mister?"

"You can just call me Mr. Spivey; this is my store."

"Well Mr. Spivey, do you carry any cooking utensils?"

"Yes, right this way." He led the way to the back of the store.

Walking along the rows of pots and pans, she spotted two things she needed. "Mr. Spivey, I need that wooden flour bowl there," she pointed, "and that Dutch oven sitting up there on the top self."

Putting the wooden bowl and the iron oven in the aisle, he took a flour sifter she handed him. Looking around, she pointed to a small stack of iron skillets. "I'll take two of those, and I could use a good butcher knife."

"I keep those behind the counter," he said, as he placed the wooden bowl on the Dutch oven. Taking the two skillets in his other hand, he headed to the front of the store, and she followed with the sifter.

After stacking the supplies on the floor, Spivey walked around the counter and reached underneath, bringing out a small wooden box with several sizes of knives. Putting the box on the counter, he said, "Just pick out the one you want."

Reaching inside the box, she picked up a twelve inch blade by the smooth wooden handle. Then she picked out an eight inch, narrow bladed knife. "This one will do me fine for boning meat. That's all I'll be needing for now."

The sun was casting long shadows when Ed drove the wagon across the bridge and past the stock yard, and they traveled another four miles before they decided to stop for the night.

~

It was early afternoon when Ed saw Jessie, Red Sun, Big Cypress, Silent Stalker, and Spirit Snake working their way up from the wetland prairie into the slash pine forest, scouting for cows and a place to build the branding pens. Spirit Snake saw the wagon top the hill and start down into the valley. Shouting to the others, he spurred his horse into a gallop, waving as he headed toward his new friend who was driving the wagon. As he rode closer, he saw the two strange looking people sitting on the seat next to Ed. He had heard of the people whose skin was black, but he had never seen one and wondered where Ed and Justin had found them. Ed saw his friend racing toward him and waved back. Turning toward Franklin and Sara Mae, he eagerly explained to them, this is my new Indian friend Spirit Snake, and we are close to home now.

"Lawd, I's never seen an Indian before," Sara Mae exclaimed.

"I's ain't never seen one neither," Franklin agreed. "Is they wild?"

"No," Justin assured them. "They are people like you and me. They just live a different life than us and are peaceful people when they are left alone. They are a fierce people though when they have to fight for their life."

"I can sure understand that," Franklin replied. "This will be most interesting." He watched the Indian come close enough to see the strange clothes he was wearing.

"What are ya'll doing out here?" Ed asked, seeing the other riders coming their way in the distance as Spirit Snake slowed his horse to a walk and came alongside the wagon.

"We've been searching for cows and a place to build the pens. There are cows everywhere when you look for them. I think I have seen a thousand myself!" Spirit Snake's eyes never left the two people sitting next to Ed. "Were you born with your skin that color?" he asked as his curiosity got the better of him.

"As much as you were born the color you are," Sara Mae answered, smiling at the boy's innocent curiosity.

"Where is your tribe?" asked Spirit Snake. "Are there more of you?"

"That's enough questions for now," Justin spoke up as he spurred his horse forward to meet the oncoming riders, leaving the two excited boys to see who could out talk the other. He slowed his horse to a stop as Jessie approached.

Greeting Justin, Jessie asked, "Did you have a safe trip?"

"Yes, I have all the supplies except for the nails. They only had about half of what we needed, but there should be more the next time we are there. We have all we will need for now." Seeing the questions in Jessie's eyes as the wagon approached, Justin began to explain.

While everyone sat and listened, Justin described how he had found the Reverend Ike and explained to him his need for a trail cook. He told them that Reverend Ike had introduced him to Franklin and Sara Mae, and repeated the story of their back ground on the plantation, before it had been burned down during the war. Then Justin went on to say that they had been homeless ever since and how the people of the church had taken care of them.

As Ed brought the team of horses to a halt, Justin rode along side of the wagon next to Franklin, who was in a state of anxiety and total confusion. Franklin wasn't sure what to expect when he left Tampa, but it had nothing to do with what he was seeing now. Wild Indians! Franklin was trying not to jump out of his skin.

Seeing fear in the man's eyes, Jessie rode up to the wagon and dismounted. Reaching up to shake their hands, he said, "I'm Jessie Tucker, and I sure am glad Justin had the good sense to find you both and bring you here. You will be most welcome here, and I hope you can bring your selves to tolerate and put up with all of us, because we sure are going to need your help."

Relieved at the welcome, Franklin hopped from the seat, swinging his legs out and landing on his good leg. Putting his hand out to Jessie, he said earnestly, "Mr. Tucker, you won't ever have to tell me to do my job; all you have to do is tell me what you want."

"I believe that," Jessie answered back, squeezing the man's hand and feeling the strength in Franklin's handshake. Looking up at Sara Mae, he smiled and said, "Ma'am, you will certainly be welcome here and I know someone who's going to be glad to meet you."

All the doubts she had since she first climbed up on the wagon vanished, and she smiled. "God bless you Mr. Tucker. I should have known you would be a good man after meeting your son here," she said, patting Ed's knee and making him blush.

Jessie mounted his horse and turned to face the wagon. "Let's get this wagon to the barn and unloaded and get you and Sara Mae a place for yourselves. Don't worry about these wild Indians. You will soon learn to love them."

When Franklin climbed back up on the seat, Ed flicked the reins across Dolly's hips and followed the riders. He was hoping they would travel through the village, so he could catch a glimpse of Little Otter. Spirit Snake was riding alongside the wagon asking a dozen questions, and Ed wanted to ask him about Little Otter, but he didn't want to sound too anxious.

Twenty-Six

The warm March winds blew across the fields where more than five acres had been cleared and plowed. The fields were laid out in neat rows, waiting for the seeds to be planted. The families wouldn't plant until the moon was right, and everyone was confident that there would be no more freezes. Jessie asked Justin and the Indians from the village to start cutting the poles they would need to build the branding pens. Once they were finished building the pens, they would go and round up some cows. He had left Ed in charge of clearing the land to be planted.

Franklin was put to work helping Ed and even with his bad leg, he turned out to be more valuable than Ed could have imagined. Every morning by the time the light was good enough for them to see, Franklin had both oxen ready with their pulling harnesses and chains and was leading them to the fields. Horace came to help, and the three of them began pulling felled trees to the edge of the field. Later they would be cut into cook stove lengths, then split into fire wood and stacked to dry. After clearing the field of all the trees, they started on the palmettos that grew in small clumps around the yellow pines that they had removed.

Then came the task of pulling the tree stumps; with the oxen as one team and on some mornings, using Preacher and Dolly before they were needed for the wagon. Even with the two teams pulling together, it took much yelling at Dolly and Preacher along with a lot of whip cracking over the oxen heads, to remove a few of the larger stumps. It took Ed another two days to clear the limbs before Franklin started behind him with the cutting disk. In order to have enough weight to cut the turned up clods of dirt with the harrow, all four of the young boys had to sit on a board that spanned the width of the disk, two on either side of Franklin. It would be the first of many times the disk would be pulled back and forth, until the planting rows could be turned and worked with hoes.

When the field was cleared of all the larger limbs, Franklin built a sled, fifteen feet long and eight feet wide with two foot high sides that he pulled behind one of the oxen. Belle and the women and children from the village walked beside the sled, loading it with the smaller limbs. The winter cold snaps had killed most of the grass and roots of the turned up weeds. They threw the larger roots into the sled with the small tree limbs. Jessie had ridden over to see John Campbell at his sawmill and bargained for the lumber that Franklin used to make the sled. For the price of twenty dollars, Jessie brought back more than enough lumber to build the sled and a twenty by twenty foot house with a front porch for Franklin and Sara Mae. The small house sat between Jessie's place and the village, under a small stand of live oaks at the edge of the garden. Franklin and Sara Mae were truly home.

Jessie rode ahead and waited, holding open the gate to the branding pen as the riders herded twenty head of the most stubborn creatures he had ever seen. It had taken them two days to keep enough cows together, to make it worth driving them to be branded. After being branded, they were turned loose only to be rounded up again later. Jessie stood shaking his head as one cow after another broke away trying to reach the pine thicket. He listened to the yelling of the men and the popping of the whips. The men had been practicing all winter and had become really good at cracking the whips. They had endured several welts from back lashes in the learning stage, but by now everyone could cut a pine cone from its limb, or cut an ornery cow from the thickets with a few well-placed stings from the popper.

As the others dismounted, Jessie closed the gate behind the milling cows and turned to the men with a worried look on his face. "If it's going to take this long to roundup twenty head of these God awful creatures, we'll starve to death before we have enough to drive to Tampa. If it takes all six of us to roundup twenty head, then there is no way we are going to split up into two different groups as we planned," Jessie said, with frustration in his voice.

"We need some cow dogs like we used on the ranch I worked at a while back," Justin spoke up. "It would take me a while, but I could take a trip back there and see if I could get us a few," he offered.

"No, I think I know where I might be able to get a couple. Justin, you and the others see if you can round up what we have branded. I'm going to take a ride." Mounting his horse, he headed toward the lake, leaving the men eating smoked ham and hoe cake under the tall yellow pine.

Jessie sat at the edge of the field being plowed, thinking about the dogs and waiting for Franklin and the boys to reach him. As he got to the end of the row, Franklin brought the oxen to a halt. "Good afternoon Mr. Tucker, is there something I can do for you?"

"I need Horace to come with me. I'll send him back to you in a while." Lifting Horace up behind him on the horse, Jessie said, "I am going to need you to pick me out three of those pups of Dixie's to take with me."

"What are you going to do with them, Pa?" Horace asked with concern in his voice.

"I need me some cow dogs to help round up those stubborn cows, or we ain't ever going to be in the cattle business. The pups will be in good hands. I'll see if I can get John Campbell to trade me for a couple of his cow dogs he brought with him from Georgia."

"I remember them," Horace answered. "They are pretty mean dogs. I remember when they tore up those hogs that time on the way here."

"They're tough animals," Jessie explained, "but they're not mean, just protective. John said they were good cow dogs, and that's what we need right now."

Leading the way into the barn, Horace opened the door to the stall where Dixie was lying on her side, patiently letting all seven puppies feed. "Which ones do you want Pa?"

"I'll let you pick them out for me. Just pick me out three good ones, ones you would be proud to give to a friend."

Horace picked the biggest male of the litter and handed it to his pa then, picked another male and a pretty little female from the feeding litter. Holding the two squirming puppies he said with a plea in his voice, "Pa let me go with you; I want to see where they are gonna live."

"OK, go down by the lake and pick one of the Marsh Tackies and saddle him up. Tell Franklin you won't be back today. I'll go tell your Ma where we're going," he yelled, smiling at the boy already running toward the lake.

Jessie checked the cinch on Horace's saddle and laid the saddle bags behind it. Then he stuffed a piece of a blanket in each bag, put a puppy in each one, and after helping Horace up into the saddle, he handed him the big male. "Can you handle the pup and the horse at the same time?"

"It's no problem Pa; he'll just lay right here on the saddle in front of me. He won't be no trouble; we'll be just fine," he grinned.

John saw the riders as they crossed the shallow stream of the Little Withlacoochee River, and after making the last cut on the cypress log, he shut down the steam engine that ran the saw. Walking away from the noise the steam engine made as it settled down, he told the boys to take a break and get themselves a drink of water.

As Jessie brought the horse to a halt, John walked over next to Horace's horse and said, "You must be Ed."

"No Sir, I'm Horace," he said drawing himself to his full height with a grin.

"Why you've grown so much I thought you were Ed," John said smiling as he reached up, lifted him out of the saddle and put him on the ground. "What have you got there?" he asked, seeing the pup Horace was clutching to his chest.

"It's one of Dixie's and Rebel's puppies, and we brought more." He pointed to the small head sticking up out of the saddle bag. "There are two more," he said proudly.

"Well is this part of their training?" John asked Horace with a hint of a smile in his voice.

"No Sir," Horace said, "we brought them to trade you for cow dogs, cause Pa's trying to round up cows to sell. But I don't think he's doing very good."

"Well let's get the other two down and see if they're worth trading for," John said as he reached in the saddle bags and took both puppies out. Holding them up in front of him and turning them for a closer inspection, he said, "These are some fine looking hounds." Then he placed them on the ground to watch them play.

"They are the best puppies in the world!" Horace exclaimed.

"Well I reckon they are if you say so, cause you seem like a real dog man to me," he said, grinning. "Let's take them up to the house and see if we have anything worth trading for these world's best puppies."

Holding the reins of the two horses and walking slowly, Horace called to the puppies as they played, and followed his pa and John to the house while Jessie explained what he needed.

Twenty yards from the house, John let out a loud whistle and all six dogs came around the house, barking as they ran to John. As soon as they saw Jessie, they all stopped and the hair stood up on their backs. They gave Jessie a low growl while they waited for John's orders. Jessie stood still as John knelt on one knee calling them to him. They bounded forward, almost knocking John to the ground. "Easy,

easy!" he said, soothing them as they took turns sniffing Jessie, until each one recognized that he was no danger.

Horace stayed back with the horses and called out, "Mr. Campbell, they won't hurt the puppies will they?"

"No," he answered, "just bring them here slowly." Turning to the dogs, he said, "Sit!" Following his orders, they all sat watching as Horace slowly walked the puppies over to them. As the puppies played around the dogs, Horace could see the large dogs' tails wagging in anticipation. John walked along in front of each one, giving a pat on the head and saying, "Easy now, don't hurt the puppies," giving them permission to sniff and lick the strange little animals.

John's three youngest boys came running up from the creek and seeing Horace with the puppies, they all started talking at the same time. "Hey Horace, can I play with one of the puppies?"

Without waiting for an answer, they started crawling on their knees and rolling in the grass with the pups. Sitting on the porch with John and his oldest boy Frank who had joined them from the mill, Jessie finished explaining to them what he had in mind. Then he asked John if he could spare a couple of his dogs to trade.

"Well looking at those kids of mine playing with those pups, I wouldn't be very popular around here if I didn't!" John said laughing. "But from what you're telling me about the way you're splitting up into two groups, you're going to need two dogs to each group, if they are going to do you any good. With those three pups of yours, I'm going to be overrun with dogs. Four of those dogs I brought with me from Georgia, but those two smaller ones there are not quite a year old yet. I'll send two of those grown males along with the two young ones. You can put one of the young ones with one of the older dogs and they will be quick to learn. They will make you some fine cow dogs as they get older. I'll keep the other male and bitch. They'll give me all the dogs I'll need in the future. Tomorrow I'll send Frank to you with the dogs, and he will stay until you get used to them and know how they work. It'll only take a few days."

Jessie swung up onto his horse as John lifted Horace up and sat him in his saddle on the Marsh Tackie. "Well," Jessie said, smiling, "it looks like I got the best of the bargain."

"Well, we'll see when they get big enough to hunt," John said and laughed, as Jessie turned his horse and headed back to the lake.

~

"Bring 'em Boy, bring 'em!" Jessie called to the two dogs as he sat on his horse. He was astonished as he watched the younger of the two dogs help work a cow out of the brush. The young dogs were this good, and it was only the fourth day of working with the older dogs. Frank had amazed everyone at his skill to get the dogs to work. By pairing a younger pup with an older one, on the second day each of the younger pups was working a cow's hind leg as the older dog worked the other side. The hardest part for Jessie was getting the dogs to follow him or the others on their command, but with a handful of pieces of smoked ham, by the end of the second day, they would follow anyone who waved a piece of ham. They were responding better to Jessie and the others now, so they had sent Frank home the day before, feeling confident they could handle the dogs on their own. Jessie also knew that Frank's help was needed back at the lumber mill.

As Jessie, Red Sun, and Silent Stalker worked their thirteen head of cows towards the branding pens, they saw Justin, Big Cypress, and Spirit Snake penning the last of their small herd and closing the gate. Jessie rode ahead to the pens. "It don't look like there's enough room left for thirteen more head," Jessie said to Justin.

"You're right," Justin answered. "Why don't we move them on down to that wet land for the night? They will feed on the salt marsh grass and we can bring them in tomorrow after we brand and get some of these cows out of the pens."

Jessie gave a sharp whistle, and the two dogs that had been working with Justin and his crew sprang to their feet and ran ahead to join the others. Riding back to the herd, he stopped and told Red Sun where to take his cows. Then turning back to the pens, he saw Big Cypress and Spirit Snake bringing large limbs while Justin started the branding fire. He rode past the pens for another hundred yards and dismounted next to the work wagon that Franklin had turned into a chuck wagon. There, Sara Mae kept the men fed by day, and at night she slept in it.

"There is no way I'm going to sleep on no ground with any rattle snake!" she had declared.

Lifting the lid off the water barrel, Jessie reached in and filled the dipper with water. After drinking his fill and wiping his chin with his sleeve, he put the dipper back. Then he turned to Sara Mae and said, "We will be heading back to the lake tomorrow after we finish branding these cows; so after feeding the boys their noon meal tomorrow, go ahead and pack the wagon and I'll drive it back."

It was late afternoon the next day when the riders started down the valley to the lake. They were tired, bruised, and dusty from head to toe, but every one of them was happy at what they had accomplished. After five days, they had rounded up and branded over eighty cows. Riding on the wagon with Sara Mae, Jessie smiled as he watched the two puppies chase each other under the horses' feet. Between the small cow ponies and the dogs, he knew that now he had a chance to round up enough cattle to drive to market. Tomorrow they would spend time with their families and rest for a couple of days.

Twenty-Seven

It was close to the end of June, and there were more than six hundred head of branded cattle feeding in the bottom of the valley. The valley covered more than eight hundred acres in wet prairie grass that reached to their knees. It had been three weeks since they finished rounding up all the branded cattle, pushing them into the valley to feed on the rain soaked lush grass. The cows had no interest in moving any further. You could almost see them getting fatter every day. Jessie planned to start the herd moving in another week, slowly heading south and west toward Tampa, letting them feed for at least another month to six weeks so they could put on more weight.

Justin, Big Cypress, and Silent Stalker sat just inside the shelter of the red gum trees, enjoying the June breeze. The red gum trees grew along each side of the clear, spring fed stream that ran through the bottom of the valley. Watching the cattle feed, the three men ate their noon meal of venison stew and hoe cake, washed down by the cool water. Even the four dogs had taken shelter from the sun, as they kept an eye on the feeding cattle.

They all sat and listened as Sara Mae's voice carried across the valley, singing about her lord, song after song. She was sitting on her stool, mending a shirt for Justin, whom she fussed over like a son since he had brought her and Franklin to the lake. Jessie knew as far as she was concerned, he was sent to them by the Lord and it was her way of thanking him. She had set the cook wagon up a good fifty yards from the men's camp where she had some privacy. Dolly and Preacher grazed along with the cattle until Sara Mae needed them every few days when she drove the wagon back the three miles to the lake and checked on Franklin. While she fussed over Franklin, she also picked up more supplies. She had insisted that Ed teach her how to handle the wagon and horses. Like Ed had taught her, she learned to handle Dolly and let Dolly handle Preacher.

They had been rounding up and branding cows all winter and spring, except when the cold fronts came through bringing their freezing winds. Then everyone hunkered down inside by the fires, enjoying the break and letting the bruises and sore muscles heal from being thrown from horses, slammed into fence rails by cows, being run over and kicked at least ten times a day while branding the meanest bunch of critters they had ever seen!

Belle watched as Raven added coontie flour to the large pot of venison, making the stew thicker as it came to a boil. She had come to love the new tastes that the women of the tribe had introduced her to. Sara Mae had cooked a large pan of biscuits from the supply of flour she brought from Tampa. Belle contributed an iron cook pot full of Jessie's favorite blue berry cobbler. Belle figured it would be another hour before they were ready to call the kids up from the lake where they were all swimming, while Little Otter and Little Moon watched over them. Since the hurricane, Little Moon had become so concerned for their safety, that she would not let Little Wolf and Spirit Dancer out of her sight.

The men gathered under the shade of the large oak branch in front of Two Worlds lodge, where they were discussing the cattle drive from the prairie to Tampa. There was only enough grass to feed them for a few more days. Everyone had come in for the meeting, leaving the cows on their own to feed for a couple of days while they prepared for the drive to Tampa. For the next few weeks, they would move them slowly, from one feeding ground to the next. It was not that far to Tampa, but it would seem like a long trip.

Jessie decided to leave Franklin and Ed to tend to the garden; it wouldn't be long before the women and children would all help with the harvesting and canning of the vegetables. Then they would store the corn to dry. Jessie was about to ask Ed if he had any objection to staying behind, but then he looked over at Ed who was staring at Little Otter playing in the water, laughing and splashing. As he turned, he saw the other men smiling knowingly at him, and he knew there would be no objections from Ed.

"I thought you was going to need me on the drive," Franklin said. "If it's because you think I can't do my job," he started to protest.

"It's got nothing to do with your leg Franklin. There will be plenty of time for the men to gather fire wood and keep the water barrel full as slow as we will be moving, and somebody is going to have to keep Ed's mind on what needs to be done," he laughed.

Looking over at Ed's gaze, Franklin chuckled, "You might be right, Mr. Tucker, you might just be right."

"OK, tomorrow we will gather the equipment we need for the drive along with the extra horses. Franklin, I will leave the loading of the wagon to you and Sara Mae. I want everyone carrying pistols and rifles; there will be extra ammunition in the wagon. There are still men roaming around out there who will kill all of us for those cows. Red Sun, will you and your people use the saddles on your horses so you can keep a rifle in a scabbard, and will you carry a pistol on your side?"

"I will speak with the braves later, and we will decide."

The big orange ball was just dropping behind the sky line when Jessie and Belle started back around the lake. Horace and Jenny were waving good bye to their friends from the back of the wagon. Ed decided to stay with Spirit Snake and do some hog hunting in the garden after dark.

Ed and Spirit Snake slipped silently through the stalks of corn, now full and within days of being ready to pick. They both stopped, listening to the sound of grunting hogs, rooting up bushes of squash. This was the third night the wild hogs had invaded the garden; destroying corn, beans and pumpkins. Tonight it was the squash they were feeding on, and this was not the first night that Ed and Spirit Snake had waited on the deer and hogs that came to feed in their garden. They had supplied meat for their families several times since the seeds began to sprout. The deer loved the three to four inch, tender sprouts. Then the hogs began their invasion, as soon as the small pumpkins and squash were two inches long.

That night, the boys decided to test their skills with their bows. Ed had become good with the bow Big Cypress had given him, and with it he used a quiver of arrows that Silent Stalker had made from hickory branches. By the light of the almost full moon, they silently moved towards the grunting sounds. Ed's heart began to beat faster when he saw the huge boar within twenty feet of them. The boar suddenly looked up at the two of them who were standing frozen in awe. Before Ed could bring his bow up and pull the arrow back to shoot, he saw Spirit Snake's arrow bury itself half way through the boar's neck.

Whirling in a circle and letting out a loud squeal, the boar charged straight at Spirit Snake as Ed's arrow buried itself in the boar's shoulder with no effect on his attack. The boar charged straight at Spirit Snake, head low, still squealing while slinging his head back and forth, spit flying. Spirit Snake faced the charge and tried to place another arrow on the bow to shoot again, but the boar was on him too fast. Thinking fast as the boar moved in to make its kill, Spirit Snake jumped straight up as the hog ran under him. He was not fast enough though, as one of the slashing, razor sharp, eight inch tusks ripped down the side of his leg, leaving a six inch gash down to the bone. Spirit Snake came down on his back; the ground knocked the air out of him, and he didn't see the boar whirl eight feet behind him to charge again, while trying to get air back into his lungs.

Ed reached behind his back, pulling the .44 caliber pistol from his waist band and started firing as the boar made his turn. The boar stumbled from the first bullet that broke his front shoulder, but it came right back up charging again, squealing in his madness of pain. The second bullet tore off the side of the monsters head, and now honing in on Ed, he was shaking, slinging blood, and coming in a blind charge. Jumping up and sideways, Ed fired as the boar ran under him and he saw the top of the beast's head explode as it stumbled, then lay quivering as the last breath left him and he lay still.

Ed stood, trying to stop the trembling in his legs so he could move; he needed to help Spirit Snake. He watched the blood pouring from his friend's leg, knowing that if they didn't stop the flow of blood, he would bleed to death. Walking as fast as he was able, he reached Spirit Snake still trying to catch his breath. Ed removed his shirt, kneeled down and pinched the gash together with his fingers, then wrapped the shirt as tight as he could around Spirit Snake's leg.

"Where did the gun come from?" Spirit Snake asked, still taking short breaths.

"It don't matter now; we have to get you to Woman of the Wind before you bleed to death. I'm going to get Franklin to help me; can you keep that shirt tight until I get back?"

Not waiting for an answer, he turned and ran through the garden towards Franklin's house, jumping rows of bean and squash bushes and hollering, "Franklin, Franklin!"

He kept yelling at the top of his voice until he saw the glow from the lantern through the window. Then Franklin was on the porch, holding the light above his head with Sara Mae standing behind him, trying to see who was running at them. Coming off the porch he met Ed in the yard.

"Hold on son," Franklin said, grabbing Ed by the arm, "slow down now and tell me what's happening."

"It's Spirit Snake. He's been hurt bad and bleeding to death; I need your help getting him to the village, or he's going to die!"

"OK," Franklin said, "show me." As he started to follow Ed, he turned to Sara Mae and said, "You better go to the village and wake them up."

"Hold up son," he called to Ed, "I can't move as fast as you can on this leg."

"My God Almighty!" Franklin exclaimed, coming upon the boar. Looking down at the dead hog, he turned to look at the two boys, blood splattered across their faces and all over their clothes. "You both should be dead. I've never in all my born days seen anything like this!"

Ed stood next to Spirit Snake, and watched while Franklin knelt down; looking at the blood soaked shirt, wrapped around his friends leg and said, "We got to hurry. So Ed, you carry him by the legs and I'll carry him from the front." Lifting Spirit Snake under the arms while Ed gently lifted his legs, they started down the row of squash toward the lake and the village.

Ed saw Two Worlds leading the way with Woman of the Wind on one side and Sara Mae on the other, followed by Big Cypress, Little Moon and Little Otter. As they met Franklin and Ed carrying Spirit Snake, Big Cypress stepped forward between the two men, lifting Spirit Snake in his big arms and carried him to the village. He placed him inside Two Worlds' lodge on some hides that Woman of the Wind had laid out. She turned to Little Moon, trying to get her attention and had to call her twice.

"Go and put water on the fire and bring it to me when it is hot. Go on now!" she said again, raising her voice to get her attention.

"I'll help you," Little Otter said as she took Little Moon by the shoulders and pulled her through the lodge door.

Squatting next to the lodge door, Ed saw Woman of the Wind unwrap her bundle of hides, choose a small gourd, and removing the stopper, she poured a little bit of powder into a drinking gourd. She turned and held the cup up as Waiting Owl poured a small amount of water from the skins into the gourd. Lifting Spirit Snake's head, Woman of the Wind poured the mixture into his mouth until he drank down the last drop.

"That will make you sleep while I begin the healing of your leg." He heard her say. Removing the small needle bone and the deer sinew,

Ed watched as she prepared to sew the terrible gash together once she was finished cleaning it. By the time Little Moon returned with the hot water, Spirit Snake was in a dream world, where he felt no pain.

Looking at Spirit Snake's closed eyes, she asked in a panicked voice, "Is he dead?"

"No," said Waiting Owl, taking her by the arm and leading her to the entrance. "Now you must go and leave your Grandmother alone."

He saw Woman of the Wind adding powder into the steaming water, Woman of the Wind stirred the liquid, letting the powder dissolve. She slowly un-wrapped the shirt, a little at a time until she could see the wound. As she began pouring the hot water over the deep cut, Waiting Owl began wrapping a narrow, two inch strip of leather around the wound, pulling the flesh together after the cleaning. The last two inches of the cleaned wound were left open, and Woman of the Wind began sewing the deep wound closed. Finishing, she mixed a paste from a different powder and after covering the wound with it, she wrapped the leg with a clean cotton cloth.

"That is all we can do for him; it is up to the Great Spirit now," she said as she rolled up her medicine bundle. "I will make him a drink, so he will feel no pain later. Little Moon can keep watch over him now." Ed stood and moved away from the opening when Woman of the Wind headed for the lodge's entry.

"I don't think we will have to worry about that," Waiting Owl smiled. "I will see to it." Little Moon was waiting outside and almost ran over her Grandmother, coming though the opening.

While Ed stood outside Two Worlds lodge, Jessie rode up and was off of his horse before he came to a halt, crossing the short distance between him and Ed. Seeing Ed's face and clothes still covered in blood, he asked, "Are you alright? Where are you hurt?"

He looked down and saw the side of Ed's brogan split open, like it had been cut with a razor. Following his fathers gaze Ed looked down and caught his breath when he saw the cut in the boot and the torn and bloody sock. Sitting on a log, he removed his boot and sock and gingerly touched the thin razor cut, running from his ankle bone seven inches up his shin. His face was pale as he looked up at his father and said, "I didn't even know!"

Squatting down, Jessie took Ed's foot by the heel, and looking closely, he saw that the cut was only skin deep. He let out the breath he didn't realize he had been holding. "We'll get something from Woman of the Wind to wash it in, and you will be alright."

Ed could hardly breathe as he sat watching Little Otter, who was holding his heel in her soft hands and washing the cut with a warm water mixture, made up by Waiting Owl. She began wrapping a piece of thin, soft leather around his foot and slipped his boot back on, gently tying the leather boot string. She looked up at him with a small smile on her face.

"Does that feel better?"

"Yes, that does feel better," he replied, smiling down at her.

The next morning, Jessie and Ed rode up to see Two Worlds, who was resting in front of his lodge. Jessie dismounted, giving Ed the reins and squatted in front of Two Worlds, greeting him.

"How is the boy's leg this morning?"

"He has lost a lot of blood, and it will take time for him to renew what he has lost, but he will keep his life for a while longer."

"Will he be crippled from the wound when it heals?"

"We can only wait. He is young and strong, and he will not want to be left behind by the other warriors or be less than a man for the woman he will marry. I have seen men recover from battle wounds that were worse, but it will be a long time before we will know."

Ed walked over to Two Worlds and squatted on his heels next to Jessie. "Can I speak with him?"

"He has drunk the medicine Woman of the Wind has prepared for him, and he is still awake, but not for long."

"I won't be long," Ed said, rising and heading for the opening in Two Worlds' lodge.

"He has been moved to Little Moon's lodge," Two Worlds said as Ed reached the opening. Turning, Ed hurried toward her lodge.

Entering the dimly lit lodge, Ed knelt down next to his friend. Spirit Snake opened his eyes slowly and reaching for Ed's hand, he clasped it tight and said in slurred words, "You saved my life, I will never forget."

His eyes closed as his hand fell away. Ed felt his chest tighten as he rose to leave. That was foolish, he said to himself, and almost cost us our lives. From now on, I will always have a gun in my hand when I am hunting anything. He swore under his breath as he ducked through the lodge opening.

Jessie stood as Ed walked toward him. "You will have to take his place on the drive. Franklin will have to handle the crops with Horace's help."

"I know Pa; we were foolish, doing what we did."

"You are both brave young men," Two Worlds spoke up, "and you must put this behind you. You have learned a lesson that will help you in the future; you will both be wiser from this. You have to think of what's ahead of you. And a word of caution from an old man, don't hunt the hogs with a bow unless you are close to a tree!" he said, laughing.

Jessie turned as he heard the sound of horses behind him and greeted Red Sun, Silent Stalker, Big Cypress, and Justin as they all rode up, sitting in saddles. He saw the rifle butts sticking from their scabbards and the .44 revolvers riding on their hips. Their whips were coiled and hanging from the rifle butts. Red Sun and the others said nothing as Justin explained to Jessie that Franklin and Sara Mae were finishing loading the wagon, and they would be ready to go when he was.

"You and the others can go ahead when you are ready," Jessie said, looking from one to the other and nodding slightly, acknowledging their decision. "I have a few more things to do before Ed and I will be ready. I will ride with Sara Mae and the wagon when I come."

As they turned their horses to leave, Justin looked down at Ed and smiled, saying, "Maybe you will try some of those oysters with the fish this time."

"I still don't know about those oysters, but I can't wait to eat some more of those fish!"

Ed was standing with his horse next to the wagon as Jessie was saying good bye to Belle, Horace and Jenny. Lifting Jenny up into his arms, Jessie said, "You be a big girl and help your mommy while I am gone. OK?"

Holding back tears, she wrapped her arms around his neck and said, "I will Pa, I'll be a big girl if you promise you will come back soon."

Setting her down he said, "Not only will I promise to come back, but I will bring you a pretty present."

"OK," she smiled, running to her mother's side.

Jessie turned to look at Horace, ruffling his hair. "You have a big job on your hands, but I know you will make me proud."

Standing as tall as he could, Horace said, "I'll make you proud of me Pa, I promise."

"I know you will son, I know you will."

Walking over to where Belle was standing, Jessie smiled and put his arms around her. "I'll be back before you know it," he said, trying to keep the mood light.

"I know, but I'm beginning to wonder what happened to that quiet, gentle farmer I married. Seems to me you go looking for danger," she said, looking in his eyes and smiling.

Stepping back and still holding her by the shoulders, he laughed. "I don't have to look for danger, it seems to look me up, but I promise I will do everything I can to keep away from trouble."

She reached up to kiss him on the lips. Looking at him from those hooded eyes, she said, "I'll be waiting."

"You look at me with those eyes like that, and I'll be waiting another night before I go," he said, smiling as he pulled away and mounted his horse.

Riding the Marsh Tackie he had picked out for the drive, Jessie rode to the wagon, where Franklin was making sure everything was tied down. Jessie spoke to him as he tugged one more time on a rope. "I'm leaving my riding horse, and in case anything happens and you need help, you send Horace to get Bill Walsh. He knows the way there. If you can use the oxen to hang that boar, I want him cut up and ground into sausage, then hung in the smoke house. That's all he'll be good for."

"Don't you worry yourself none," Franklin said, "you just get them cows to the market. Everything will be fine here, and that sausage will be ready for breakfast when you get back."

"Is the wagon ready?" Jessie asked.

"It's ready as it will ever be!" Sara May said from the seat, "and if we don't get going, Franklin will have them ropes so tight, I'll never get them loose to feed you all." Looking over at Ed waiting to climb up on the wagon, she said, "Don't want to hear any more from any of ya'll wanting to know if I want one of you driving my wagon!" Saying that and releasing the brake handle, she flicked the reins gently across both horses' rumps and started out for Tampa, anxious to see her friends again.

Twenty-Eight

It was late afternoon when Red Sun saw the wagon leaving the pine strand and starting down into the wet prairies with Ed riding on one side of the wagon and Jessie on the other. Sara Mae kept to the outer edge of the wet land, making her way toward the red gum trees where she would set up her camp for the night.

Jessie could hear the crack of the whips and the barking of the dogs, as the few cows that had wandered off were being brought back to the herd. He and Ed headed toward Red Sun, who was riding the outer edge of the herd to keep them bunched up and ready to move. As Jessie and Ed rode up, he asked Jessie, "Are we going to start the herd moving today?"

"No, we only have a few hours left in the day, so we'll just get them ready and start out early in the morning."

Turning to Ed, Jessie said, "Ride the herd with Red Sun, and get them bunched up as tight as you can; I don't want to have to hunt any of them up, come day light tomorrow."

Nodding his head in acknowledgement, Ed turned the big roan heading in the direction of Red Sun, and saw his pa headed for the sounds of the whips and dogs.

A quarter of a mile inside the pine strand, working his way around the large clumps of palmettos, Jessie spotted the four cows. They were heading for a large palmetto thicket away from the riders, where it was almost impossible to get them out, even with the dogs. He turned the Marsh Tackie, giving him his head, and the small horse did what they were famous for. Seeing where the cows were headed, he set out on a dead run, working around small palmetto patches. The little horse was outrunning the cows as Jessie uncoiled his whip and began popping it over his head. The cows started to turn and he heard the barking of the two dogs as they caught up with the four cows, turning them toward the rest of the herd. As Jessie slowed the Marsh Tackie to a walk, Silent Stalker rode up beside him.

"That should be all of the strays. We have circled the marsh and this is the last we have found."

"Good, we will keep the herd together tonight and move out tomorrow," Jessie replied, following the dogs as they moved the strays through the brush back to the marsh.

They sat on logs or leaned against their saddles, eating stew and biscuits that Sara Mae had made before leaving the lake. When Jessie finished his bowl of stew and carried the empty bowl to the wagon, he stood facing the men and spoke as they finished their meal.

"Even though it's not much more than two weeks to the cattle pens in Tampa, I figure it's going to take four to six weeks of slow travel to fatten these scrub cows and make them worth any money. Within the next month, the rainy season will be on us, and by that time we need to be on the south side of the Withlacoochee River before it floods. We will head more south than west, until we cross that river and then turn west to southwest. Then we'll work our way to the Hillsborough River and follow it to the stock yards.

"We've been lucky so far. There have been plenty of wild animals for the panthers, bears and wolves to feed on, but that don't mean when they see a bunch of slow moving cows, they won't try for that easy meal. The problem is not the one or two cows that they kill to feed on, but they can scatter these cows to hell and gone. We'll set up two men on three hour watches, using two of the dogs at a time on the watch with us. If there is any hint of trouble, crack your whips three times in a row. During the rainy season, when a lighting storm moves in late in the evening or during the night, we will all stay with the herd until it has passed. If we're lucky, we can keep them more afraid of us and the dogs than the storm.

"There are several valleys with good grass and water between here and the Hillsborough River, so we will keep them moving slow from one valley to the next. There will be enough grass for them to feed on for several days, and we can better keep them from scattering if anything happens. I know that most of you have been around cattle before, but this is the first time for Ed and me, so we will count on the rest of you to keep us from making too many mistakes until we learn more." Looking around at the men sitting quietly, Jessie said, "If any of you have anything to add, say so now."

Silent Stalker slowly stood to his feet, holding his rump in his hands, drawing his face up in a grimace and asked, "Am I going to be able to move my legs more than a little at a time after riding in that saddle all the way to where we sell the cows?"

After the laughter settled down and Jessie could speak again, he said, "If not, when we get the cattle to market, we can tie your legs to two horses and stretch them back in place." Laughter broke out again and Jessie could see the built up tension being replaced with a sense of adventure; then they stood up to take their empty bowls to the wagon.

Sara Mae took their bowls and said, "When you men wake up in the mornings, you bring yourselves on over to the wagon where there will be hot coffee, smoked bacon and grits with gravy to go with your biscuits or hoe cake. When you get hungry during the day, there will always be something to eat on the wagon. Woman of the Wind has sent potions to fix cuts and keep infections out, so if you gets a cut you come to me right away and let me fix it before it gets bad. If I needs your help, I'll surely ask somebody, but don't you go making no fuss over me just cause I's a woman, and that's all I's have to say!" As the men nodded and moved on, she started gathering up the empty bowls to clean.

The cows were slow to move as they milled around in a circle, not understanding what they were supposed to do. The whips cracked over their heads, and the dogs nipped at their heels until slowly, they began to move south out of the valley. Justin and Red Sun rode at the front on either side, trying to keep them going in the right direction. Silent Stalker, Big Cypress, and the dogs moved up and down the herd keeping them together until they began to follow the leaders. Jessie and Ed followed behind the herd, making sure they were all moving forward.

They had barely made two miles at the end of the day as the cows were reluctant to leave the valley and move into the open pine forest. They had to work them all day, moving up and down the stretched out herd, working with whips and dogs, chasing the stubborn ones that kept breaking away and making a mad dash for the brush and palmettos. Once they were recovered, the cows had to be moved back into the herd. At the end of the day when they felt they could go no further, they made camp a little ways away from the herd. Taking their turn at the water barrel, they didn't realize how tired they were until they sat or lay against their saddles; laughing at how awkward they all were, trying to move 600 head of stubborn scrub cows.

"Is it going to be this hard all the way there?" Ed asked, lying stretched out with his head on his saddle.

"No," Justin answered, "the cows will start moving on their own once they figure out what they need to do. The only problem is by the time they figure it out; we'll be at another feeding ground where they will feed until we decide to move on. Then we'll have to go through this again, but it won't be as bad after the second or third time, when they will be fatter and lazier and less likely to run off."

Jessie leaned back against his saddle, observing the tired men waiting on their supper, and watched Sara Mae as she filled the wash pan with water and set it under the edge of the wagon. He looked at the four dogs as each took their turn at lapping up the water, until they had all finished and lay under the wagon where it was cooler, panting and waiting on the leftovers from the mens' supper.

The sounds of the whips cracking and the occasional bark of the dogs could be heard across the open grass land as they kept the strays from leaving the moving herd. It was the fourth day, and the cattle kept on a slow move as they fed on the carpet grass that covered the vast expanse of open flat land and rolling hills. Then they grazed on the wire grass, which covered the longleaf pine forest that broke up the open miles of grass land.

Jessie and Red Sun rode ahead of the slow moving herd to check out the cypress hammock that they would be approaching by early afternoon. The water covering the hammock was shallow, maybe two feet deep as they cautiously moved further into the cypress shaded water for a quarter of a mile. There they came to the steady flow of the Little Withlacoochee River, flowing southwest where it would join the larger Withlacoochee River. As they sat on their horses, they discussed the idea of letting the cattle work their way through the shallow water hammock. The cows could feed on the water lilies and the alligator weed that covered the half mile wide hammock.

"This would be a good opportunity to drink their fill of water after the last two days crossing dry open land, but we will need to move them out and across the river before night fall," Red Sun said to Jessie as they steered their horses back toward the slow moving herd. "I have not seen any alligators yet, but that does not mean they are not around."

Jessie looked back over his shoulder at the giant live oaks that shaded the banks on the other side of the shallow stream. His gaze followed past the oaks to the open grass land, stretching at least a mile where he saw the land rise, forming another valley on the other side. "We can push the cows on through this hammock into the open, and tomorrow we should reach the next valley," he said as they reached dry land.

The cows started a low bellow as they got within a quarter mile of water. They began to pick up their pace as the cows in the back pushed the front of the herd on into the hammock. Then they all settled down and fed on the wet lilies and alligator weed. The men sat on their horses letting them drink their fill, not daring to leave their saddles to wade in the stirred up, muddy water, where there could be angry moccasins. The dogs drank from the edge of the hammock and decided that they didn't want anything to do with the stirred up, muddy water either.

After two hours, the cows, which were now full of water, began to wander across the shallow stream through the oaks to feed on the lush carpet grass. Justin and Red Sun, along with the two dogs they were working with, rode on ahead to keep the cows bunched up as they left the hammock. Big Cypress and Silent Stalker moved across with the other two dogs, as most of the cows crossed the stream, moving with the rest of the herd to feed. Justin heard the cracking of Jessie's and Ed's whips as they moved the slower ones on across the stream to catch up with the rest of the herd, slowly feeding as they moved forward. As the last ones caught up with the herd, Jessie and Ed turned back to where Sara Mae was waiting on the edge of the wet hammock. Reaching the horses, Jessie rode up next to Preacher and leaned over, taking him by the halter, as Ed took Dolly by her halter; and they started the wagon through the now muddy water and across the shallow stream into the giant live oaks, where Sara Mae stopped for the night to set up to cook.

After unhooking the two horses from the wagon and offering their help which she refused, they rode to catch up to Justin and Red Sun at the front of the herd. As Jessie reached Justin he said, "Let's circle the cows for the night and tomorrow we'll move the herd into that valley ahead of us."

Then turning, he rode back to meet Big Cypress, slowing his horse as he approached the big man and said, "I want to take the cattle into that valley ahead of us, but I need to know if there's water there before we move them. I need you to ride over and see what's there."

"I'll ride with you if Pa don't need me," Ed spoke up.

"I don't need you for now, so go ahead with Big Cypress," Jessie answered as he turned to help circle the herd and settle them down for the night.

Big Cypress and Ed rode through the scattered long leaf pines, growing along the sandy soil. They topped the outer ridge and looked down on miles of rolling hills, covered with more long leaf pine. Now that they were in rainy season, the land got watered every few days, and it was covered with carpet grass, over shadowed by the yellow of the goldenrod and the bright purple of the milkweed flower. Ed sat in awe as the scene in front of him took his breath away.

"You could sit and look at this all day!"

"Yes," Big Cypress agreed, seeing the small lakes dotted throughout the valleys. His eyes followed the creek that ran through the bottom of the valley from the overflow of a large spring fed lake, which he could just see in the distance to the east. Red gum trees lined the banks, two to three hundred yards wide on both sides of the creek, as it wound its way through the bottom, filling a shallow bowl and creating one of the smaller lakes, before over flowing and winding its way on across the vast valley floor as far as the eye could see.

Watching the dark rain clouds moving their way, Big Cypress looked at Ed, and turning his horse back down the slope, he said, "I think we are going to get wet before we get back to camp."

"I agree," answered Ed as he dismounted and removed his home made canvas slicker from behind the saddle. Then he waited on Big Cypress, who had stopped and was removing the skins he used to keep dry.

There was just enough light for Jessie to see the riders leaning forward over their saddles as Big Cypress and Ed rode into camp.

Tying their horses to the rope, they brought their saddles with them to put under the canvas shelter, stretched out and tied to low hanging branches of the giant live oaks. Then they could sit on their saddles to keep dry.

"Before you get settled," Jessie said to Ed and Big Cypress, "you might want to grab a bowl of food from the wagon. Sara Mae has been keeping it warm for you."

"Good idea!" Ed said, leaning forward and running for the wagon. Sara Mae was sitting on a small stool under the canvas that she had stretched from the side of the wagon to a low hanging oak branch. Big Cypress followed Ed under the shelter, and he watched Sara Mae already filling the tin plates with venison stew. She added wild greens that she called poke salad. She had picked the greens earlier by the water's edge after setting up her camp.

Back under the stretched out canvas sitting on his saddle, Ed asked no one in particular, "Are we going to eat venison all the way to Tampa and back?"

"When we move these cows into that valley tomorrow, maybe you could take the 12 gauge and see if you can hunt up some rabbits or a turkey or two," Jessie said. "I think we could all eat something different and if we need to, we can slaughter one of the young calves."

"I don't think we'll have to," Ed replied, excited about going hunting. "I know I can kill something!"

Looking out from under the canvas shelter, Jessie watched as the rain moved off in the distance. Speaking to the men sitting around the small fire, drying out their damp clothes, he said, "The rains are starting to come every two to three days now and so far the sandy soil has absorbed the water almost as fast as it hits the ground. I figure we have another week, maybe two, before the real rains start coming every day and the rivers begin to swell. Soon they'll be too deep and running too fast for the cows and the wagon to cross safely. Once we get the cows settled into their new feeding grounds, I want to take Red Sun and find out just how far away we are from the Withlacoochee River and find a good place to cross. Then see if the rains are having any effect on the river yet. I don't want to get caught on this side when it starts to flood."

The cattle fed along the clear stream in the valley that Ed and Big Cypress had scouted two days earlier, and the men stretched canvases from the limbs of the red gum trees. There they would camp for the next few days while Jessie and Red Sun traveled ahead to check on the Withlacoochee River.

It was still an hour away from daylight when Ed walked into the glow of the fire, leading his horse and tying him to the back of the wagon.

"Good morning Miss Sara Mae."

"Good morning, young Mister Ed; aren't you up a little early?"

"No Ma'am. I'm going hunting this morning for turkey or rabbits, and I need the shotgun from the wagon."

"Well just go and pull back the canvas, and you will find it under the shelf on the left along with the bag of shells where your pappy put them. The biscuits will be done in about five minutes, so have yourself a cup of coffee. Then I'll make you up a couple with smoked bacon to take with you."

As Ed mounted his horse, Sara Mae placed the biscuits which she had wrapped in a small sack in Ed's shell bag with the shells and patting him on the leg, she said, "I sure am fond of them wood ducks if you happen to see any. I sure would be happy to roast any you brought back."

"Yes Ma'am," Ed answered as he set out for the far end of the valley. He moved toward the spring that fed the cool, clear stream. They had moved the cattle there the day before, to feed off the rich and lush grass for the next week or more until it was time to move them across the Withlacoochee River.

It was just breaking day light as Ed took the shotgun and shell bag, looping it over his shoulder. He hobbled his horse and removed the bridle and saddle to let him feed until he returned. Slowly easing into the hardwood forest as the gray began to disappear and the trees began to take shape, he stepped carefully on the soft leaves, still wet from the rains. Cautiously, he avoided any small sticks that could snap and spook anything within a hundred yards. He was a quarter of a mile inside the forest, and the sun was creeping up the eastern horizon, when he heard the familiar barking sound of squirrels talking to each other and the caw, caw! from the crows as the forest began to come alive.

Staring through the trees and myrtle bushes twenty feet away to his right, he was beginning to think he was wrong about the movement he thought he had seen. It was just a flicker, but then he saw it again. His heart stopped and his breath caught in his throat, as his brain began to take in the large shape almost hidden behind the myrtle bush. Again he saw the flick of the reddish orange tail, and his eyes followed the fur shape until he was staring into the intense and hypnotic eyes of a huge male panther. Unable to look away from those eyes, he began to get control of his senses and slowly started to raise the shotgun, but before he got it to his shoulder, he realized he was not going shoot. The fear released its grip on his heart, and he slowly released the breath caught in his throat. As he stared into the panther's eyes, he wondered how long the big cat had been following him before he let him know he was there. Ed knew he was seeing the cat only because it wanted him to.

Not knowing what else to do, Ed began walking slowly, not worrying where he stepped now or how quiet he was. He realized that he had been walking for more than an hour, and the panther had gotten no closer or any further away but kept a silent pace with him. Ed came to another small spring no more than ten feet wide, with a small stream running south down a slight slope out of sight. He had forgotten all about why he was here or why he had kept walking in this direction, except he couldn't turn back. Suddenly realizing how dry his throat was, he sat the shotgun down and removing the shell bag from his shoulder, he sat it down next to his feet. As he took one more look, he saw that the big cat was gone.

Kneeling down on his knees, he felt no fear as he leaned forward on his hands, placing his face in the cool water and drinking his fill. Then he placed his head under the water, and raising his head, shaking the water from his long reddish hair, he suddenly froze. The panther leaned forward on the other side of the spring, ten feet away, and crouched between huge shoulders, lapping water with his tongue. His eyes never left Ed's. The panther's eyes hypnotized him until it finished and turned and walked away. It disappeared as silently as it had appeared, leaving Ed on his hands and knees and staring into the forest for another five minutes.

Ed could just see the pasture of grassland through the end of the trees, when a noise coming through the tree tops startled him, disrupting the image of the eyes that had hypnotized him. He stopped and stood still as a flock of more than a dozen turkeys landed and started scratching in the leaves and feeding, no more than twenty yards in front of him. Moving very slowly, he cocked both hammers as he raised the gun to his shoulder, picking two large hens. He fired the first barrel and turning slightly to his right, he fired the second barrel as the flock scattered back through the trees. Seeing the two dead turkeys brought him back to why he was here. Tying their legs together with strips of leather, he threw them across his shoulder and headed back to camp knowing that somehow he was different now.

Sara Mae was squatting down by the stream washing pots from the morning meal, when she saw Ed riding toward her with the two turkeys hanging across the horse, behind the saddle. Reaching back behind him, Ed removed the turkeys and handed them down to Sara Mae. Without a word spoken, he dismounted and put the shotgun and shell bag back in the wagon. Then he swung back up into the saddle and rode off, leaving Sara Mae completely dumb founded. What in the world happened out there? she asked herself, watching him. Whatever it was, she would have to wait to find out.

Justin watched as Ed walked along the stream almost out of sight and felt completely puzzled by his actions. He had tried to talk to him earlier but only got short answers to his questions, and he gave up as Ed wandered away.

~

It had been a week since Ed had been to the spring where he encountered the panther, and the rains were coming most every day now. The ground could no longer absorb the water as fast as it fell, and it was beginning to puddle, which that meant the rivers would begin to swell. Jessie told everyone at supper that it was at least four days moving at a slow, steady pace, before they could get the herd to the Withlacoochee River, and they would start out in another two days.

Sara Mae watched Ed as he silently slipped the shotgun in the scabbard and secured the shell bag with the two biscuits and smoked bacon, she had placed in the bag on the saddle. He didn't say a word, even when she had handed him his cup of coffee. She felt concern now as she stood next to the horse. "Mr. Ed, is you sure you want to go wherever it is you going? You ain't been yourself, ever since you came back with them turkeys. Maybe somebody ought to go with you."

"No Miss Sara Mae, I'll be OK. Nothing bad happened out there," Ed assured her. "I'll try to find you some of those wood ducks you like this time." He turned the horse and headed to the far end of the valley, arriving as daylight broke the spell of darkness. Hobbling the horse and removing the bridle and saddle, he started into the forest at the same place he had entered before, moving slowly until there was more light. The shadows and leaves flickered in the light breeze, playing tricks on his imagination as he moved further into the forest of hardwood and myrtle bushes, not worrying about sounds of twigs breaking under his feet. He felt let down and disappointed when he reached the small spring and had seen no sign of the panther. There was no fear now, just disappointment at the thought of the panther being miles from here by now. Maybe it had only been fate that they had been in the same place at the same time.

Leaning the shotgun against a small gum tree growing next to the spring, he removed the shell bag from his shoulder and sat in the grass at the edge of the water. He removed the biscuits with the smoked bacon and began to eat as he watched the small minnows swimming in the cool fresh water.

A chill went down his spine, freezing him in place as he heard the low throaty purr that came from behind him. Slowly turning his head, he looked once again into those eyes that hypnotized him and kept him from moving. The big cat stood no more than a foot away, his long tail swaying back and forth, and he leaned forward, just inches from Ed's face. Ed could smell the wildness of the panther's breath, and as he slowly released his pent up breath, he saw the nostrils flair slightly as the big cat took in his breath. Seconds felt like a life time before the panther slowly backed away and disappeared into the brush, leaving Ed stunned and breathless.

The sun was rising above the trees before Ed took a drink of water and dunked his head under the cool water, letting it run down his neck and between his shoulders, bringing him back to reality. Gathering his shell bag and shotgun, he made his way slowly back through the forest trying to understand why this was happening to him. Reaching the open pasture where he had left his horse, he removed the hobbles and then saddled his horse and started back the way he had come.

Sara Mae stayed busy as she watched Ed return the gun and shells back into the wagon and walk away, leading his horse without saying a word. Lordy, Lordy, something done gone and happened to that boy and it ain't natural, she thought to herself, watching him walk away.

The days had been slipping by and everyone was feeling lazy, but it would only be a couple of days now, before they would start the herd moving south again. Justin was looking forward to more oysters and beer, and maybe he'd see his lady friend. The half-moon was straight above Justin, as he followed the handle of the big dipper and found the North Star. Smiling, he searched the sky until he found Orion, his favorite constellation. He always felt that he knew where he was when Orion moved with him across the Gulf, as he took his turn on watch while crewing on the supply ships.

His mind became alert when he noticed the cattle beginning to move about nervously, pushing and shoving against each other. A small knot of fear started in the pit of his stomach. Justin had seen this before when he worked on the ranch after his wife and son had died from the fever, and he knew that the cows were spooked about something. He could feel them getting ready to bolt from whatever danger they felt. He had just started to uncoil his whip and give a warning sound, when he heard the three rifle cracks of Big Cypress' whip on the other side of the herd. Kicking the big Morgan in the ribs, he started toward the front to try and stop the cows from stampeding, when he saw the shadows coming up from the stream. Wolves, his mind said as he swung his whip overhead, giving three more cracks to let the others know how urgently they were needed.

Jessie, Red Sun, Ed and Silent Stalker were trying to buckle on their pistols as they ran for their horses. Outlaws, Jessie thought as he pulled the cinch strap tight on the saddle and mounted his horse. Kicking him in the ribs, he followed Silent Stalker, already ahead of him, toward the panicked cows as they started breaking away in small groups. He saw Red Sun and Ed start around the opposite side with whips cracking, when he heard the first rifle shot followed by several others. Urging his small horse to move faster, he forgot about the panicked cows and headed to where he heard the fighting going on. He saw Justin in the distance, firing his rifle, but he could not see who he was shooting at. Then he saw the wolves running, scattering the herd. They were the smaller, red wolves he had seen before always in the distance, and he knew they ran in large packs of twenty to thirty, but he could only see eight or ten. He wondered where the rest of them were when he heard the snarls of the two dogs as they bolted towards the moving shadows.

Ed saw Red Sun ahead of him, cracking his whip overhead as he rode, when he felt his saddle begin to slip sideways. It was too late to stop from going off the side of his horse, and pulling his feet from the stirrups as he fell to the ground, he saw his horse dragging the saddle under him in a panic. Ed saw the rifle fall from the scabbard, and the fear built up in his chest as he heard the bellowing of the panicked cows. As his chest tightened, it was hard to breathe as he started towards his rifle, and then he saw the wolves coming up from his side and cutting him off. He tasted the panic in his throat as he made a run for the rifle, and pulling his pistol from his holster, he began firing at the wolves closing in on him. He heard the high pitched whine as a bullet struck one of them, while the others kept coming.

He heard the growls behind him as he went down on one knee to grab the gun, but he knew it was too late. He saw the shadow pass over him, and he heard the throaty growl and then the high pitch yelp of another wounded animal. Looking up with the rifle in his hand, he began firing and watched in awe as the huge panther slashed open the throat of another wolf. He heard rifle fire behind him as the wolves began to scatter. Looking back, he saw Red Sun firing as he rode hard toward him. He turned to locate the panther, but he had disappeared.

Riding up, Red Sun dismounted. "I saw your horse come by, dragging your saddle. Are you OK?"

"Yes," answered Ed, "but if it had not been for the panther, I would be dead now." Red Sun said nothing as he looked at the dead wolves, with their throats and stomachs slashed open.

Turning to Ed he said, "The cows have stopped scattering now; we need to find the others."

Ed rode behind Red Sun, and they saw Ed's horse up ahead, standing with his foot caught in a stirrup, still quivering from fear. Ed slipped off the back of the horse and slowly approached the frightened animal. Taking the reins in hand, he calmed the horse down while Red Sun removed his foot and slid the saddle back in place, tightening the cinch strap. Sitting on his horse, Ed saw cows scattered as far as he could see. Seeing the other riders headed their way, they started forward to meet them.

Relieved to see Ed and Red Sun, Jessie asked, "Are you alright? I heard gun shots; did you kill any of those devils?"

Red Sun looked at Ed and said, "We killed some."

"Well there is nothing more we can do tonight. I'm sure Sara Mae has hot coffee by now, tomorrow we will start rounding them back up," Jessie said. Later as they all sat under their shelter drinking hot coffee, Jessie asked Big Cypress, "Why didn't the dogs warn us about the wolves?"

"They did, but by the time I realized what they were warning me of, the wolves were already attacking the herd."

"Where were the other dogs?" Justin asked.

"They came with me," Jessie answered. "They were tearing up wolves like lions; I think they were enjoying the whole thing."

"Tomorrow we will take their pelts, they make warm clothing," Silent Stalker said.

"I do not believe the cows will have scattered too far," Red Sun spoke up.

Jessie felt concern as he looked at Ed who sat holding his still full cup and staring out into the darkness. "Are you ok?" he asked Ed.

"I was scared Pa," he said. "I made a foolish mistake," he continued, explaining what had happened with the saddle.

"You're not the first one to make that mistake; it happened to me more than once," Justin laughed, trying to lighten the mood.

"We were all scared," Jessie said. "You have to let it go. I've been scared many times, and it will hang over you like a dark cloud if you don't."

"You did fine tonight, you fought as well as any brave I know," Red Sun said to Ed.

Jessie didn't miss the look between the two of them. "Let's get some rest now, we have a tough job ahead of us tomorrow," Jessie said, drinking the rest of his coffee and then stretching out on his blanket.

~

It had been almost two weeks since they crossed the Withlacoochee River. They kept a slow steady pace until they reached the Hillsborough River and turned west. From there they would follow the river until they reached the cattle pens, sometime the following day.

As they sat around the fire finishing their meal, they all felt impatient to have the cattle drive over with and be back home with their families. It had not been a hard drive, once they had gotten used to the pace of the cattle and adjusted to the saddle. However, they were a little anxious to reach the end of the drive the next day, and they were excited about finding out just what was going to happen to all the cows that they had been fattening up for weeks.

They were a mile away from the cattle pens, which were built next to the river where the ships waited at the docks. More ships were anchored out in the river ready to take their loads. Jessie rode forward to the head of the herd, catching up with Red Sun and Justin. First he spoke to Justin.

"I want you and me to ride ahead and talk to the buyer and find out where they want the cows." Turning to Red Sun he said, "I want you to just keep the herd moving slow until we get back."

Twenty-Nine

Jessie and Justin rode up to the small building sitting next to the dock, where two ships sat waiting to be loaded. They dismounted and walked through the open door, stepping into a dimly lit room, where a man was sitting behind a small desk. Two more men sat in chairs leaning back against the wall. The man behind the desk looked up as Justin stepped forward.

"Mr. Marshall, I'm Justin Hannah, and this is Jessie Tucker."

"Ah yes," Tom Marshall said as he stood up, "I remember you and a young man was in here a few months ago, asking about selling some cows. I hope you have brought me some. I've got two ships sitting at dock, waiting for a load to take to Cuba."

"Yes Sir, we have," Jessie spoke up. He stepped forward to shake hands as Tom stood and walked around the desk. "I have a herd no more than two hours away that we have been feeding on the way here for the past seven weeks. I need to know how much you are paying, how you are paying and where you want to put them, when they get here."

"Put them in the holding pens next to the dock here, and if they are in good shape, I pay fourteen dollars a head, and I pay in Spanish gold doubloons," Tom answered.

Jessie and Justin sat on their horses, turning the cows into the holding pen as one of the two men that he had seen inside held the gate open. Then he hollered to the other man to open the gate and put the rest of them in another pen.

The smile on Tom's face changed to wonderment as Red Sun, Silent Stalker, Big Cypress, and Ed rode up behind Jessie and Justin.

"Where the hell did those redskins come from?" asked one of Tom's men.

Turning his horse to face the man, Jessie let the whip uncoil to the ground.

"You don't even want to get into that."

"No Sir!" the man said, looking in Jessie's eyes and backing up a step.

"Mr. Tucker, you've done a real good job, fattening up that bunch of yellow hammers, and I'll be glad to take them off your hands. Randy, you and Hank start getting a head count of those cows, while I talk to Mr. Tucker and don't let there be any trouble! You understand?" Tom said to the two men.

"Yes Sir," they both answered as they moved toward the pens. Ed followed the two men as Red Sun, Big Cypress and Silent Stalker turned their horses and headed back to where Sara Mae waited with the wagon. She had set up the chuck wagon by the river a half mile back and was gathering wood for a cook fire.

More than an hour had passed by the time Ed followed the two men into the small office where Tom was still discussing cattle with Jessie and Justin.

"There's 621 cows, and they are all in good shape," Randy said, smiling at Jessie and Justin.

"Great!" Tom said. "Now Randy, you and Hank go and get the crew off the ship and get those cattle aboard. I want to get those cows to Cuba."

"Yes Sir," they both said as they headed for the door.

"Now let's see how much I owe you," Tom muttered as he pulled a pencil and a piece of paper from his desk drawer. While he was working the figures, Jessie and Justin sat and held their breath.

Looking up just as they were letting their breath out, he said, "That comes to $8,694." Pushing the pencil and paper toward Jessie, he said, "Check these figures to make sure I'm right." Jessie looked at Ed and nodded his head as Ed took the pencil and started checking the figures.

After a minute of silence, Ed looked at his father. "I got the same figure Pa!" he exclaimed, stunned at what he was seeing. Ed had never heard of that kind of money.

"The money is in the back in a vault. They are 20 dollar gold doubloons and there is $1,000 dollars to a sack. Do you have something to carry them in?" Tom asked.

"Yes Sir," Jessie answered, "we'll put them in our saddle bags." He was still staring at Tom as if he were playing a joke on them. It was not until Jessie, Justin and Ed had all looked in the bags of gold, before they were convinced that this was all real.

"You can count it on the desk if you want to," Tom said, smiling to himself as he had seen this same reaction from everyone the first time they brought cattle in. It was the excitement in that look and the realization of what they had accomplished that kept most of them coming back every year with more cows.

"There's no need to Mr. Marshal," Jessie said, still a little stunned, "and I'll be back next year with even more cows." As they each picked up three bags of gold to put in their saddle bags, Jessie turned and set one sack back on Tom's desk. "This one has too much money in it." He started to open the sack when Tom reached over and stopped him.

"Don't worry about it," he said. "They're worth every bit of gold in those sacks." He followed them to their horses, watching as they put the sacks of gold in their saddle bags and mounted their horses. Then he shook hands with each of them as they turned and headed back down the river, where Sara Mae was waiting with hot food. Heading back into his office, Tom shook his head and wondered, what in the world is he doing with those Indians, and where did he get that scar? Shaking his head and chuckling to himself as he remembered the look on Jessie's face at Hanks remark, he thought wherever Jessie got them, I ain't asking!

Walking the horses over to where the other men sat under the shade of a large hickory tree, they removed the saddles, hobbled them and turned them loose to feed with the rest of the horses. Everyone sat quietly as Jessie removed a sack of gold coins from his saddle bag, untied the string and set it on the ground in front of the men.

"I never dreamed we would actually get this much money from that bunch of scrub cows, so I am not sure just what to do at this point. I think we should wait until we're back at the lake and have time to think on this. I want to take what we need for supplies and whatever else we want to do before heading back." He removed a small money pouch from his pocket and filled it with coins.

Turning toward the wagon, Jessie called to Sara Mae, asking her to come join them. Balancing three bowls in her hands, she brought the three men food as she joined the discussion.

Setting his food aside for the moment, Jessie said to Sara Mae, "I know we need supplies to take back with us, and there is still time today to go into Tampa. Ed can go with you."

"I'll ride in with them too," Justin said. "There are a couple of things I want to do before heading back."

"Mr. Jessie," Sara Mae spoke up, "if you don't mind, I sure have a hankering to go by and see my friends before we go back, but I'm not sure there is enough time left in the day to do all that and get back before night fall."

"We're not in that big of a hurry," Jessie replied, so if it's safe where you're going, just keep the wagon, and Ed can come get you tomorrow. We are going to move the camp a mile or so on up the river and get away from the smell of those cattle pens. I would like to sleep tonight without smelling or hearing any cows."

Jessie turned to Ed and Justin and said, "Just put the bags of gold next to mine and Red Sun's saddle bags before you go. You can take as many of these gold coins as you need, Justin. We will settle up back at the lake."

"A couple of these will do just fine." Justin reached in the pouch that Jessie held and removed two of the shiny gold coins, placing them in his pants pocket. Jessie removed five more and put the pouch back in his pocket.

Jessie walked back around to the front of the wagon where Sara Mae sat on the seat, holding the reins and waiting on Ed to finish saddling his horse. He handed her one of the gold coins and said, "This is for you; Ed will have money for the supplies."

"Oh Mr. Jessie," she said, catching her breath, "this will feed so many of the children in the quarters; we will all say a special prayer for you and all of mine and Franklin's new family. God bless you Mr. Jessie, God bless you!" Jessie smiled at Sara Mae and walked over to Ed, who was just mounting his horse.

Handing Ed the four gold coins and a piece of paper, he said, "Stay with Sara Mae until she gets all of her supplies and that is a list from me and your Ma ... and Ed, find something purty for your ma and Jenny."

"OK Pa." Ed was grinning as he rode toward where Justin was waiting. Thinking of beer and fried fish, Ed looked back at his pa with a grin on his face. As he left, he said, "I may not be back tonight, but don't worry if I'm not." I wonder what that's all about, Jessie thought smiling, proud of the man his son was becoming.

They were half way down the hill to the lake, when the villagers started shouting and waving. The small ones were already running towards the group and quickly caught up with the riders. Silent Stalker, Big Cypress, and Red Sun reached down to them, each taking an arm and swinging the boys up behind them.

"We are glad you are home father," Snake Handler said.

"I am glad to be home also," Silent Stalker said to his son.

"Are you going to stay now?"

"Yes, until we get a herd ready for next year."

"Maybe I can go with you next year; I will almost be a man by then," said the twelve year old.

"Yes you will, but someone has to take care of your mother; that is a very important job, and you are the only one I trust to do that," Silent Stalker said to the boy as he squeezed the arm around his waist.

Jessie dismounted in front of Two Worlds, who sat leaning on his fur covered back rest.

"I hope the trip went well, although I do not see Justin with you," Two Worlds said as Jessie squatted on his heels.

Jesse grinned and said, "I think he got an invitation from a pretty woman he couldn't turn down. He will come later."

"That is always good for a man," Two Worlds said, smiling.

Jessie spent the next several minutes telling Two Worlds about the drive and how to their amazement, the buyer bought all the cattle. "He wants all we can bring him every year. He paid in gold, more gold than any of us has ever seen, and you and I will have to discuss how it will be shared along with the other men, perhaps when Justin returns."

"That is good then," Two Worlds answered. Jessie saw the relief in the old man's face and realized how worried Two Worlds must have been, not having any word all this time.

"I will return soon," Jessie said as he stood and walked back to where Ed and the others were unloading supplies for the village. Jessie approached Ed, who was helping the others and Sara Mae. She was still sitting on the wagon.

"Get Franklin to help you unload the rest of the supplies in the barn, so Sara Mae can rest now; it's been a long trip for her. I will see you at the house," he added as he mounted his horse and started around the lake.

Ed stood next to the wagon wearing a big smile as he watched Spirit Snake, walking slowly with a limp to greet his friend, Little Moon by his side. They had come from her lodge where he stayed now while he healed.

"How is your leg?" Ed asked as they came closer.

"Woman of the Wind said it will heal, but it will take more time and Little Moon is taking good care of me," he grinned, looking at Little Moon. "You will have to tell me about the trip. Did anything exciting happen?" he asked.

"When I get the wagon unloaded and see my family, I will come back and tell you something you're not going to believe," Ed said. Looking around again, he asked, "Where is Little Otter?"

"She is with your mother," answered Little Moon. "She stays with her a lot since you have been gone."

"I have to go now," Ed said as he saw Sara Mae driving the wagon toward the barn, "but I'll be back." Then he mounted his horse and started to follow the wagon.

Ed kicked the little Marsh Tackie in the ribs, putting him into a run when he saw Little Otter leave the yard and head for the village. He brought the horse to a halt in front of her, his face flush with excitement.

"I'll give you a ride to the village if you want." Little Otter looked him straight in the eyes as she raised her hand to take his, and placing her foot in the stirrup, she swung up behind him, wrapping her arms around his waist and pulling herself tight against his back.

Softly, she spoke in his ear, "I have missed you. I am glad you are back. I thought of you each day while I have waited."

"I thought of you all the time I have been gone," Ed spoke as he slowly released his breath, afraid he would break the magic of the moment. Steering his horse, he turned back, sitting up straight and proud as they made their way to the village.

Thirty

Jessie sat at the table along with Two Worlds, Red Sun, Justin, and Ed, who were sipping on coffee as Jessie explained his thoughts about dividing the money from the sale of the cattle.

"I have never been in a situation like this before, and I will need all of your thoughts so we can make this fair. We are all starting out at something new so I will give you my thoughts first. Since Two Worlds and his tribe are now part of this family, I will divide the money in half between my family and Two Worlds' family, after the cost of supplies and help. If it is OK with Justin, he will get two dollars a head for each cow that reaches the market. He will take charge of the cattle and become the foreman over any cow hands we hire in the future. After the success we had with this cattle drive, I am hoping we can drive more and more cows to market each year. With a little extra help I think we can. There are thousands of wild cattle out there for the taking and people will always be eating beef."

Turning to Two Worlds, Jessie asked for his thoughts. Slowly as he looked at Jessie, he began to speak.

"Red Sun and I have discussed this with the rest of the tribe and these are our thoughts. Our fear is losing this land and having to go back into the Everglades to be safe. We as a tribe do not need very much money; we hunt for the food we need and the furs as we always have. We cannot own any land, and in the future you will need to buy this land, or one day someone else will and we will all have to give up our homes and villages. Red Sun and the rest of the braves will continue to work with Justin, to round up and drive the cows to market, and we will take one dollar for each cow that reaches the market. That will be more than enough for us. I have spoken for our tribe."

"Justin?" Jessie asked.

"This is the first time since I lost my wife and son that I feel I have family again," Justin said, looking around the table. "The offer you have given me is more than fair; I would stay here for room and board, but I will take the money," he added, grinning from ear to ear.

Looking at Two Worlds, Jessie said, "You are right. If we don't buy this land, we could lose it, but that will not happen. You and your people will always have the land you are on now as long as this family exists." Then he turned and said, "So will you Justin, as long as you want to stay. For one more year, I would like to round up all the cattle we can before we hire any help. I think with what we have learned this year along with help from the dogs, we should have over a thousand head next year. We can add to the herd as we are fattening them at the feeding grounds. We can also start branding and moving them earlier into salt marsh valleys, where they will feed without scattering too far. But for the next few weeks, we will spend time with our families."

The sun was just coming up over the lake when Justin was about to take over watching the yearling cow, which was roasting over a bed of hot coals. Franklin had been up all night keeping the fire going. Jessie sat on his horse, speaking with Justin when Franklin walked by on his way home to get some rest.

"How is it coming?" Jessie asked as Franklin drew close.

"Just fine, just fine, it will be ready to eat by about noon. I'll be back before then, I's just gonna get me a little rest now," he said as he started toward home. Jessie knew Franklin was tired, as he watched him limp more than usual.

"You take your time now, there will be plenty help coming."

Jessie rode to where Justin was adding more oak limbs onto the hot coals. "You want me to send you some help?"

"That won't be necessary; there will be more people here in the next hour than I'll need," he chuckled.

Jessie turned and rode a couple of hundred feet to the small stand of huge water oaks, where several tables had been built under Franklin's supervision. The wood had come from a wagon load of lumber that Big John had sent over with his oldest son Frank and two of his brothers. Jessie had visited him, Bill, and Dave, inviting them and their families for a get together. They were all excited, especially the wives who were longing for female gossip. John had volunteered the lumber when Jessie explained to him what he needed.

It was October now, and the days were getting cool. To Jessie, this looked to be a perfect day. As he turned towards the village, he saw the small kids putting wood together for the fires. The women would be cooking all morning and Jessie's mouth watered at the thought of eating venison stew cooked in coontie flour and roasted turkeys stuffed with wild herbs. He was smiling when he rode up to where Raven was already stuffing the three turkeys, readying them to be slow roasted over the fire.

"Good morning, is Two Worlds up yet?"

"He is down by the lake," Raven answered.

"Thank you," he said as he turned back toward the lake. On the way, he saw Spider Woman and her nineteen year old daughter, Dancing Sun, carrying a large pot between them. He knew that they would cook the venison in it.

Dropping the reins at the edge of the water, he let the horse feed as he removed his clothes, waded in knee deep and sat next to the old man. Two Worlds' face was turned upward as he chanted a prayer to his ancestors. Jessie leaned forward and began splashing cool clear water over his head while waiting for the old man to finish his prayers.

"I had a vision last night," the old man suddenly spoke as he leaned forward and began pouring water from a gourd over his frail body. Jessie was always amazed at the strength that Two Worlds' body carried. "This will be an important day for all of us. Again before the sun goes down, the white man will be part of our future."

"What do you mean? Is it good or bad?"

"We will have to wait and see, but we will still be here as a people in the future."

"OK," Jessie said, "we can handle anything else." He pushed himself forward, swimming under water as long as he could hold his breath. Coming up for air, he saw Two Worlds wrapping his loin cloth around his waist as he headed back to the village to ready himself for the day.

Jessie swam for a while longer, letting his mind try to figure out what the old man meant. Still puzzled, he swam for shore as it was time to go and see about his family, knowing that Belle would be in a frenzy. She had all the children running errands for her until they could sneak out and play with their friends. He smiled with pleasure when he thought about Belle's excitement last night after everyone had gone to bed. This morning, as he had stood in the doorway watching Belle add wood to the stove, she looked up and flushed when she saw the smile on her husband's face.

"You better not stand there smiling like that if you want me to cook," she warned, remembering last night.

"I was just thinking, maybe we should have these get-togethers more often." he said as he backed out the door, grinning.

It was still an hour or so before noon when Jessie saw the three wagons start down the valley, heading for the lake. He rode down by the lake where all of the kids were playing hoops that the Indian kids had made. They had taught Jenny and Horace how to roll the hoops with a stick. He called Horace and all the other kids to him. They rolled their hoops up next to him and stopped. Looking down, he spoke to Horace and Jenny as they all looked to where he was pointing.

"I want you to introduce all of your new friends to your old friends who are coming around the lake now."

"OK Pa," said Horace, "it sure will be fun to play together again."

"I sure miss Sara and Lilly," Jenny spoke up, "I bet they will like our new friends, just as much as I do."

"I bet they will," Jessie said smiling. "Now why don't all of you go and meet them."

Jessie met the wagons as they came to a stop under the oaks. Walking over, he greeted Bill with a hand shake and went around the wagon to help Martha down, just as Belle come walking up. He left Martha in Belle's arms and went to greet Dave and Bonnie, whose girls were already playing with Jenny and the other kids. Giving Jessie a quick hug, Bonnie headed toward Belle and Martha. Jessie reached John's wagon as he brought it to a halt, helping Myra down first and receiving a quick hug from her. Then she was off to see Belle and the other wives. After receiving a hug from everyone, Belle started towards the village to introduce them to her new family. The men gathered around Jessie, and Justin walked up smiling as the men came to greet him.

"Sergeant Hannah, It's good to see you again," John said, shaking his hand with that big bear paw of his.

Shaking hands with each one of the men, he laughed and said, "I'm not a sergeant anymore, just Justin the cowman.

"You've done well with the cattle business," Bill said to Jessie.

"It has been a learning process," Jessie answered back, "but it could never have happened if not for Justin and the Indians and a good pair of cow dogs from John! You should have seen us trying to pop those cows out of the palmettos before the dogs," he chuckled. "I think we got about eight cows a day."

"How many did you push to market this year?" Dave asked.

"We had over six hundred head this year, and I think we can round up even more this coming year."

"Are you going to hire any help?" Dave asked.

"No, we will round up what we can get with just us. I don't want any outsiders yet. How are you coming with your farm?" Jessie asked, changing the subject.

"I've got over fifteen acres cleared and plowed under," Dave said.

"I've got almost twenty acres planted," Bill spoke up. "We are working together to grow tobacco. We think it is our best money crop, we have built a curing shed between me and Dave," Bill went on. "The problem is being able to get it all cut and hanging in time, before the frost comes."

"When will you start cutting?" Jessie asked.

"When we get back, we will start with mine," Bill said. "John is going to send his boys to help, so maybe we can get it all cut and hanging in time."

"I guess I have been so busy with what I have going on, I haven't paid any attention to what my friends are doing," Jessie said.

"We all know that you have had your hands full, probably more so than any of us," Bill said.

Jessie looked over at Justin and said, "We are at our waiting time now and won't start with the holding pens and cows for another month or more. There is no reason that we can't bring everyone in my family, and I will talk with Two Worlds and the others. I think they will be glad to help."

"Any help we get now will be heaven sent," said Dave.

"When will you be ready for our help and what tools will we need? Jessie asked.

"We can be ready to start in two days. If you could bring your wagons, we have cutting knives." Bill answered. "Thank you Jessie, you have always been a good neighbor."

"I want to thank you too," Dave spoke up.

"I should have already offered my help; I will make it a point to keep up with my friends and neighbors."

"And how is the saw mill coming, John?" Jessie asked.

"Me and the boys have sawed most all the timber into lumber that we cut down. By the time a cold spell comes and drops the sap in the pine trees, we will be ready to cut and haul enough by the end of winter to keep us busy all summer."

"Where are you selling the lumber?" Justin asked

"Well so far, we have hauled most everything we have cut to Brooksville. They are growing pretty fast now. We have hauled several loads to Fort Dade, which is southeast from here. There is a settlement growing around it. I believe there is going to be a big demand for everything we can produce. From what I've seen, there are a lot of families moving into Florida, mostly from the war torn southern states. It seems the northern carpet baggers are taking over the large plantations. They are taxing the land and when the owners can't pay they take them over. There are a lot of locals who don't want to work for them and they are leaving and moving this way. At some point in the near future I've got to find me some help if I am to produce all I can sell, but that is not going to be easy. There are not many men who can or wants to cut timber, it's a hard job."

John stopped talking when he saw the group of Indians led by Two Worlds, coming from the village. Frank had told John and Myra about being around the Indians when he had brought the dogs to Jessie. They were not what John had expected; walking proud dressed in their deer skin clothes, decorated with beautiful bead work. He watched the old man walking slightly bent over, with a light red cotton blanket covering his frail shoulders.

When Two Worlds arrived with his group, he stopped in front of Jessie. The men all stood, now waiting with anticipation to meet these men they had heard about, who had saved Jessie's life. Looking at the men standing together, Jessie turned back to the Indian men standing behind him and spoke.

"These are my friends that came here with my family to get away from the war. I am glad it is over now and maybe we can live in peace." He introduced each man and then turned to Two Worlds and the small band of men and introduced each of them to John and the others.

Big John walked up to Two Worlds, taking his small hand and shaking it gently.

"Speaking for all of us, we want to thank you for saving our friend and you will always be our friends." Turning next to Red Sun, Big Cypress, and Silent Stalker, he thanked them as he shook their hand. Bill and Dave did the same until everyone had met.

The men sat at the benches, talking about crops and cows until they saw the women bringing food and setting it all on the tables around them. They were talking and laughing like they had known each other for years. Belle and Waiting Owl had been smiling knowingly at Little Moon, Little Otter, and Dancing Sun as they watched Ed and Spirit Snake showing off for the girls. They were trying to teach Frank how to shoot a bow. Calling the three girls to her, Waiting Owl asked them to go get the kids. The boys were down by the lake, trying to catch minnows by hand while the girls were picking flowers for the tables. Belle and Waiting Owl saw Spider Woman stop and watch as the three girls took the long way around to the lake, passing in front of the boys shooting the bows. Spider Woman saw Dancing Sun look back over her shoulder and give a small smile to Frank, whose face turned into one big smile.

"You had better learn to shoot that bow, Frank, if you ever want to impress a girl." Ed said as he and Spirit Snake began laughing at Frank, who was standing frozen with a big grin on his face.

Thirty-One

Ed, Spirit Snake, and Frank sat with Little Otter, Little Moon, and Dancing Sun in the grass by the lake, watching the little ones splash and play in the cool clear water. The women were covering the leftover food on the tables, when Jessie saw the soldiers as they started down into the valley. Two Worlds made a hand motion to Woman of the Wind, and Jessie watched as she spoke quietly to the other women and started toward the village, taking Belle and the other wives with her.

Jessie, Justin, John, Bill, and Dave moved into position between the Indians and the soldiers and standing almost shoulder to shoulder, they waited for the captain and the six soldiers with him to stop in front of the men.

"Good afternoon," John said, recognizing the captain from Fort Dade. "What can we do for you?"

The captain was looking past John at the Indians, who were now standing, except for Two Worlds.

"I am looking for the owner of this place."

"That's me," Jessie spoke up, "what can I do for you?"

"We understand you are letting Indians stay on this land, and it is illegal to harbor Indians," he said, looking again behind Jessie. "All Indians are supposed to be on the reservation."

Jessie stepped forward and took the captain's horse by the bridle. He looked up at the captain and said, "I have fought one battle already and I don't want to fight another. These people saved my life when I was left for dead to rot, and they are my family now, and no one," then lowering his voice, "no one is going to make them leave. They have not fought in any wars against the white man. They are Creeks, not Seminoles, and they are not your enemy."

"It doesn't matter; they are Indians." the captain said.

John stepped forward, putting his hand on Jessie's shoulder and said to the captain, "Tell Major Johnson that Jessie and I will come to the fort in the next few days and talk to him. I'm sure we can work something out besides going to war over a few Indians. As you can see, there is nothing short of going to war with all of us, that's going to solve this today. You men must be tired and hungry and the food is still warm."

One of the soldiers spoke up, "I could sure use some warm food and rest my behind ... that is if we could," the soldier added as the other soldiers shook their heads in agreement.

Looking down at Jessie still holding the bridle, the captain said, "If Mr. Tucker doesn't mind."

Jessie moved his hand away from the bridle and stepped back. "We are always glad to share our food with hungry men."

It was mid-afternoon when Jessie and John crossed the small stream that ran from the spring by the fort and rode through the opened gates to the major's office. Dismounting and tying their horses to the hitching rail, they walked onto the porch and knocked on the door.

They heard a voice call out, "Come in." As John and Jessie entered the major rose from his chair and came around to greet them.

"John, it's good to see you again," he said, coming around the desk to shake his hand.

"Major, this is a long time good friend of mine, Jessie Tucker."

"Glad to meet you. Please sit down," he said as he returned to his seat. "I am glad you came in because this could be a serious matter. Indians are supposed to be on a reservation, and I understand you have several living with you, Mr. Tucker."

"I do," Jessie answered.

"Well, can you tell me how they came to be there?" the major asked.

Jessie explained the whole story, as the major sat and listened while looking at the scar on Jessie's forehead.

When Jessie finished, the major nodded saying, "The war was bad for everyone on both sides, but it is over now and we have to rebuild. There is still a lot of resentment out there and your Indians could be in danger, being at your place unprotected."

"They are under my protection," Jessie said, "and like I told your captain, the Indians stay where they are."

John broke in when he saw Jessie begin to stiffen up. "Major, let me make a proposal. Jessie and his Indians are rounding up cows every year to move to market. Now you need meat other than deer, which your soldiers are probably tired of by now. You buy whatever half-starved cow that is brought to the fort, and you don't ask if they are stolen or not."

"I buy whatever we can and don't have any choices," the major broke in.

"I understand that," John went on, "but Jessie and I have discussed the possibility of Jessie and his Indians bringing you 30 or more head a month of well-fed cows. The people building homes in this area will need fresh beef too."

"But I can't even think about that without the Indians," Jessie added.

"Well if the Indians were working through you for the army, then that would be a different matter," the major said, smiling. "I will pay eighteen dollars a head for thirty cows a month on a standing order."

"You will have them here. In the next two weeks I will bring in 30, but they won't be as fat as in the future when they have had more time to graze," Jessie said as he stood to go.

The major stood and reaching across the desk, he shook their hands. "But I have to tell you again, I can't protect your Indians if something goes wrong."

"I don't need your help, we take care of our own problems," Jessie said.

"My soldiers found and buried five men a while back; would they have been a problem you fixed?"

"Like I said Major, we take care of our own problems."

"I understand," the major said as he walked them to the door. As they started toward the gates, Jessie recognized one of the soldiers walking toward them. He pulled up as the soldier reached his horse.

"Mr. Tucker, me and the other boys want to thank you again for that fine food the other day."

"Glad you enjoyed the food." Jessie shook the man's hand as he reached out to him. "Stop by any time you are in the area," he added, and giving the horse his leads, they started home.

The next day Jessie gathered everyone at the village and explained to them what had happened at the fort. Jessie could see the worry leaving their faces as he explained.

"You will be safe here as far as the army is concerned. We still need to travel in groups, because there are still people out there who don't care who you are. You are Indian and that's all the excuse they need to harm you. Anytime you leave the village, make sure you are armed and never just let someone harm you; always defend yourself, and we will take it from there. Justin talked to you about helping gather the crops for Bill and Dave. Do you have an answer yet?"

"They are your friends, and now they are our friends," Red Sun spoke up. "We will help all we can."

The next morning at sun up, Red Sun heard the wagons, and then the big work wagon appeared, being driven by Franklin with Sara May sitting next to him. The wagon had been stripped and was ready to haul a big load. Horace drove the buck board with Jenny sitting between him and Belle. As the wagons pulled to a halt in front of the village, all of the women climbed in except Woman of the Wind, who would stay behind to take care of Two Worlds and the children. Red Sun and the other braves gathered around Jessie and Ed, who waited on horseback.

Two Worlds sat leaning on his fur covered back rest under the shade of the big oak, watching as everyone gathered together. Woman of the Wind handed Two Worlds a bowl of warm soup for his breakfast and went back to sewing beads on a new, soft deer skin shirt. As he sipped the warm soup, he paid attention as Ed and Spirit Snake rode by, sitting proudly with Little Otter and Little Moon behind them, snuggled tightly against their backs, with their arms wrapped around their men's waists. He watched as the two girls looked at each other and shared a smile. Looking over to where Woman of the Wind sat smiling at the same things he saw, he was at peace and thought to himself, it's a good day to be alive.

Thirty-Two

The sun was starting its final decent when Warrior Spirit saw White Crow emerge from the cypress hammock across the opening and pump one hand up and down. This was the signal that it was clear for the small band of survivors that he led to move out of the small stand of pines they were hiding in. Now they would cross the clearing to the cypress strand where they would hide for the night, as they tried to stay ahead of the Seminole braves who had been tracking them for the past two weeks.

Warrior Spirit knew he was the one they were searching for, to revenge the two Seminole warriors he had killed in a fight. He had encountered them when they were drunk on the white man's whisky, returning from a hunting trip. First they had taunted him, calling him woman names and accusing him of having no courage, because he would not fight the white man with them. Warrior Spirit had tried to pass around them. He wanted no fight with them; in the past they had killed several of the Creek braves who did not want to fight the white soldiers. The small band of Creeks wanted only to be left alone, to live as they once had. The two Seminole braves were too drunk on the white man's whiskey to fight, but they had attacked him with knives and he had killed them both.

Two weeks before, a group of Seminole braves had attacked their camp and had killed men, women and children. Warrior Spirit and the small band had fought a running battle for two days, losing his father and mother as the women and children fled ahead of them.

They had out-distanced the Seminoles by traveling day and night, but they knew the warriors were still pursuing them, aware that there was nowhere for the small starving group to go. It was just matter of time before they ran them down and took their revenge by killing the small Creek band.

As Warrior Spirit roused the exhausted group, they gathered their small belongings and followed him across the palm dotted opening to the cypress strand. White Crow led them deep inside to a small spring of fresh water, bubbling up from the earth. Warrior Spirit knew from the tracks surrounding the small spring that this was used by a lot of animals.

Warrior Spirit called his wife Dancing Turtle to his side as the others quenched their thirst from the cool water of the spring. "When the women and children are through, tell them to move away from the water; then gather dry wood for a fire and palm fronds for bedding. I will take White Crow and Broken Arrow to hunt for food. Shadow Walker will stay behind, to protect you from any animals that might come to drink at the spring."

Dancing Turtle saw the strain on his face from bearing the burden of their losses and asked, "How much longer do you think we can go on like this? There is not much strength left in anyone. The children will become sick soon if this goes on much longer."

"I know, but if we stop now, we will surely die. I hope we will find Two Worlds and the others. Last time Red Sun was at our village, he told me that their village is west toward the great waters. We have to keep moving until we can find them."

Dancing Turtle reached out and touched his arm saying, "I see the hope fading from their eyes, but I know we will find Two Worlds soon; I do not feel that this is the end of our lives. I will go and talk to the others, and when you bring food back, we will eat and rest. Tomorrow we will be ready to go on."

The small Florida deer was almost finished now, and everyone was feeling better as they rolled out what skins they had left. Spreading them over the palm fronds, they lay exhausted, watching with curiosity as Spirit Warrior gathered more dried wood and placed it on the fire until it was waist high. Stripping down to only a loin cloth, he moved into a slow dance around the fire and began a low chant. Each time he circled the fire, the chant grew louder as one by one, the others joined in the dance and took up the rhythm of the chant. They had heard this chant since childhood and the stomping of their feet began to sound like a drum, keeping rhythm with their voices. The sound awakened the memories of the children, who were sitting silently on their furs, watching.

Two Worlds took one more, long draw on the ancient pipe he had prepared earlier. Setting it aside, he poured water over the hot rocks and heard the steam hiss as the heat wrapped around him. The sweat ran down his small body, which was covered with only a loin cloth. Even if his eyes had been open, he would not have been able to see in the darkness of the sweat lodge. His body swayed with the rhythm of the drums, and his voice rose as the sound of the chanting grew louder around the fire outside. Two Worlds knew he would need the power of the whole group, if he were to accomplish what he had to do tonight.

Ed sat next to Justin on the log outside of Justin's lodging that was complete now, except for a woman to warm his nights. In silent fascination, Ed watched his Father sitting in a circle with Red Sun and the other braves, wearing nothing but a loin cloth. Jessie was keeping rhythm with the others, beating on a large, skin covered drum. He used a small limb that was covered with tightly wrapped skin two inches thick on one end, and on the other was a fur wrapped handle decorated with hanging feathers. Then his eyes found Little Otter, holding the hands of the women on either side of her. Together they swayed, chanting and softly stomping their feet, in perfect timing around the large fire that was over five feet high.

The smoke from the pipe took its effect on Two Worlds, freeing his spirit from his body. He felt himself floating through time as he sensed the spirits of his ancestors around him.

"Fathers of our Fathers, I need your help in carrying a message to one of our people before they become memories as the rest of their families are. I must send them to a place where they are safe until our warriors can reach them and bring them to the rest of their families."

Spirit Warrior felt the presence of Two Worlds at his side as he danced around the flames. He heard him speak to his spirit, showing him the way and what he must do to keep them safe until the warriors came for them. He must go in haste, but without fear. Spirit Warrior did not know when the dancing had stopped and the others had gone to their sleeping mats, only that he sat alone in front of the dying coals trying to understand what had just happened. He had never had an experience like this before, but he knew that Two Worlds had been by his side and had spoken to him. He wondered if any of the others had seen him.

Woman of the Wind finished bathing Two Worlds' small thin body and handed him a small gourd filled with nourishing broth. She had seen this before and knew it would be several days before he would regain all his strength. She watched him drink from the gourd as he sat back against his fur covered back rest. Once he had taken a few sips, he asked her to send in Red Sun.

Red Sun sat across from Two Worlds, waiting in silence for his father to finish his broth. Red Sun knew after last night's gathering that something important was happening, and he would wait. Two Worlds finished the last of the nourishing broth and slowly set the gourd down. He paused a moment before he began to speak.

"A terrible tragedy has happened to the people we left behind." Slowly he explained to Red Sun what he knew. "If we do not get to the ones who have survived, we will lose them all. You must take the braves and go to the place where the big storm came and bring the survivors back with you, but you must hurry or it will be too late. You must leave as soon as you can."

"We will be ready; we knew that you would need us," Red Sun said to his Father. "They have already packed the supplies we will need to move fast. Waiting Owl has packed my things and the braves are gathering the horses as we speak."

"Take extra horses with you. You will need them. Take also the guns and extra ammunition; you will need them too." Speaking quietly, he leaned forward so Red Sun could understand what he said. "Use the guns as you need to."

Red Sun nodded his head in understanding. As Two Worlds lay down and stretched out on his sleeping furs, Red Sun stepped through the opening. The sun was just reaching over the horizon as the other braves were saddling the horses, tying their rolls of skins to the back of their saddles. Red Sun saw Spirit Snake as he threw the saddle over one of the Marsh Tackies in front of his lodge.

Walking over to the lodge he said to Spirit Snake, "Go and bring four more horses to take with us; I will finish here."

Red Sun sat on his horse looking at the mounted braves, packing rifles in their scabbards and wearing holstered pistols. With them was Justin, holding the lead line of one of the extra horses. Red Sun knew that Justin wouldn't question his reasons.

Explaining to them where they had to go, Red Sun said, "We must travel hard and rest only when we have to. Our brothers' lives depend on us." Red Sun turned his horse and put him into a fast paced trot. He knew the little MarsTackies could keep up for hours before they had to stop and rest.

The sun was below the tree tops when Spirit Warrior and his small group began to work their way through the broken branches, trying to reach the long cypress strand before dark. They had all become quiet as they worked their way closer to the foreboding forest of broken trees. Spirit Warrior stopped the small group at the edge of the strand.

Feeling uneasy, he spoke to the stragglers, "We will make a small camp here in the opening, and tomorrow we will go around this place that feels of death." No one argued with his decision, feeling the same fear of death around them.

Red Sun's group had crossed the Caloosahatchee River earlier that morning. As they sat around the small fire watching the millions of fire flies light up the darkness, eating smoked meat and biscuits and drinking from their water skins, Red Sun knew that they would reach the cypress strand tomorrow. Thinking about the place where many of their people had died from the great winds, he felt the dread build up in his stomach at the thought that they had to pass by there to get to their old village at the edge of the great waters.

Tomorrow he would send Silent Stalker ahead with an extra horse so he could travel faster without resting. Red Sun knew Silent Stalker was the right brave to scout for the small band that they were hoping to find by tomorrow or the next day. Still he worried, afraid that the

Seminole warriors would reach their people before he got there. Soon exhaustion overcame him and he lay back on his furs and slept.

Silent Stalker left camp at daylight while the others were getting ready. He took an extra horse and started out at a run. Heading south and east, he hoped to pick up the trail he knew the Seminoles would be tracking. He rode without saddle and would ride one horse until it tired and then would switch horses and travel at a fast run until he could pick up Warrior Spirit's trail.

Red Sun and the others could just see Silent Stalker in the distance when they set out at a fast trot, hoping to reach the camp of the great storm before the sun went down and the Seminole braves caught up with Warrior Spirit.

Jumper, their leader, stood and faced the other six Seminole braves who had been following him for days. "The trail is new; they are only hours ahead of us. We will catch them before this sun has gone down, and this time we will kill them all." Turning, he started at a fast pace trot. The others followed keeping pace, wanting this hunt for revenge to be over so they could go back to their families.

Justin watched Red Sun and the others glance repeatedly toward the hammock of death. They kept more than a half mile to the west of the place where so many of their people had lost their lives in the great storm. They were more than half way past the hammock, when Justin looked back and saw Silent Stalker moving around broken branches scattered across the palm dotted opening between the smaller hammocks. He was catching up with them as fast as he could move.

"There are seven braves in the war party," Silent Stalker said, speaking to Red Sun. "They are less than one hour ahead of us and no more than three hours behind the others. They are moving at a fast trot, but are slowed by the tree limbs scattered by the great winds. We can reach the camp of the great storm before them if we stay to the west and travel fast."

Without speaking Red Sun and the others turned their horses and started forward as fast as they could travel through the broken limbs, until they came to the fresh water stream that had flowed through their old camp.

Warrior Spirit and the others heard the riders coming before they saw them. Sending the women and children to hide; Warrior Spirit, White Crow, Broken Arrow, and Shadow Walker turned to face their enemy. There was nowhere else to run. Relief swept over them when they recognized Red Sun and the other braves, as they rode into the opening that had once been their home, but was now unrecognizable.

Red Sun slipped from his horse and went to greet Warrior Spirit and the others. He saw the relief on his face and confusion on the others.

"We have been sent by Two Worlds to bring you with us where it is safe. But we have to take care of the Seminole warriors who are no more than an hour away." Warrior Spirit saw the pistols they carried on their waist and the rifles on their horses.

"Give us rifles," Warrior Spirit said, "and we will meet them and get our revenge! They have killed enough of our people. It will be our time now! We will let the animals eat their bodies, and they will bother us no more!"

"No," said Red Sun, "we will go and meet them. We will kill only if they force us to. It is the wish of Two Worlds."

Warrior Spirit stopped and looked at Red Sun, thinking for several seconds. "We will come with you."

Red Sun turned and pointed toward the extra horses saying, "Use the extra horses we have brought for your people, but there will be no killing unless I say so. Where are the rest of your people?" Red Sun asked.

"Hiding in the woods," Warrior Spirit said, as he turned and pumped his fist up and down above his head.

Red Sun and the others saw the tears of relief as the women recognized them. Big Cypress stepped forward when he saw his little sister, Spotted Fawn. She was staring at him, clutching her small child in fear. Then she ran to him, and he put out his giant arms and took her to his chest until her crying stopped.

"You and the others are safe now," he said, loud enough for the others to hear. "You will come with us to your new home."

Spotted Fawn stepped back and looked up into his face. She held out the small child and beaming at him, she said, "This is your nephew."

Seeing the others mounting the horses, Big Cypress smiled and said, "I will see him better tonight; I have to go now," and turning, he moved to his horse that spirit Snake was holding for him.

Red Sun and the others had traveled for a half an hour when they came to the edge of what was left of a small stand of mixed pine and cypress. Slowly they rode within twenty yards of the edge of the stand and stopped. They sat their horses for a minute, waiting before Red Sun called out.

"Your hunt is over. The fight ends here today. I speak for Two Worlds our leader. We will not fight unless you force us to do so. That is the word of Red Sun." He moved his horse forward a few paces as he held his hand up to the others to stay. Justin and the others sat their horses waiting with their rifles laid across their saddles. Warrior Spirit sat his horse with the other three braves from his tribe, trying to control the anger building up inside him. He could see by their faces that the others were doing the same. Red Sun saw Jumper and the other braves slowly rise up from behind broken branches and warily make their way forward until they stood outside in the clearing, no more than fifteen feet away.

Red Sun spoke first. "You have killed more than enough of our people for your revenge. You will kill no more. You will only die trying and your people will have seven warriors less to protect the women and children, hunt for food, and fight the whites you war with."

Jumper stepped a few paces forward before he spoke. "We have come for revenge. I see your guns, but we are not afraid to die. We will not go back like cowards."

"I do not ask that you go home as a coward, but as a wise leader who puts his people first."

"How can that be so if we do not fight, even if we die?"

Red Sun looked down at Jumper and said, "Two Worlds has sent a message for you and your people through me. We have rifles and bullets that you could use to feed and protect your people, but you must go and give your word, that there will be no more killing of our people. I will take your answer back to Two Worlds."

Jumper paused for a few moments, thinking about Two Worlds' offer. "All of our people know of Two Worlds and his great medicine. He speaks only words of truth. I will give you the word of our people. It is with the wisdom of our ancestors that I accept your offer from the great leader of your people. I will take your offer to our people and will be grateful for this gift. I will tell them of my promise I have made to you for our people. There will be no more war between our people and yours; before the white man came, we were all brothers."

Red Sun slipped off his horse and reached into his saddle bag, bringing out two boxes of ammunition and offered them to Jumper, who took them and handed them to one of his warriors. As Red Sun's band slipped from their horses and reached into their saddle bags to bring out boxes of ammunition, the other Seminoles accepted the guns and boxes with looks of amazement on their faces. Jumper removed his knife from its leather sheath and pulled the sharp edge across the palm of his hand before holding it out to Red Sun. Red Sun pulled his knife and did the same. As they clasped each other's hand in a tight grasp their blood flowed together.

"We are brothers again," Jumper stated, "and we will fight each other no more."

It was late afternoon when Horace and Snake Handler, who were fishing along the lake's edge, spotted Red Sun and the others as they started down into the valley. Red Sun saw the two boys running toward the village waving their hands, shouting to the others and pointing to him and the other braves. Then Horace turned for home to tell his father that they were back. Looking back at Warrior Spirit and the others, Red Sun saw the bewilderment on their faces as they looked down, seeing the village and further around the lake, the wooden houses of the white man. Red Sun had tried to explain once where they were going, but he realized he was only confusing them. The story was too long and complicated for them to understand, so he had assured them that they would be safe at their new home.

Warrior Spirit rode his horse forward next to Red Sun, and with a look of confusion asked, "How is it that you live next to the white man's trading post. Does he not make you leave, when you are through trading for his goods?"

Red Sun felt amused at Warrior Spirit's confusion. "Two Worlds will explain everything to you later," Red Sun answered, "after you and the others are welcomed. You are safe now with us and our white brother."

Thirty-Three

Ed, White Crow, and Broken Arrow were no more than a mile from the holding pen with more than sixty head of branded cows. They were moving them more than four miles to the valley of wet prairies feeding and holding ground. Already there were over five hundred head of cows feeding contentedly and getting fatter by the day. This year, with the extra help of the survivors now settled in with Two Worlds and the others, the goal was to gather 800 to a 1000 head before starting the push to Tampa. They planned to add to the herd as they moved, taking time to let the cattle put on weight. Red Sun had left for the village the evening before, leaving Ed and the others to move the cows the next morning.

Ed whistled, then turned the Marsh Tackie and started after the three cows that had made a run for the thicket, when he felt the shock of the bullet as it tore through his shoulder. He felt the small horse drop when its legs buckled beneath it from the bullet that tore through its head. As the Marsh Tackie landed across his leg, it slammed him to the ground, knocking the air from his lungs and he blacked out.

Ed heard his name being called as he slowly opened his eyes and felt the pain in his shoulder. Everything was blurry as he tried to recognize the face above him, calling his name. Slowly he recognized White Crow.

"What happened?" he asked. "Is Broken Arrow OK?"

"No, he is dead and I have been shot through the leg but I will be OK. We have to get your leg from under the horse. Can you move your leg if I can lift the horse some?"

"I'll try," answered Ed.

Kneeling down on his good knee, White Crow ignored the pain in his other leg as he shoved his hands as far under the dead horse as he could. Straining with all the strength he had left, he barely moved the horse. Trying once again while Ed waited, he was not able to move the horse enough for Ed to move his leg.

"I will have to go and get help, but we must stop the bleeding from your shoulder first."

Taking the cotton sleeping blanket from behind Ed's saddle, he cut a four inch wide strip. Tearing it in half, he helped Ed rise up enough to lean on his good arm, as he put a folded piece on both sides of his shoulder over the wound. Then cutting another four inch strip, he rapped it around his chest as tight as Ed could stand it. While retrieving the canteen of water from the saddle, he found some smoked meat in the saddle bag. Laying them in reach of Ed, he cut more strips from the blanket and did the same to his leg as he had done to Ed's shoulder. Lifting a six foot long limb, White Crow tested it to make sure it would hold his weight as he leaned against it and hobbled to where Ed lay.

"I will send help as quickly as I can." Turning, he started a slow hobble toward the village, ignoring the pain he knew he had to endure if Ed was to live.

Big Cypress looked up as he heard the faint yell and saw White Crow crumble to the ground no more than a hundred yards from where he stood. Reaching for his whip he cracked it three times over his head giving the signal for help. He saw others look around as he ran toward White Crow, who was trying to get to his feet. Big Cypress caught him as he was falling, lifted him in his big arms and begin to trot toward the village. As he got closer to the village, he saw Woman of the Wind and Waiting Owl standing together, surrounded by all the women in the village, and carried White Crow to where they stood.

"Take him to Two Worlds lodge; Waiting Owl and I will bring the medicine bundle," Woman of the Wind told Big Cypress. He laid White

Crow on the bundle of sleeping furs next to where Two Worlds sat on his fur covered back rest. Red Sun knelt down to look at White Crow.

"What happened and where are Broken Arrow and Ed?" he asked.

Woman of the Wind and Waiting Owl knelt down and started removing the blood soaked rag from the wounded leg, as others gathered close enough to hear. After swallowing the liquid from the small gourd Waiting Owl held to his lips, he spoke softly.

"Several white men on horses were waiting in ambush, I heard the rifle shots and then I saw Ed and his horse go down. I was hit in the leg, but I managed to pull my rifle and dove into the thicket. I didn't see Broken Arrow until it was over. I kept firing my rifle until they had run the cows off with the horses. I found Broken Arrow dead, then I went to find Ed, but I couldn't lift the horse high enough for him to pull his leg from under it."

Spirit Snake, running as fast as possible, met Jessie and Franklin half way between the village and the barn. Jessie was working with Franklin, adding on to the barn when he had heard the rifle cracks from the whip and started on a run toward the village, Franklin started out as fast as he could, following behind Jessie.

"Red Sun said to hurry, Ed and White Crow have been hurt, Broken Arrow is dead. They were ambushed by some white men outlaws."

"Is Ed at the village now, and is he hurt bad?" Jessie asked.

"He is still in the woods trapped under his horse, and he's been shot," replied Spirit Snake.

Jessie broke into a run and looking back, he hollered to Franklin, "Hook Dolly to the buck board and bring it to the village." Still running with Spirit Snake by his side he saw Red Sun leaving Two Worlds lodge. Seeing Jessie, Red Sun started toward him.

"What has happened?" he asked, reaching Red Sun.

"They were attacked by some white outlaws. White Crow thinks there were five or six of them, and he thinks he hit one of them."

Turning toward the lake, Jessie saw Silent Stalker kicking his horse in the side riding fast and he saw the young boys bringing horses up from the lake on a run.

"Silent Stalker has gone ahead to start tracking the men and the herd," Red Sun explained. Looking around, Jessie saw the braves coming from their lodges, carrying their rifles. Then he saw Franklin trying to stay on the seat of the buck board as he raced Dolly across the rough ground.

Facing Red Sun, he said, "I'll follow with the buck board, and when you find Ed, send someone back to show me the way." Turning he started toward Franklin and the buck board at a fast walk. Climbing up on to the wagon seat, he saw his shot bag under the seat, and looking back he saw his saddled horse with the shotgun sticking from its scabbard. He looked again at Franklin, who just shrugged his shoulders.

"I didn't know just what all you wanted, Mr. Tucker."

"You did fine Franklin, you did fine."

He was over half way to the holding pen when he saw Justin riding toward him.

"I will show you the way," Justin said as he rode close to the wagon and saw the worry in Jessie's face.

Red Sun and the others rode past the holding pen and picked up the trail of the herd. Riding fast, they came upon the downed horse lying on Ed's leg no further than a mile from the pen. The two dogs stood on either side of Ed, wagging their tails when they saw the men sliding from their horses and rushing to Ed. Spirit Snake got there first, saw that Ed was barely conscious and going down on both knees, he lifted Ed's head. Ed saw the worry in Spirit Snake's face, and licking his dried lips, he tried to smile. Spirit Snake grabbed the canteen of water and held it to Ed's lips. He let water run slowly into Ed's mouth and that brought a bigger smile. Ed felt the pressure of the horse's weight leave as Big Cypress and the others lifted it off his leg. He winced as Red Sun reached under his shoulders and pulled him from under the horse.

"Can you move your leg?" Red Sun asked.

"I don't have any feeling in it."

Spirit Snake started rubbing his leg and looking at Ed he said, "You're going to be all right just like me; my leg is as good as ever and you will be too." To prove his point, he started lifting his leg up and down.

Silent Stalker rode in just as Jessie pulled up in the wagon. Jumping down, Jessie ran to Ed and kneeling down, seeing the soaking wet shirt from sweat and blood, he knew Ed was in a lot of pain.

"Son, we are going to take you home, so bear with me now."

Big Cypress knelt down. Putting his big hands under Ed, lifted him easily off the ground and walked to the wagon. He waited until Jessie made bedding from the tarps Franklin had thrown in. Jessie lifted Ed from Big Cypress' arms and gently laid him to one side. The others brought Broken Arrow's lifeless body and handed it to Jessie. As he laid the lifeless body next to Ed, he saw the two bullet holes in his chest. Anger shot through his body like a lightning bolt, consuming all thoughts except finding the men who did this. He jumped down from the wagon and walked to where Silent Stalker was talking to Justin and Red Sun.

"How far have the bastards gotten?" His face was red with anger.

Silent Stalker turned to face Jessie and said, "They are driving them hard, losing a few as they push them. It looks like they are headed towards Fort Dade."

"To sell them to the army," Justin broke in.

"They are a day ahead of us," Silent Stalker went on, "but we can catch up with them before the sun comes up tomorrow. They have to stop before long to rest and let the cows feed and water. If they keep pushing them, they will be at Fort Dade before the sun goes down tomorrow."

"If they reach Fort Dade, we will never see those cows again, and the bastards will be gone," Justin added.

Walking back to the wagon, Jessie saw Franklin wiping Ed's forehead with a wet piece of cloth. He walked to the side of the wagon and spoke to Franklin.

"You take Ed on back to Woman of the Wind, and then go get his mama; she is going to be worried. Tell her I'll be back when we get this taken care of." Untying his horse from the back of the wagon, Jessie slipped his foot in the stirrup and swung up in the saddle, heading to where the others were waiting.

Riding up next to Silent Stalker, with fire in his eyes and anger in his voice, he said, "Take me to the bastards." Turning, he followed Silent Stalker on a run. He would run his horse until he dropped if he had to, but he would catch those bastards before they reached the fort.

Franklin started down the slope where the whole village was waiting for word of what was happening. As he came closer to the light of the fire in the center of the village, they all started for the wagon. That's when Franklin saw Mrs. Tucker in front with Waiting Owl. Not waiting for the wagon to stop, Belle ran over and looking over the side boards, she saw Ed lying on the tarps with his eyes closed and covered in blood.

"Oh God!" she sobbed, turning to Franklin, "is he dead?" she asked, gripping the side of the wagon to keep from falling.

"He was alive a couple of hours ago when I checked on him. It's been a rough ride in this buck board," answered Franklin.

"Bring him to my lodge," Waiting Owl said as she took Belle by the arm. Little Otter took the other arm and followed the wagon. Looking at Little Otter, Belle saw the pain and fear in her eyes and she reached and squeezed her hand. Franklin lifted Ed under his arm pits while Waiting Owl and Belle lifted a leg each. Together they carried him inside the lodge and lay him on a bed of furs. Woman of the Wind knelt down next to Ed, putting her face close to his mouth. Belle saw her slowly sniff.

"He is alive," she said sitting up. "Hand me my medicine roll."

Belle let out a sob as she went to her knees and began praying to her God. As she prayed, she heard the women outside chanting together to their God as they lifted the dead body of Broken Arrow from the wagon to prepare him for burial. After Franklin finished helping carry the dead body to one of the women's lodge, he went to find Two Worlds.

Spirit Snake had been riding next to Jessie all night, and it was still an hour before daybreak when they spotted what was left of the small bunch of cows. Pulling up, they stopped and sat on their sweat soaked horses, watching the cows feed on the lush grass by a small stream. The fact that the cows and horses were feeding this late told Jessie that they had been pushed most of the night. They couldn't spot the men yet, but they saw the horses hobbled and still saddled, feeding closer to them.

Moving closer to Silent Stalker, Jessie spoke in a whisper, "We will wait here while you go on foot and find where they are sleeping."

Silent Stalker slid from his horse and began slipping quietly just inside the red gum trees until he came to the opening, two hundred yards from where they had stopped. Half way between the trees and the small stream, he saw the outline of five bodies wrapped in blankets. He saw movement to his right and noticed the rider slowly walking his horse around the cows, keeping them bunched up while they fed. Easing back through the gum trees to where Jessie and the others waited, he explained what he had seen.

Red Sun said, "One of us will go and take out the rider before we attack the others."

"I will take out the rider," Spirit Snake answered.

"That's fine," Jessie spoke up, "but you come back here when it is done." Before Jessie could finish, Spirit Snake was already out of sight, moving through the trees. Jessie just shook his head.

"They killed his friend and tried to kill his spirit brother," Red Sun spoke up.

"I know," Jessie spoke quietly, "let's move up to the edge of the opening, and we will attack from there when Spirit Snake returns."

Easing forward to the edge of the opening, they saw the men wrapped in blankets as they sat their horses and waited.

Spirit Snake crouched low and came out of the trees no more than twenty feet behind the rider leaning forward on his horse dosing. Knife in hand ten feet from the horse, he sprinted forward on silent feet, leaping over the back of the horse. He grabbed the riders head, pulled it back and reaching around; he drew the knife from ear to ear. Frank Bormann was dead before he could ever figure out what had happened. With knife in hand, Spirit Snake threw the body from the horse and charging the sleeping men; he let out a pent up, blood lust, war cry, bringing the men scrambling up from their blankets in confusion, trying to find their guns.

Sitting on his horse Jessie heard the war cry, and saw the men scrambling from their blankets. "Oh hell!" he said, kicking his horse in the ribs and letting out a yell that joined the others. He brought his 12 gauge shotgun up and headed for the scrambling confused men, who had found guns and turned to face the oncoming, screaming riders from hell. Thirty feet from the men and hearing the guns firing from the other riders, Jessie raised the barrel of the shotgun and pulled the trigger on both barrels, almost cutting the man in front of him in two. They were past the men on the ground when they slowed their horses to a walk. Looking back, they saw Spirit Snake sliding from the still running horse in the middle of the dead men, looking for someone to kill. Riding back toward the outlaws, Jessie saw Spirit Snake check each man before raising his hand in the air, shaking the knife with anger and letting out another war cry.

Walking back slowly, Jessie dismounted in the middle of the dead men. He was still angry and looking at each man, he wondered which one had shot his son.

Justin, who was still sitting on his horse asked, "What do you want us to do with the dead men?"

Facing the mounted men, Jessie said, "You men gather their horses and gear; leave the sons of bitches for the wolves and buzzards; I don't care. Red Sun and I will start back to the ranch, and when you men get some rest, round up what cows that's left and move them to the feeding area."

"I want to go with you," Spirit Snake spoke up, holding the reins of his horse that one of the riders had handed him.

"They will need you here," Red Sun replied.

Looking at Spirit Snake's face, Justin said, "Let him go; he won't be any good to me here." Justin watched the three men ride away with Spirit Snake already out front. He knew he would not wait for Jessie or Red Sun, but would push the little animal as hard as he could, to get back and check on his spirit brother.

Justin looked at the remaining men and said, "Silent Stalker, take Warrior Spirit and go get the horses, while me and the others gather up the dead men's belongings. We'll start moving the cows a couple of miles away from here, and then we will get some rest."

Thirty-Four

Jessie and Ed sat their horses at the top of the ridge looking down at the herd of cattle. There were about a thousand head milling around, feeding on the lush pickerel weed, growing fatter every day as they fed in this wet bottom land. This was the first time Ed had been away from the lake since he had been shot over six weeks ago. Although he carried his arm in a sling, the wound was healing from the medicine that Woman of the Wind kept putting on it. She also made sure he kept stretching his arm and shoulder every day, to keep it from becoming stiff. Most days now he kept his arm out of the sling, working it slowly up and down and only used the sling when he was doing some kind of chore.

"I want to go with you on this cattle drive," Ed spoke to his father.

Jessie looked at Ed's arm in the sling and said, "Son, I don't think your arm is ready yet, to use on a drive."

"I know White Crow can't ride yet, and if I don't go, you will be shorthanded. I can ride just fine, and I can stand watch." Looking seriously at his father, he said, "I have reasons to go on this trip." Seeing the earnest look in Ed's face, Jessie knew this was something beyond his understanding, but knowing Ed was determined to come on this trip, he nodded his head.

"Then we better get this herd started," Jessie said, turning back toward the lake. Ed felt his heart beating faster with anticipation as he followed the man he admired so much.

Belle, Waiting Owl, Little Moon, and Little Otter, along with the other wives, watched as the men rode out to start the drive to Tampa. Sara Mae sat and waited patiently until Franklin finished checking the ropes and came around to tell her to be careful.

"You just be ready for me when I gets back," she beamed down at Franklin, putting a big smile on his face before she flicked the reins across Dolly's and Preacher's rumps, to start the long trip ahead of her. It was well before noon when they started down the slope where the cattle fed.

Speaking to Justin and Red Sun, Jessie said, "Let's get the strays rounded up and get these cows moving. It's going to be a slow process, getting them away from their feeding ground, but I would like to have them on the move before dark."

"I'll take Spirit Snake and a couple of dogs and bring in the strays," Justin spoke up. As Justin and Spirit Snake rode toward the tree line, Jessie and Red Sun heard the rifle crack of whips and the yelping of the dogs as they nipped at the cows' feet, trying to get thousand head of lazy cattle to move away from good grass. Over an hour later as Justin and Spirit Snake moved the handful of strays toward the herd, Justin saw that they were finally starting to move forward as the yelling and cracking of whips had their effect.

As they sat around the camp fire eating the meal Sara Mae had made for them, Jessie spoke to Justin. "The herd will be moving slowly for the next several days, so I need you to take the men and cut out fifty head of the fatter cows, for you and Ed to take to the fort. Tell the major that this will be all of the cattle until we return from Tampa in six to eight weeks. While you are cutting out for the fort, pull another hundred to leave here in the wet land to feed, so when we return there will be fat cows to supply the fort."

For over a week they moved slowly, letting the herd graze as they kept a steady pace heading south and west until Justin and Ed returned from the fort.

Jessie saw Silent Stalker riding toward him, crossing the small stream a half mile away. Red Sun and Justin, seeing the rider, rode over by Jessie and waited until Silent Stalker met them.

"About two miles beyond this valley, there is a large forest of pines with at least two hundred cows."

"What's beyond this forest?" Jessie asked.

"It is flat with good grass but no water."

"OK," Jessie said. "We will leave the herd here to feed; there is enough water in those two small lakes for the cows to water." He looked around at the men and said, "Ed and Shadow Walker will stay with the herd. The rest of us will take the wagon with the tools, to build branding pens. When the wagon is unloaded, Sara Mae will drive it back here, and we will return to the herd at night. I won't leave only two people with this herd at night, where panthers and wolves could scatter them to kingdom come."

By the second day the branding pen was complete and would hold up to forty head of cows. They returned each night to the herd, and Sara Mae set up her wagon next to one of the small lakes, making sure there was always hot coffee and food in the mornings. She also provided a sack of biscuits and leftover meat, which the men would take for dinner.

It was more than a week before they had rounded up, branded and moved over a hundred and seventy cows into the slow moving herd; the rest had scattered from the pine forest into thicker brush. Ed recognized the stretch of knee high grassland they had camped in last year. Looking out past the open land and seeing the edge of woods where he had gone turkey hunting, he felt his breath shorten and his heart beat wildly. Heading back to the herd more than two miles back, he rode hard until he could see his father. Pulling up short before he reached him, Ed walked his horse slowly until he rode next to his father. Calming himself as much as he could, he announced that he had found a good spot for the cows to feed for a couple of days, and that they could make it there before dark. Jessie saw the excitement in his sons face and knew that whatever Ed's reason for wanting to come on this trip, this was part of it.

Riding back to the wagon, Ed told Sara Mae to follow him; he knew where she needed to set up camp. She kept watching Ed ride out a ways and then ride back to the wagon. Shaking her head, she kept Dolly and Preacher at a steady pace until she recognized the spot where she had set up the wagon the previous year, and she remembered Ed's strange ways when he had come back from turkey hunting. Lawd, Lawd, she wondered, what in the world was going on with that boy?

It was still an hour before daylight when Ed saddled his horse and walked him to the wagon where Sara Mae had hot coffee waiting.

"I been expecting you," Sara Mae said, not looking up as she poured him a cup of coffee. "While that's cooling enough to drink, I'll fix you some food to carry with you." Opening the shot bag for the shotgun, Sara Mae placed the cloth sack with two biscuits and smoked pork in it and closed the bag. Looking up at Ed, she said, "I still haven't tasted those wood ducks you was going to bring me."

"Yes ma'am, I'll try again," he said as he rode off still leaving her puzzled. Ed didn't wait for daylight; he felt his whole being anticipating what he hoped to find at the spring. Unsaddling and hobbling his horse, he started into the woods. The trail was familiar now and he made himself slow down to keep from becoming lost and losing time. Day was breaking when he saw the light reflect off the crystal clear water of the spring. Reaching the spring, Ed knelt down on both knees and scooped water into his closed hands. Bringing them to his mouth, he sipped the cool water to wet his dry throat.

Looking at his reflection in the spring water, he saw the image of himself lying under the horse, trapped and in pain. The image was so vivid; he could even feel the rough moist tongue as it moved the bandage away from the still bleeding wound. He smelled the wildness of his breath, and he opened his eyes to stare into the face of the huge panther as he licked the wound closed and stopped the bleeding. He watched through what seemed to be a hazy fog as the big cat stood and moved away, when he heard the riders coming to take him home.

Ed heard the soft sound of lapping water on the other side of the spring, and even before he looked up, he knew the big cat was there. He cupped another handful of water and drank it before leaning back on his knees. The panther was watching him. The hooded eyes hypnotized Ed as the big cat leaned forward between huge muscular shoulders and drank.

"Why me?" Ed asked silently, staring into the panther's eyes. The big cat turned and began walking into the forest of red gum trees. He had gone no more than twenty feet when he stopped and looked back at Ed, slowly moving his tail back and forth and waiting. Ed slowly came to his feet, and leaving everything where it was, he started around the spring to follow the panther. He followed the big cat at a fast pace for more than two miles. They were trotting through thick pine and red gum trees, when the panther stopped and looked back at him. Walking to where the cat stood, he stopped and stared in awe as he stood on the rim of the biggest hole in the ground he had ever seen. Ed had seen sink holes where the earth had fallen in, leaving deep holes in the ground. Most of them looked like bottomless pits.

Ed felt as if he were looking at a different world as he measured the rim of the hole. It was about a quarter of a mile across and looked to be at least sixty feet deep. Thick brush grew around small scrub oak and gum trees, growing out of the jagged walls and turning upwards, trying to find sun. Looking across the bottom, he saw several, huge magnolia trees in full bloom and myrtle bushes, full of pink flowers. A large water oak leaned toward them, its great branches pushing against the wall. He watched as squirrels sat on branches, chattering back and forth at one another, announcing his arrival. Blue scrub jays and red cardinals sang their unique songs as they fluttered from tree to tree, and a mocking bird practiced various tunes from its collection of sounds.

Ed followed the panther as he started down an invisible path. Rabbits scurried across the path no more than a foot in front of the cat, without a second thought. The panther worked his way back and forth, in a zigzag until they reached the bottom.

Following the big cat's gaze across the bottom, he saw the spring bubbling clear cold water and creating a small pool. The panther moved to the pool, lowered his head and drank. Ed stood looking around the giant hole and felt as if the world had shrunk. Why has he brought me here, he thought again as he watched the big cat turn away from the spring. Ed followed until they came to the large water oak, leaning away from the ragged wall and watched the cat disappear among its limbs. Ed waited until he saw the head reappear between the branches and started making his way through the thick limbs. Pulling back one of the smaller limbs, Ed froze when he saw the huge cat standing in the mouth of a cave, which was big enough to walk into, standing up.

Stepping through the cave opening and turning around, he saw that the opening was completely invisible from beyond the tree. Enough sunlight filtered through the branches into the mouth of the cave, allowing Ed's eyes to adjust to the dim surroundings. He followed the dark shape as the big cat took him further into the cave, which then opened into a huge cavern, a hundred feet in diameter and at least forty feet to the dome ceiling. Ed felt surely that he was in another world, a world he kept trying to understand. He still wondered why he was brought here.

Looking around the cavern he saw the several cave openings of different sizes: some had only a large enough opening to crawl through, others you could bend over to enter, still others were big enough to walk through standing. The big cat stood and watched as Ed took in the surroundings and then followed him to an opening, which Ed stepped through. It was only a moment when Ed stepped back out, his face ashen, staring at the big cat. The panther walked forward and pushed against Ed's leg, making him step backwards into the cave's mouth. Slowly, his eyes followed the outline of the cave. Ed took in the eerie sight of human bones, lying on a ledge, protruding from the earth wall. On the earth floor next to the shelf, he saw the perfectly shaped bones of an animal lying on its side. Looking at the bones more closely, he knew it was the skeleton of a large panther. He didn't know how he knew, but he knew. Walking over to the skeleton on the ledge, he saw: an ancient knife, made with a flint blade attached to a bone handle, and a spear, made of the same type of blade with only small pieces of fur and hide left, wrapped around the deteriorating wooden shaft.

Stepping back out into the cavern, he walked eight to ten feet further along the wall until he came to another entrance high enough to walk through and stepped inside. It did not surprise him this time as he looked at the skeleton lying on the ledge, but it did surprise him when he saw the same animal skeleton, lying on the floor next to the ledge. Looking further into the cave he saw another ledge protruding from the wall. It was too dark to see anything but the outline of the ledge, but he knew what he would find there. Ed spent more than an hour, checking the different caves and finding the same in each cave. Some caves went much deeper than he could see in the dim light, but he knew that they served the same purpose.

Following the big cat, Ed worked his way back through the oak limbs, careful not to break or disturb the branches that hid the entrance to the ancient cave opening. Standing still as his eyes adjusted to the light, he looked up through the oak branches and saw the osprey. Puzzled but not surprised, he glanced around and saw four does drinking from the spring and eating the tender grass while keeping an eye on their young. The spotted fawns were running and playing, getting used to their new legs, and they stopped to watch a mother raccoon lead her little ones to the berries hanging from the blueberry bushes.

His mind suddenly began to understand what he was seeing; he looked up in the trees full of bird nests and saw the small new born squirrels sitting motionless, blending into the moss or knots on a limb. As he followed the big cat to the spring, the does only gave a quick glance at them and went back to their feeding. Squatting next to the cool spring water, Ed scooped up several hands full of water and splashed his face. Standing and taking one more look around, he now understood that this was not just a place of death as he had thought while in the caves, but a haven where all animals could come to give birth in safety. He also knew that he had just been made the caretaker of a sacred place of life on this earth. Then the big cat led them up and out of the giant hole. Ed knew what he must do.

As Ed rode toward the wagon sitting under the large oak shade, he saw his father and Red Sun riding toward him. Pulling up as they got close, he heard his father ask him where he had been, they were about ready to come looking for him. Not looking at his pa, he kept riding toward the wagon.

"I just got turned around; I'm ok now," he said over his shoulder as he rode on by, leaving Jessie and Red Sun looking at each other in utter confusion. Not understanding what had happened, but seeing him safe, they turned their horses and headed back to the herd.

Jessie saw Silent Stalker as he came out of the tree line a quarter mile away and head toward him. Jessie whirled the whip over his head and cracked it twice, and saw Red Sun and Justin steer their horses in his direction. They rode up next to Jessie just as Silent Stalker slowed to a halt in front of them.

"The water of the Withlacoochee River is still barely low enough to cross, but with the rains it will be full in another two days."

"How far away from the river are we now?" Jessie asked.

"We can be close by dark if we keep the herd moving," said Silent Stalker.

"Alright," said Jessie, watching the dark clouds forming no more than two miles away, "let's keep them moving and we will take them across the river in the morning, and then we can let them feed slowly again, between there and the Hillsborough River for the next two weeks before we reach the stock yards in Tampa."

All of the riders were on alert as they tended the herd. Watching the sky turning black and moving fast their way, they saw the lightning inside the huge black clouds and heard the rumble of thunder.

Ed rode up alongside Jessie, fear showing in his face and said, "Pa, those clouds look real bad, what are we going to do?"

"I don't know yet son." He uncoiled his whip and cracked it twice over his head and watched Justin and Red Sun start towards them on a run, pulling up as they reached him and Ed.

Looking at Justin and Red Sun he said, "This storm coming at us is going to spook the cattle all over hell and back." Justin was listening to the low moaning of the nervous cows as they started milling about bumping into each other, wanting to get away from what was coming.

"You are right," Justin said, "I have seen this happen before on the ranch I worked and when they panicked they tore down fences and it took us weeks to round up cows and mend fences."

"Does anyone have any suggestions before we have to get out of their way?" Jessie asked. "Because I would say we have no more than ten minutes before they panic and I don't want anyone close when they do."

Red Sun spoke up saying, "The river is not that far away and if we panic them ourselves, they may run themselves out and the river will slow them down."

"I think that might work," Justin spoke up, "but even that will be dangerous."

"I agree," said Jessie. "Justin, you and Red Sun spread the word to the others and tell them not to take any chances; if the herd gets out of hand, get out of the way and let them go. Red Sun, when everyone is ready crack your whip three times, and use your whips and your guns, I want to panic them more than the storm does. Ed, you go back and tell Sara Mae to stay where she's at; we will be back for her. If she needs you, stay with her."

"Ok Pa," Ed answered as he turned his horse, kicking him in the ribs and starting on a run back to the wagon.

Jessie saw the riders stretched out along the herd, when he heard Red Sun's whip crack three times. In seconds, the herd was stampeding toward the river as the crack of whips and pistol fire overrode their fear of thunder. The black clouds unrolled, blanketing the sky and drenching them with rain that stung their faces as they rode hard, keeping the herd bunched together. As the lightning flashed, lighting up over a thousand set of horns with blue fire, they panicked even more. The riders saw the horns light up, but there was nothing for them to do with the fear they all felt. They had to keep pushing the cattle forward or lose them.

Warrior Spirit rode at the head of the panicked herd, Big Cypress and Justin riding close behind, one on each side, keeping them headed in the right direction, when Big Cypress' horse plunged into the river almost throwing him off. Keeping his balance, he kept cracking his whip, driving the cattle head first into the water, while his horse fought the current to carry him across to the other side. Coming up the sloping bank on the far side, he looked back at the struggling cows, which were fighting the current as they made their way out of the water, still panicked and being pushed by the other cows, plunging in the river behind them. He saw Warrior Spirit and Justin riding back and forth in front of the tired cattle, cracking their whip and turning them in a circle, as they slowed to a walk and moved out of the way.

Big Cypress stayed close to the river, cracking his whip and keeping the cows moving, as Red Sun on one side of the herd and Shadow Walker on the other reached the river, swimming across with the cattle, still cracking their whips. As Red Sun and Shadow Walker rode past, Big Cypress waited for Spirit Snake and Silent Stalker to reach the river. He could hear the yelling of Spirit Snake even above the gun fire and cracking whips, and he knew there was no fear in him. Big Cypress watched for Jessie and Ed, who had pushed his big roan harder than he ever had, to catch up with his father and the stampeding herd of wild cattle. Sara Mae said she didn't need any help, and now he was keeping up with the herd. He and Jessie plunged their horses into the river, fighting to stay in their saddles as they pushed the last of the panicked cows, fighting their way through the current to the other bank.

Jessie watched a large paddle boat about to plunge head long into him and the cows, as the current carried some of the weaker ones toward the boat, and he saw some disappear under it. As the boat slowed to a stop, he and Ed rode up the bank on the other side. Jessie stopped next to Big Cypress and watched as some of the cows came out from under the boat and fought their way to shore. Others had drowned and were floating past the boat. Turning they started toward the herd, where the others were keeping them bunched up as they walked off their fear. The blue fire was gone now and they began to graze as the squall spent itself out futher east.

Capt. Russ Gober stood at the helm of his paddle wheel steamer as he made his way down the Withlacoochee River. He had been up and down this river dozens of times, but today he kept a nervous eye everywhere on the river, not wanting to run over a floating branch or one of the many sand bars. This was the most important trip he would ever make, taking the governor and friends on a hunting trip. As the governor was touring the state, he had made arrangements with Major Johnson at Fort Dade for a hunting trip down the river, where they had been shooting everything that moved in the river or on land. At times it sounded like a war going on when they passed a group of thirty or forty wild hogs left here by the Spanish, or when they had flushed a flock of turkeys roosting in the cypress trees that grew along the banks. The governor was red with excitement as he shot gator after gator, watching them thrash about in their death roll, or when he knocked a turtle off a log while sunning itself.

Captain Gober kept a close watch on the huge thunder heads building to the west, while he tried to decide if he should turn back toward the fort. At this point, he knew that they were going to get caught by the summer squall that was building, no matter what decision he made. Calling his first mate up to the helm he said, "Get the other crew together and prepare to tie off to shore when that storm gets close, it's too late to turn back now and from the looks of those clouds it's bringing heavy wind and rain with it. I am going to try to get us to a place where the bank is clear of tree roots; I don't want my boat pounding against trees and roots."

"Yes Sir Captain," answered the first mate as he turned and took the steps down two at a time, calling his crew to get ready to secure the boat.

Looking out of the back of the boat, the knot started building in the captain's stomach as he saw the lightning, flashing inside the thunder heads. He watched them come together, forming one huge black roll, shutting out the sun as it covered the sky. Everyone was so busy killing anything that moved; they didn't see what was coming at them faster than the paddle boat could travel. Looking down on the deck below the helm, Captain Gober yelled down until he got the major's attention and pointed behind them.

Turning, the major saw the black cloud no more than a mile away. Fear was his first feeling as he realized the danger that the governor and his group were facing. He saw the crew gathering lines, preparing the boat to ride out the storm.

"Sergeant!" he yelled.

The sergeant, hearing the urgency in the major's voice, hurried across the deck. "Yes Sir?"

"Sergeant, take our men and help the crew with any help they need and Sergeant, hurry!"

He walked quickly to where the governor and his guests were still firing shotguns at a flock of crows so large you could not see through them and watching them fall by the dozen, unaware of the coming storm. He waited until they had finished firing the guns they were shooting and turned to the soldier attending them for another loaded gun.

Speaking to the soldiers, he said, "Take the guns and ammo below deck, now!"

Turning to the governor and his guests and trying to keep his voice calm, he said, "Governor, there is a bad summer squall headed our way. You and the others should go below until it blows over and Governor, prepare yourself for a rough ride until this blows past."

"Are we in danger?" one of the guests asked nervously.

"No the boat will be fine, but it could get quite rough before it's over."

The major watched the men scramble over each other as they looked behind them at what was coming fast, now no more than a half a mile away. He felt the first wind picking up ahead of the black blanket, which was now turning the sky dark gray. He turned to the governor, whose face was flushed with excitement from the killing.

"Sir, you need to go below for your own safety!" The knot was growing bigger in his stomach as he felt the sprinkle of rain and knew he had only minutes.

"I will not go below and shake like a coward like those wimps are doing already. You forget Major, I too fought in the war and I didn't run then and I'm not running now. Get me one of those slickers; I'm riding this out with the men!" Saying that, he turned and began helping one of the crew ready the lines, as the captain fought the wind already pushing the stern of the boat out into the middle of the river.

Captain Gober pulled back on the throttle, giving the signal to the engineer below to add steam to the paddle wheel, as he turned the rudder to bring the boat back in control before the current of the river turned him sideways. The captain knew if he lost control now, they could wind up on one of the fallen logs, ripping a hole in the bottom and if that happened, he knew he was going to lose people. Fighting the wind and current, he got the boat headed for a clear spot on the bank with enough trees to secure the boat even if he had to run her aground.

The sky came alive with spider webs of lightning, and then he saw with frightening clarity, over a thousand head of long horn cattle, their horns lit up with blue fire, heading for the river in a panic. The cattle were driven by what looked like demons on horseback, firing pistols, cracking whips over their heads and driving them into the water, where his boat was going to plow headlong into them in the middle of the river. Captain Gober pulled back and forth on the throttle three times, sending the emergency signal to the engineer below, and then yelled as loudly as possible down the brass tube.

"Reverse the engines to full throttle, now!" He turned the rudder toward the river bank. The boat was no more than fifty feet from the moving mass of cattle when he saw several cows slam into the side of the boat as they struggled to stay afloat. Then he felt bumping as the momentum of the boat pushed its way over several cows. The boat come to a halt and then slowly began to move backward, turning toward the bank as he held the wheel steady. As they got closer to the banks, soldiers and crew jumped from the boat in knee deep water, wading as fast as they could, to get to the bank as the lightning flashed all around them. Carrying lines with them as the captain tried to keep control, they wrapped the lines around trees as the soldiers and crew on board began pulling on the lines, bringing the boat closer to the river bank.

The major stood next to the governor on the front deck. Gov. Harrison Reed was confused at the sound of gun fire in the distance, mixed with the sound of thunder as lightning continued to flash above them now, with sheets of rain soaking all of them.

"Major!" the governor yelled, "what is that sound?" He kept hearing gun fire, when suddenly his mouth dropped open and his eyes widened as he saw the biggest Indian he had ever seen. The Indian's horse plunged into the river almost losing its balance. He kept popping his whip over his head as some of the cows behind him broke away and swam toward the boat. The governer felt the cows slamming into the boat and watched them finding their way around and reaching the shore. He stared as other cows disappeared under the boat while he stood frozen in place. Still more riders and cattle, their long horns shimmering with blue fire, plunged into the river and fought their way to the other shore.

The governor watched a young man and another man who had to be the father both with rain soaked red hair, crack their whips like rifle fire over their heads and push the last cows into the river, no more than forty feet away. The governor saw the confusion and disbelief in Jessie's face as he saw the boat and the two men watching the whole thing.

As the riders circled the herd to make sure they weren't going to panic again, they made their way to where Jessie sat on his horse watching, still trying to absorb what had just happened and wondering what in the world that boat was doing there. He thought he recognized the major from Fort Dade, but that didn't seem possible. Jessie waited until everyone had gathered around him, looking as confused as he was.

"Yee yeeeeiiii!"

Turning, they saw Spirit Snake racing the little Marsh Tackie from around the herd, pulling to a halt in front of the confused men, grinning and yelling, "There will never be anything that will ever be as exciting as that! I thought I might die!"

"I thought I was going to die for sure!" Ed said, as he rode his horse over next to Spirit Snake. "I don't ever want to do that again."

"We still have things to do," Jessie said. "I will take Big Cypress and Ed with me and bring Sara Mae with the wagon and cross the river before it gets too high; the rest of you keep your eye on the herd. Silent Stalker, I need you to scout the river and see if there is a shallower place to cross, this may be too deep already to cross here."

The boat was secured now, and Captain Gober came down from the helm and joined the major and governor out of the rain, under the shelter of the upper deck. The governor's guests were coming up from below, still shaken from their frightful ordeal. The captain and the major followed the governor out into the drizzling rain to the front deck as they saw Jessie and the others wading their horses back into the river, testing the depth as they crossed.

Turning to the captain and the major, the governor asked, "Do either of you know what is going on here or who these men are?"

"I've never seen them before," the captain spoke up, still trying to calm himself.

"The man up front is Jessie Tucker," said the major. "The young man is his son; they own the Double T Ranch, and the Indian is one of several who works and lives there." The major walked across the gang plank to shore as the riders were leaving the water, waving his arms at the men. He saw them turn and ride toward him and the governor who had joined him. Walking over to where Jessie and the others sat their horses, the major spoke to Jessie.

"I never expected to see you here, you scared us all half to death," he chuckled.

Stepping down from his horse, Jessie held out his hand to the major, "Sorry Major, I don't think you could have been more afraid than the rest of us."

"Mr. Tucker, I want you to meet the governor of Florida."

The Governor stood rooted in place staring at Big Cypress, sitting his horse next to Ed, not quite beliving what he was looking at, when he heard the major calling his name.

Governor Reed, taking his eyes off the two men sitting their horses and staring back at him, stepped forward to grasp Jessie's hand and said, "That was the damnedest sight I have ever seen; I would like to know more about you and your men."

"I would like to talk more with you and the major, but we have to go and bring our wagon and cook and try to cross this river before it gets too high, if it's not already."

"I understand," the governor said, "how far away are you?"

"An hour and a half there and two hours back," Jessie answered. "It will be close to dark by then," Jessie stated, then quickly mounted and rode off at a gallop.

"I didn't think Indians were allowed to live in Florida," the governor stated, still amazed at what he was seeing as he watched the riders disappear in the distance. The major began to explain what he had learned from John Campbell after they had all met at the fort. After the Major finished, the Governor said, "That is one hell of a story, and you gave permission for all of this?"

"Yes sir," the Major answered. "We needed meat and lumber and these men are the only ones left who are capable. We had no building materials for a growing community, and the only beef we were getting was a few scrawny scrub cows, that had been run all the way to the fort by some outlaws. These are Creek Indians; they have nothing to do with our war with the Seminoles."

"I want to talk more with these men. This country is going to need men like you are talking about, before the carpetbaggers get here and take it all. Florida is still a wild country and it's going to take tough men like this Jessie Tucker, and I am not worried about a few Indians. You give what protection you can, although I am not sure they are the ones who will need protection," the governor stated.

"Sir," the major said, "we need to leave now so we can get back to the fort before dark. It is dangerous for the captain to navigate the river at night."

"OK Major," the governor said as he headed back to the boat, "but I want to know more about these people."

"Yes Sir," the major answered, "the next time you are in this area, I will take you to their ranch."

Silent Stalker had found a more shallow area not much further down river to cross and rode out to meet Jessie and the others. After crossing the river, Sara Mae drove the wagon and stopped beneath a large water oak not far from the river bank.

Calling Ed over, she said, "I have a kettle of stew I made earlier, but I am going to need some dry fire wood if you can find some, to heat it up."

"Yes Ma'am," Ed said, "I'll find you some; I'm starving."

There was only a reminiscence of light left in the western sky as the men sat around the fire, drying out and eating warm stew under the large canvas shelter they had stretched between the gum trees. They were all releasing their tension by talking and laughing about how frightened they all were, when a thousand set of horns lit up with blue fire.

The night was absorbing the last light of the day when Jessie rode to take the first watch. The herd was still feeding on the lush grass when Ed rode up along side of him.

"Aren't you supposed to be on the next watch?" Jessie asked his son.

"I wanted to talk to you about something Pa, before we get to Tampa."

"I have been waiting since we left home," Jessie answered, seeing the seriousness in his face. "How is your arm?"

"Its fine Pa," he said, lifting his arm up and down without wincing, "but that's not what I want to talk to you about."

"I didn't think so; go ahead, I'm listening."

"Well Pa, I been thinking. If we don't buy the land we are living on, one day someone else will buy it and then what? What if they tell us to move?" Jessie just kept quiet and listened as Ed went on. "One day the cows will all be gone. Justin said we will need to raise our own cattle like they do on the ranches he worked on. He said there are better cows to raise than these scrub cows, which take too much time to round up out of the palmettos and scrub oaks. What do you think Pa?"

"I think you are right," Jessie answered. "Your ma and I have talked about the same thing, and unless there is another war where they can take our land, we intend to stay right here. There are too many people who depend on that land to lose it to someone else. We will take the money from the sale of the cattle and go to the land surveys office and see just how much land we can buy." Watching Ed ride back to camp, Jessie wondered what that was really all about. He would wait and see.

Thirty-Five

It had been more than two weeks since the storm when they reached the Hillsborough River and turned west toward Tampa and the cattle pens. Reaching the river, Jessie called the men together around the fire as they ate their supper that Sara Mae had fixed for them.

"We are only a couple of days from reaching the cattle yard and getting rid of these bunch of stinking cows and going home!" Jessie said. Looking at Red Sun and the other Indians, he continued, "If you all need anything from town, Sara Mae can bring it back for you, and if you tell Ed, he can write it down for you and give it to her."

Jessie and Ed rode up to the small office at the end of the holding pens and dismounted. Walking up the steps, he looked into the open door of the office where Tom Marshal was looking over some ledger books. Looking up when he heard footsteps and seeing Jessie and Ed, he stood up and coming around the desk to meet them, he smiled and said, "I hope you brought me some more fat cows."

"We have over a thousand head." Ed answered proudly, and they are all fat as ticks on a hound," he grinned. "How much are you paying this year?" he asked before Tom could say anything.

"Top money this year for prime beef on the hoof is sixteen dollars a head," Tom answered Ed and seeing the grin spread across his face, offered them a chair. "Sit and have a drink," Tom offered.

"We have to get back to the herd," Jessie said. "We should have the cows here before noon tomorrow, and then I'll have that drink."

"Me too," Ed spoke, up looking at his pa.

Grinning, Jessie headed for the door, saying, "I will see you by noon tomorrow."

"We'll be waiting," Tom said with a wave.

Tom heard the crack of the whips and looked out his door. Seeing the herd less than a half mile away, hollered to his two men, "Get the gates open and help turn those cows into the pens." Tom watched in awe as the Indians with their whips and cow dogs, moved the cattle into the pens with the ease of any cattlemen he had ever seen. One day, when he knew Jessie better, he would ask him if he would tell him the story of the Indians and the scar across his forehead, but he knew it wasn't the time now.

When the gates were closed behind the milling cows, Jessie gathered everyone together. Sitting his horse, he said, "I will ride back to camp when I have settled business with the buyer. Ed will come with me." Looking at Justin, he asked, "Do you have things to do in town? If you do, we will be fine without you now, so take your time if you do."

Justin saw Ed looking at him with a big knowing grin on his face. Smiling back at Ed, he said, "I have a couple of things to do before heading back." Then speaking to Ed, he said, "Why don't you join me for a while before you head back to camp?"

"OK," Ed grinned, "I can't wait to eat some more fish and drink some..." Ed stopped in mid-sentence, smiling. "Well, I'll meet you there anyway as soon as Pa and me are through, you don't care do you Pa?"

"No," Jessie answered. "You're man enough now to do as you want. Are you coming back to camp tonight? Sara Mae needs to go to town, and you and I have business to do."

"I'll be back tonight," Ed answered. Turning the big roan Ed started towards the holding pens to help count the cows.

Jessie and Tom were talking about raising cattle in the future, when Ed came in with the two men after counting the penned cattle. "We counted 1,127 cows," Ed said to his pa and Tom with a big grin on his face.

"Great," said Tom as he took out his paper and pencil and began his figures. After he had finished, he handed the paper to Ed and watched the grin come over his face as he finished checking the figures and handed the paper back to Tom.

"Pa, it's over eighteen thousand dollars!" Ed said in disbelief. They both waited in shock as Tom brought the gold from his back room and counted the bags while he placed them on his desk.

Their saddle bags were heavy as they placed them behind their saddles and turned to shake Tom's hand.

"I will be looking forward to seeing you next year," Tom said, watching them mount their horses.

"Same here," Jessie said, as he and Ed started for the camp where Sara Mae had set up in the same place as last year.

It was early morning as Sara Mae drove the wagon down the main street of Tampa. Jessie and Ed rode their horses, one on each side, until they reached the street that the land surveyor office was on.

Turning to Sara Mae, Jessie said, "You go on and see your friends and take care of your shopping with the lists you have from Belle, Red Sun and the others from the village. You should have enough money for everything, and I know you gave away your money last time to the preacher, to share with everyone. This time you give that twenty dollar gold piece to the preacher for me and Ed."

"Yas sir Mr. Tucker, it sure will be appreciated. God bless both of you," she smiled as she flicked the reins across the horses' rumps.

As Ed followed Jessie through the door of the surveyor's office, a big heavy set man stood up from a small desk and walked over to the counter next to where Jessie and Ed set their saddle bags on the floor.

The big man asked, "What can I do for you fellers today?"

"I want to buy some land," Jessie said.

"Well you came to the right place. You've homesteaded you a little place have you?" the big man chuckled. "Well it's good you can buy you a piece of land, because one day all this land will be bought up by them carpet baggers from up north. Now the only thing is you have to buy 40 acres or I can't sell it to you. Do you have that much money? It can't be that confederate stuff, it's worthless now."

"We have gold. Now can we see a surveyors map?" Jessie asked.

"Sure," the big man said. Turning and walking back to his desk, he pulled a large folded map from a drawer, and bringing it to the counter, he unfolded it, turning it toward the two men. "You want to be real careful when picking out your spot. 40 acres is hard to find on this map and if you don't get it right, somebody else may come along and buy it."

Jessie and Ed stood slowly looking over the map. Finding the Withlacoochee River, Ed ran his finger along the line on the map until he came to the Little Withlacoochee, and moving his finger north, he stopped when his finger came to a large lake.

Looking at his pa, he said, "This is our valley here."

Looking where Ed was pointing, the big man chuckled, saying, "Fellers, that's a lot more land than 40 acres. Why that lake, looking at the size of it, must be over 200 acres."

Jessie ignored the statement and asked, "What are these lines across the map?"

"Well, those are tracts. The smaller lines are 2400 acre tracts, and the larger lines are 4800 acres. Looks like the lake you're looking at is almost in the center of a 2400 acre tract. That tract stops at the Little Withlacoochee River."

"What about the tracts joining it to the west?" Ed asked.

"That would be a 4800 acre section," the man said, looking again at Jessie and Ed. "If you are serious, it is cheaper if you buy the whole section, but, that takes a lot of money, and I have to say I haven't seen that kind of money since before the war."

"Well you're going to see it again," Jessie said, looking the big man in the eyes. "You said it was cheaper if I bought the whole section; how much will it cost?"

"Well in that part of the state, there's nothing going on so I can sell you that for, let's see." Getting a pencil and a piece of paper, he started writing down figures. "Mister: that would cost you 60 cents an acre, $2880.00. Looking up, he asked, "Seriously, you got that kind of money?"

"I do," Jessie answered, "and I want the two sections next to that one."

"Are you boys fooling with me?" the big man said in astonishment, taking a step backward. Ed was still studying the map as Jessie reached down and lifted the heavy saddle bag. Opening one flap, he started placing bags of gold coins on the counter.

Looking in one of the bags, the big man looked up at Jessie with renewed interest. "The only place you can get gold like that is from selling cows; you must have had a pretty big herd to get that kind of money. Well you can't go wrong buying land and it's safer than a bank these days."

"Pa," Ed spoke quietly, "there's one more piece of land I want to buy.

Jessie looked puzzled by the piece of paper Ed was holding next to the surveyor's map. Looking at the lines on the piece of paper Ed had drawn next to the surveyors map, Jessie slowly began to recognize the piece of land that Ed had gone hunting on both times they had stopped to let the cows graze. The place always left him confused when he came back, acting strange for days.

"How much of it do you want?" Jessie asked

"This whole 4800 acre section that this valley is in," he pointed to the map.

"Add that to the sale," Jessie said, asking no more questions and seeing relief in Ed's face. After a second thought, he told the surveyor to put that in Ed's name.

"Sure," the big man said, "but as you can see the back part of that section is part of a swamp that is several miles big."

"That's fine," Ed said.

After adding the figures on a piece of paper, the big man looked up. "That's going to cost you $11,520.00." He watched in amazement as Jessie took out 11 bags from his and Ed's saddle bags. Pushing eleven bags toward the surveyor, he opened the twelfth bag, and dumping it on the counter, he counted out $520.00 in more gold coins.

Pushing them across the counter, Jessie asked, "When can we pick up the deeds?"

"I can have them later this evening by about five o'clock," the big man said, putting the bags of gold coins in a safe next to his desk.

"We'll be back then," Jessie said, heading for the door with Ed following right behind him, wearing a big grin on his face.

Outside, Ed said with that grin still on his face, "Pa, if we don't have anything else to do, I know where we can find Justin and get some good food. I promise you will like it."

"That sounds good to me," Jessie answered, stepping his foot in the stirrup and swinging up into the saddle. "Lead the way," he said, looking at Ed's grinning face.

It had been more than a week since Ed had been back from the cattle drive, and at least once a day, he pulled the deed from the metal box where his ma kept her important papers and looked at it once more. Most of the garden had been picked and put away for the winter. The men were enjoying some time with their families and hunting for meat and hides for the coming cold weather.

As Ed and Spirit Snake rode out around the lake, their saddle bags had enough food for several days.

Spirit Snake, seeing the direction they were headed in asked once again, "Why won't you tell me where we are going and why?"

"It's not something I can describe to you, but you will be glad you came, I promise you," Ed replied.

By late evening the second day, Ed led Spirit Snake down into the valley to the edge of the pine and red gum forest where he had entered the trail to the spring. "This is where we will camp for the night," Ed said, dismounting his horse and starting to remove the saddle.

Ed sat with Spirit Snake, sipping hot coffee, letting the sun rise up the tree line a little more before he led Spirit Snake into the forest. When he reached the spring, Ed was a bit disappointed that he had not seen the panther. He let the horses drink from the spring, as he knelt down on his knees and drank his fill. Spirit Snake did the same. The sun was well up when Ed came to the edge of the rim and stopped and dismounted. Spirit Snake slid from his horse and led him over to Ed. The first thing Spirit Snake felt was fear and awe as he stood looking down into the giant hole in the earth. Spirit Snake had never felt fear, even in the great storm he had not felt fear, but this was something that only the spirits would create.

Looking at Ed he asked, "How did you find this place?"

"I didn't," Ed answered, "I was brought to this place. I will explain to you later." Tying his horse's bridle to a low hanging branch, he told Spirit Snake to do the same.

"Where are we going? There are spirits here; I can feel them," Spirit Snake exclaimed, as Ed led him downward, explaining what he knew to Spirit Snake until they reached the bottom. Then he led Spirit Snake to the small spring. Ed saw the four does, watching their fawns running and playing. Their spots were almost invisible now, and he knew they would be leaving the safety of this haven, to the uncertainty of a world of predators. Ed reached down, tore loose a handful of tender grass and walked to where the does stood watching him. He slowly knelt in front of the does and held his hand out, waiting until one after the other reached forward and took grass from his hand. Ed looked up as Spirit Snake knelt down next to him, extending his handful of grass toward the does and waited until they took the grass from his hand. His spirit soared! He was no longer afraid.

Spirit Snake followed Ed as they worked their way through the branches of the large oak that hid the entry to the cave. Ed pulled the last branch covering the entry and froze in shock! Staring him in the face no more than two feet away, were the ageless eyes of Two Worlds as he sat cross legged with the huge panther lying next to him. Ed looked back to see Spirit Snake frozen in place as he tried to take in what he was seeing.

Two Worlds rose and with the panther beside him, turned and walked deeper into the cave. Carefully, Ed and Spirit Snake crawled through the limbs and hurried to follow the old man into the huge cavern. Two Worlds moved to the edge of the cavern wall and lifted a green limb wrapped tightly with dried moss and lit it. Keeping the lit torch ahead of him, Two Worlds along with the panther, led them into the first of several caves. Ed and Spirit Snake followed and listened as the old medicine man explained what they were seeing.

"These are the remains of the leaders who helped the people become a great nation. We would become known as the Creeks, so named by the white people because of the many creeks that ran through our land. There are no more nations left since the white man killed our people and took our land. Only a few scattered bands remain, fighting to survive and save our people from becoming just a memory."

Two Worlds led them back to the center of the cavern, and sitting down with his legs crossed, he motioned Ed and Spirit Snake to sit in front of him. They sat cross legged and watched the panther lay down next to the old man's side, his eyes never leaving theirs.

Ed's heart began to beat faster as he looked at Two Worlds and said with a new awareness, "You sent the panther to me. I thought it was just the panther and me. You sent him to protect me when I was lying under my horse, shot and bleeding. I would have died that day if he had not stopped the bleeding."

"The spirit of the panther has always been part of us. He is our path to the animal world." Ed watched in fascination as the old man laid his ancient hand on the back of the huge panther's head and slowly patted him. "Our time is limited on this earth. Soon we will be joining our ancestors in the spirit world. The world as we know it is changing now as the blood of our people mixes with the blood of the white man. The future of our people is in the hands of the two of you."

Two Worlds slipped the knife from its sheath and looked first at Spirit Snake. "Give me your hand." As the ancient hand reached out and took hold of his wrist, the knife sliced across the open palm bringing blood. Turning to Ed who already had his arm held out, he slid the knife across his hand as he held steady. Slipping the knife back into its sheath, he took Ed's hand and bringing it together with Spirit Snake's, he clasped them tightly. Ed could feel Spirit Snake's pulse as his blood flowed into his body and he listened to the words of the old man.

"From the two of you, our people will grow and become strong again long after I am gone. The ancestors will be watching and guiding you." Slowing releasing his grip on the two hands, he rose and walked toward the entry as the panther followed by his side.

Working their way back through the oak limbs, they looked for Two Worlds and the panther, but they had disappeared. They walked to the spring without saying a word and kneeling down, they slipped their hands under the cold water until the bleeding had stopped completely.

Standing up, Ed looked at Spirit Snake and said, "Are you ready brother?"

Nodding, Spirit Snake turned and began to lead the way up.

Thirty-Six

Ed and Spirit Snake sat across from one another as Ed added a few more small limbs to the fire. They were camped in a valley that contained several small lakes, which were connected by a creek that wandered by their camp. Although they had not spoken much since they left the caves two days before, each man felt the deeper bond that they now shared. More than blood brothers, they had become partners, destined to create a future together. Both young men were trying to find the meaning of what had happened and listened to the soft whispers of the water and the crackle of the fire. They each had that slow, hurry feeling of wanting to start their new life but not knowing what that was to be.

Suddenly Spirit Snake stood up, flashing a grin across his face and looked at Ed with the excitement of someone who had just found his way home.

"Tomorrow when we arrive home, I am going to make Little Moon my wife!" he announced. Spirit Snake saw the relief in Ed's whole body as he stood and exclaimed.

"That's it! It is time we make our own family."

Ed smiled as he followed Spirit Snake, dancing around the fire and chanting loudly to the ancestors twinkling in the sky. It was late into the night before either one could settle down enough to sleep.

The sun had started it's decent in the west, when Spirit Snake and Ed sat their horses and looked down into the valley. Hearing sounds of laughter drifting up from the lake, they watched as Little Moon and Little Otter sat together with their feet in the cool water. The twins watched the smaller children who were playing along the shore or swimming in the clear, sand bottom lake. Ed reached out his hand that was still sore from the cut toward Spirit Snake as Spirit Snake's hand reached out and grasped his.

Closing their fingers, their words came out in unison, "Brother!"

They started down into the valley, now knowing where their life was going.

The sisters stood, smiling anxiously as the two men approached them, and as Spirit Snake dismounted and walked toward Little Moon, Ed held his hand out toward Little Otter.

"Come ride with me."

She placed her foot in the empty stirrup and taking her hand, Ed lifted her up behind him. As she wrapped her arms around his chest and pulled herself snug against him, she felt his heart racing and wondered if something was wrong, as he had spoken very few words. Ed stayed close to the water's edge as he rode past his house and continued further around the lake to several large water oaks, growing seventy five feet from the shore. Ed helped Little Otter down and dismounting, he took her hand and walked her towards the oaks. Standing under one of the huge branches in the shade, he turned to Little Otter.

"I want to build me a house here; I think it would be cool in the summer and slow the winds down in the winter. What do you think?"

Looking down into her eyes, he waited for the answer to his deepest wishes.

"I think it is a beautiful place, but why are you asking me?"

Her heart was beginning to beat faster with the hope of what he was going to say next.

"I am a man now; I want a wife and children of my own." Taking both of her hands in his, he said, "I have loved you from the moment

I saw you standing in the barn soaking wet. Since then I have thought about you every day; most of the time I can hardly keep you off my mind long enough to do my work. I do not want to wait any longer. Will you be my wife?" She felt his grip tighten as he waited for an answer, and she waited for a moment to be sure that what she had just heard was real. Then letting out the breath she had been holding, she spoke.

"I dreamed of you when I was much younger. I did not see your face, but I knew you were somewhere waiting, and the first time I touched you, I knew I had found you. My heart has been waiting. I will be your wife." She looked deep into his eyes and smiled. He leaned down and touched her lips with his, and he knew that this moment was real too.

Little Moon watched Spirit Snake dismount and approach her as Little Otter started toward where Ed sat his horse. As he stopped in front of her, she knew something had changed about him; he had a quieter walk and a self-assurance she had not seen in him before. When he looked into her eyes, she knew what he was going to say, and her heart raced as she smiled in anticipation. Spirit Snake didn't realize how awkward this was going to be as he stood staring at that smile, which always made him feel strong and weak at the same time.

"I am going to speak to your father about you being my wife," he blurted out.

Still smiling, she said, "Don't you think you should talk to me first?"

Spirit Snake took a deep breath and in a much calmer voice he said, "Our ancestors have told me in a hundred ways over the years, even before I was old enough to think about having a wife, that one day you would be mine. Our ancestors have given me their sign, and now I know it is time to make you my wife... if you consider me to have earned the right as a brave and warrior to care for you and the children you have taken as your own."

"I do not know when the spirits of our ancestors decided I would be your wife, but I would have married you long before now if you had asked. I will try to be a strong wife for you and to raise the children you will give me also."

They were talking about Spirit Snake speaking with her father when Ed and Little Otter rode up and dismounted. As soon as Little Moon saw Little Otters face she rushed toward her, knowing that they too had spoken of marriage.

Belle watched Ed push his food around on his plate, taking a bite every now and then, and she wondered what could be wrong. She saw Jessie ignoring the whole thing and realized that he knew what was going on, but was waiting for Ed. She had seen Ed ride straight to the barn where his father was working. She was relieved he was home safe, but now she felt confused. Looking between Ed and Jessie, she wondered what happened out there on his trip with Spirit Snake. Finally, she could stand the mystery no longer, and she looked at Ed.

"Should I try to guess what you're holding back sitting there and about to bust, what you are wanting to tell me that you have apparently already told your father, or are you just waiting for your food to get cold before you eat."

"Ma," Ed hesitated for a moment, "I asked Little Otter to marry me and she said yes. I want to build us a cabin around the lake a ways and have my own family. I won't be far away." Not understanding when he saw the tears forming in her eyes, he said, "Are you upset, Ma?" Ed stood up when he saw his ma coming around the table and was even more confused when she hugged him.

Stepping back a step, keeping her hands on his strong arms she said, "Your father and I have been waiting for you to realize your own manhood for some time now. We have been waiting for this day. We all knew that someday you would marry Little Otter."

"I knew it!" Horace spoke up with a grin on his face.

"I knew it too! Does this mean she will be my sister now?" Jenny asked, with excitement in her small voice.

"When is this going to happen?" Belle asked.

"I don't know. I have to talk to Red Sun first and so does Spirit Snake."

"I should have known," Belle smiled

The next morning as Red Sun stepped through the opening of his lodge, he stopped short as Spirit Snake and Ed stood up. They had been sitting on their heels for over an hour, waiting. As Red Sun raised his arms above his head and stretched, he didn't make it easy on the two young men who were waiting nervously.

"We would like to speak to you," Ed spoke up.

"Whatever it is you have to say it will have to wait. I have to go wake the bears." Red Sun grinned as he turned and headed for the woods, knowing why they were there.

Ed turned to look at Spirit Snake in confusion.

"He is going to relieve himself." Seeing Ed's confusion, Spirit Snake smiled. Squatting on their heels again, they looked down as Waiting Owl came through the lodge opening and smiled at their discomfort.

It had been two weeks since Red Sun had gladly given his permission to Ed and Spirit Snake to marry his daughters. All of the women of the village worked together to make the wedding dresses and ceremonial robes. Belle made new dresses for her and Jenny. Word had been sent out to John, Bill and Dave, and they had started out early, anxious to visit with everyone again. The wives were dropped off at Belle's to help with the food and calm her nerves. They had not seen Belle get this worked up since they helped to deliver Jenny.

Everyone stood aside watching Spirit Snake dressed in his breech cloth and his new leather leggings and Ed dressed in his new cotton pants and white shirt. They waited for their future wives, standing tall and four feet apart. Two Worlds, draped in a fur robe, stood facing them. Ed's breath caught short as he watched the two sisters emerge from Little Moons lodge. They were dressed the same, and his heart caught in his throat as he tried to guess which one was Little Otter. As his mouth dropped open, Ed glanced at Spirit Snake and knew that he didn't know either until the sisters stopped beside them. Little Moon and Little Otter slid their arms around the arms of their men, who stood frozen as Two Worlds took a step forward and began the ceremony. Ed barely heard the words of Two Worlds as he slowly circled the couple, speaking to his ancestors in his native tongue, asking their blessing. Ed became aware of the present when Little Otter turned to face him, taking his hands in hers. He felt a blanket of soft furs being draped across his shoulders, wrapping him and Little Otter together. She released his hands so he could reach around her with his arms and take hold of the blanket as Belle and Waiting Owl handed him the edges. She was now his wife. They turned their heads when they heard Spirit Snake speak to his new wife as he held their blanket tightly around them.

"I am a man now, and I will protect you and my family from all harm. I will provide you with food and shelter. I say this as a brave and warrior for all my ancestors to hear."

Looking into his eyes she spoke as a woman now. "I have waited many years now to become woman enough to be your wife. I will care for you the way the women of our tribe have taught me. You will never have to wonder if my love for you stays strong, I will show you every day in ways you will know."

Ed realized that Little Moon had finished. He turned and looked into the depths of Little Otter's black eyes, and she showed him her soul as his heart spoke to her. "I promise I will spend the rest of my life trying to make you happy. I will care for you with all my heart and soul. Wherever you are and wherever I am, I will always be with you. Together we will teach our children the ways of your people and that of my people. I say these things to you as a man."

Looking into the heart of this man, Little Otter spoke with the strength of a woman's soft heart. "I have asked and prayed many times in the past if the love I felt toward you were acceptable to our people. Today, as I feel your arms around me and listen to your words of love, I will have no more doubts as I take care of you, our home, and the children I will give you. I say these things as a woman and your wife."

The couples stood together, each wrapped in their blankets, as everyone came to congratulate them. When all had spoken and food was offered, the wives took the blankets and folded them. Little Moon handed hers to her mother, and Little Otter handed hers to Ed's mother to keep until they came back from their marriage trip.

The women watched the children playing around the lake as the families and friends of Jessie Tucker and Two Worlds shared their food and celebrated the two couples. They didn't notice the newlyweds as they mounted their horses and started up and out of the valley.

Jessie stood apart with Two Worlds watching the future of their worlds in the hands of these young people. As they reached the ridge, they stopped to look back, then turned their horses and disappeared.

Turning to face Two Worlds, Jessie answered the question he had asked so long ago in a small village next to the great waters.

"Now I understand!"

"Yes ... and your part is not finished yet," Two Worlds replied.

The End